PAST
SHADOWS

STEVIE WOODS
CHARLIE COCHRANE
JARDONN SMITH

mlrpress

MLR PRESS AUTHORS

Featuring a roll call of some of the best writers of gay erotica and mysteries today!

M. Jules Aedin
Maura Anderson
Victor J. Banis
Jeanne Barrack
Laura Baumbach
Alex Beecroft
Sarah Black
Ally Blue
J.P. Bowie
Michael Breyette
P.A. Brown
Brenda Bryce
Jade Buchanan
James Buchanan
Charlie Cochrane
Gary Cramer
Kirby Crow
Dick D.
Ethan Day
Jason Edding
Angela Fiddler
Dakota Flint
S.J. Frost
Kimberly Gardner
Storm Grant
Amber Green
LB Gregg

Wayne Gunn
Samantha Kane
Kiernan Kelly
J.L. Langley
Josh Lanyon
Clare London
William Maltese
Gary Martine
Z.A. Maxfield
Patric Michael
Jet Mykles
Willa Okati
L. Picaro
Neil Plakcy
Jordan Castillo Price
Luisa Prieto
Rick R. Reed
A.M. Riley
George Seaton
Jardonn Smith
Caro Soles
JoAnne Soper-Cook
Richard Stevenson
Clare Thompson
Stevie Woods
Kit Zheng

Check out titles, both available and forthcoming, at
www.mlrpress.com

PAST SHADOWS

STEVIE WOODS

CHARLIE COCHRANE

JARDONN SMITH

mlrpress

Published by
MLR Press, LLC
3052 Gaines Waterport Rd.
Albion, NY 14411

Visit ManLoveRomance Press, LLC on the Internet:
www.mlrpress.com

Cover Art by Deana C. Jamroz
Edited by Kris Jacen
Printed in the United States of America.

ISBN# 978-1-60820-103-7

First Edition 2009

DEATH'S DESIRE

STEVIE WOODS

CHAPTER ONE

1785

Hugh leaned out of the carriage window and looked up the drive to the large house on the rise. It was quite an eyeful, a big sprawling house that had obviously been added to over the generations. Surprisingly, the mismatch of styles created a whole that was warm and inviting.

It had been three years since he had last seen his Simmercy relatives, though that had been in London before his cousin-in-law, William had inherited the Hall. He had never been to their country estate before and, though he sometimes felt out of place with the rather stuffy William, his wife Alicia had always been most welcoming to Hugh and his mother. He did want to see their son, Charles again; if only to discover if his inappropriate reaction to his young cousin was still in evidence. He had convinced himself he was over it, but that was when he was nearly a hundred miles away, and there was no immediate possibility of seeing the man.

The driver pulled the carriage to a halt in front of the wide stone steps and Hugh opened the door before the footman could do so. As he stepped down from the carriage a happy sounding voice called his name.

"Hugh! It's been too long," Alicia said as she hurried down the steps.

Hugh smiled at his mother's cousin, Alicia, but his eye was caught by Charles moving more slowly as he followed his mother. At twenty-one, Charles was three years younger than Hugh, yet somehow Hugh felt much older. Charles was still slim but Hugh could not fail to notice the wide shoulders and the strong thighs. He had filled out in all the right places.

"Cousin Alicia," Hugh said, and Alicia gripped his shoulders, giving him a quick peck on the cheek before moving aside to allow Charles to approach. Hugh smiled as he stretched out to

shake Charles' hand. "It's good to see you, Charles. You look..."
He had been about to say wonderful, but quickly changed it to,
"Well."

"I am. It is good to see you again too." Charles smiled.

"I'm so pleased that your mother finally persuaded you to
come," Alicia said. "I asked her to twist your arm if she had to."

Hugh felt the heat suffuse his face. "I was not being difficult
in not coming sooner, I just had..."

"No, no. No excuses, Hugh. You had your reasons, I may
not understand what they were, but I'm just happy that this
time you came. We have missed you. Haven't we, Charles?"

"Yes," Charles said, but Hugh could have wished for more
enthusiasm.

"Come, we'll have some tea while your luggage is taken to
your room, and then Charles will show you around."

Hugh had been relieved to discover that William, Charles'
father, was not going to be in attendance after all. He had been
called back to London on business the day before. William
Simmercy had a supercilious air that had always intimidated
Hugh, even though his mother had told him that Cousin
William was not at all as snobbish as he appeared. Hugh could
not deny that it was just as likely to be his own inferiority
complex at work. His own father's pedigree could not compare
with the Simmercy's.

Charles was following his mother's instruction to show
Hugh the house and as he moved along the narrow corridor
with Charles, Hugh did his best to relax and enjoy being with
the man, pleased that Charles now seemed more at ease in his
company. It was the first time they had been alone since his
arrival, and Hugh was trying to regain the camaraderie they had
shared the last time they had been together.

Simmercy Hall was full of history, both the contents of the
building and the lives of the generations who had lived within
its walls. There was pride in Charles' voice as he spoke of how
the original building had been awarded to Philip d'Simmercy in

1486 by the then new King Henry VII, for his bravery in the Battle of Bosworth Field.

"Father is already talking about holding a party next year to celebrate the family's three hundred years in the Hall."

"It is quite an achievement," Hugh agreed. "Your family has been lucky to have such a settled history."

"Settled?" Charles laughed. "Oh, you have no idea of the number of scandals in my family. Adultery and murder are not even the most outrageous."

"Pardon! Murder?"

Charles was clearly excited now and he tugged at Hugh's sleeve. "Come, my friend, I'll tell you the most salacious story, but do not let mother know I told you, she is scandalized that I even know all the details."

He laughed again, chivvying Hugh back along the corridor towards the room he was using. Two doors down from Hugh's room Charles threw open a pair of double doors. As they had bypassed the doors earlier, Hugh had assumed it must be William and Alicia's room, its location in the centre of the Hall suggesting it was the master bedroom.

"No one has used this room in a hundred and fifty years," Charles said as he stepped inside. "They say it is haunted," he added in a purposefully affected voice, making Hugh roll his eyes.

The room was dark and dusty. Charles moved swiftly to the two tall sets of windows and pulled back the drawn curtains allowing light to flood the room, the dust mites seeming to multiply even in the weak rays of the autumn sun. It was easy to see though how, with care, the room could look magnificent. There was a thick rug in the centre of the room surrounded by darkly stained wood flooring, which was echoed on the lower half of the panelled walls. The upper walls were covered with tapestries and paintings. The furniture was of thick oak and the curtains of the four poster bed matched the design of the rug and the window curtains.

Hugh was drawn to the magnificent bed and was surprised to find only the bare mattress. His hand slowly moved across the dusty material and it was only as the dust rose beneath his fingers that he realized what he was doing. He stepped back sharply, a shiver running through him which he put down to his own odd behaviour. He lifted his eyes and found Charles watching him closely, a slight smile on his full lips.

"You said it was haunted?" Hugh queried, not about to admit the strange feeling he'd had when he had touched the bed.

"I don't know the exact year, but it was somewhere around a hundred and fifty years ago, or so the story goes. Lady Maude Simmercy found her husband *in flagrante delicto* with his manservant."

"His manservant?"

"Yes, his manservant," Charles repeated with a gleam in his eye. "She brought her three brothers to the Hall and they confronted the husband. It is said he didn't even try to deny his ungodly act. The manservant was dragged in and killed before the husband's eyes – and then they killed him."

As Charles was speaking, Hugh had a strange feeling he was being watched but Charles' attention was on the bed.

"It is said it was here she found him, in bed with the servant, but I'm not even sure I believe that anyway."

"You mean you do not believe a man would indulge in such an unholy act?" Hugh asked quietly.

"Lord, no. I am not such a prude that I don't believe *that* goes on, but not with one's servant surely. There must be..."

He was interrupted by a cough followed by a footman saying, "I am sorry to interrupt Master Charles but your lady mother requests you attend her immediately."

Charles sighed with frustration but simply said, "I will be right there, Norton. Will you wait here for me," he asked Hugh, grinning as he added, "or back in your room if you prefer?"

For some reason even Hugh did not understand, he did not want to leave the room just yet. "I'll wait here for you. I want to hear the rest of the story."

"Good," Charles said and left.

Hugh turned back to the bed, looking stark in its unmade form. "Did you risk it all just to be with him?" he whispered. "Did it not matter to you that he was a servant?" He laughed hollowly. "Or was it just that he was a convenient body and you needed..."

"I did need, but I needed Thomas, he was everything to me. Your words speak of understanding."

The words were spoken close to his ear, but it was a voice Hugh had never heard before. Deep and husky. An icy chill washed over him. But when he spun around there was no one there.

"Charles?" he called hesitatingly. "Was that you, playing a trick on me?"

The door suddenly blew shut. But there was no window open. What was happening? Hugh shuddered. *Lord, I wish now I had left with Charles!*

"No, it was not Charles, it was I." As the words drifted to him, a form began to take shape by the door. A man a little older than he was, taller and heavier, clothed in very out-dated doublet and hose, the white lace of his shirt almost shining in contrast to his dark doublet.

Terrified, backing away, Hugh gasped. "What in Heaven's name!" It couldn't be real, it couldn't!

"No, I am not granted that mercy. I sometimes wonder if this is just another version of Hell. Do not be afraid, I mean you no harm. Allow me to introduce myself, Sir Adam Simmercy." The figure bowed, extending his right arm in a sweeping arc. "It is a rare gift to find someone who can not only hear me but see me. It has been... let me think, seventy-five years I believe, since it last occurred. Your name, if you please, sir?"

Hugh stared at the figure. It was hard to believe it was real and yet it did feel as if he was speaking to a normal person. A living person, not a ghost, and yet he had no doubt that this... this was an apparition. Taking a breath to calm his racing heart and attempt to steady his nerves, he replied, "I am Hugh Preston, Charles' cousin twice removed."

"Ah, Charles' cousin twice removed. I am delighted to meet you, Hugh. And who is Charles?"

"Oh, I thought you would know. Charles Simmercy, your descendant, I assume."

Adam laughed heartily. It seemed very odd to imagine a ghost could laugh like that.

"No, my wife never carried any child of mine. After my... removal, she married my cousin, my heir. It was always the title she was more interested in than me, and Cecil had always admired her. Suited them both admirably, I imagine."

"Still, how is it that you did not know he was... of the family? You must have seen him."

"Not really. I am trapped in the house but I do not manifest often, it is too hard to watch those living, loving and enjoying life when I can have none of it. I spend most of my time here, where it is very rare that anyone comes."

"Why me?" Hugh suddenly asked. The more *normal* the conversation became the more lost Hugh was feeling.

"That is something I cannot answer. Certain people can sense me, or sense something when they enter this room. But to see me, and hear me? Rare people it would seem, because it has only happened three times since I died." Adam stepped closer and Hugh shivered as it became more apparent then that he could see the door through Adam's form. "Rare indeed," Adam continued, "because you have not run screaming from the room, or called to Heaven for protection from the demon, as did the last person who saw me. You have the strength of heart to stand there and converse with me."

"I think it is more that I am too afraid to move," Hugh said quietly. But privately he acknowledged there was some truth in what Adam claimed. He was nervous of the ghost, confused by his own reaction, and intrigued by both the man's history and his own need to understand. Yet he felt no real fear of the spectre.

Adam laughed again and Hugh could not deny the man's laugh was intoxicating. As strange as it seemed, his laugh was so full of life.

"There is no tremor in your voice, no fear in your stance. No, my young Hugh, I do not believe you are truly afraid of me. Puzzled I grant, but not afraid. And for that I thank you, for I mean you no harm. It might be that you can be of help to me."

Hugh frowned, "I don't understand."

"No, but then you don't know my story. You drew me here soon enough that I heard a little of what that fool, Charles, told you and he does not know the half of it. Will you let me tell you all?"

Hugh knew in that instant he had to know everything, but at that moment he heard voices and knew that Charles was returning.

"I would, but not now, he is returning. I cannot be found talking to thin air, for I do not believe he would see you."

"No, he would not. Can you come back later, tonight?"

"Yes." Hugh said firmly.

As he stepped into the room, Charles said, "I am sorry I left you alone for so long, especially in this place."

"It was no hardship, I had a good look around." As he spoke, Hugh saw Adam's form dissipate as if it had never been, and he heard, as if whispered on the wind, "Midnight."

Charles was already speaking, "Mother has been trying to get me to allow her to invite Cecily Hampton and her parents over for dinner tonight, and I told her we should allow you to settle in quietly first." Charles glanced around before continuing, "Truth is, she and Lady Helen are trying to engineer a betrothal between Cecily and I, which is the last thing I want. Goodness, I used to chase the girl around the garden, and I can never see her as anything but a dirty child." Charles shrugged. "Anyhow, I have no wish to marry – not yet anyhow."

"No, I well understand that feeling. I am older than you and though I don't have the pressure of your family lineage, still my mother would like to have grandchildren. It is not easy." Hugh couldn't help his sidelong glance at Charles, who caught his eye and smiled.

"We have to stand together – bachelors together!" Charles raised a hand in salute and Hugh laughed.

"Together forever." Hugh grinned back at him, wishing it could really be like that. Three years apart, and already Hugh knew nothing had changed for him. He wanted Charles now as much as he had three years earlier.

CHAPTER TWO

Dinner had been a long drawn out affair, Cousin Alicia wanting to know everything that had happened to Hugh and his family in the intervening years. Hugh's comment that he knew his mother wrote to her monthly had little effect, unless one counted Charles' peel of laughter. It was worth it for that alone.

Charles walked Hugh to his room after they had partaken of brandy and cigars, and Hugh didn't have to fake his yawn as they reached his door.

"Have a good night's sleep, Hugh," Charles said as he turned away. "I have plans for tomorrow."

"Plans?" Hugh queried.

"You will see tomorrow," Charles called over his shoulder. With a wave of his hand, he added, "Sleep well."

"You too, Charles, you too."

Closing the door, Hugh leaned against it and blew out his breath. As if he did not have enough on his plate with unrequited feelings for his friend, he had an appointment with a ghost. Was it possible he was losing his mind?

He eyed the bed longingly, but it was already almost midnight and he dare not lie down, for he would most likely drift off. He paced up and down, keeping an eye on the mantle clock over the small fireplace.

Hugh was almost surprised that he wasn't even considering backing out of the meeting. *With a ghost, dear Lord!* But the truth was he was filled with an urge to know Adam's story. It might be because the man's death had been caused by the same unnatural urges that drove him. He knew he ought to be ashamed of the way he felt about other men, yet somehow he wasn't. He had tried to fight his nature and be interested in a woman but it never happened. He found himself attracted to various men who crossed his path, though he never felt for any of them the way he did for Charles.

The clock chimed midnight. He carefully opened his door and checked that the hallway was empty. Quickly covering the short distance between his room and the master bedroom, he slipped inside.

The room was empty. Quietly, Hugh said, "Adam?" Immediately he felt it, a slight change in the atmosphere in the room. If anyone asked him to describe it, Hugh wouldn't know how.

"You came," Adam said, materialising by the bed. "I was uncertain you would come." He smiled. "I am glad I was wrong. You are the best chance I have ever had to end this."

"Start at the beginning, Adam, please."

"Thomas, oh my Thomas," Adam said, flopping on his back still happily experiencing the after effects of their love making. Thomas was curled up along his side, his long fingers moving languidly over Adam's chest.

Thomas leaned up and kissed his cheek and then captured his mouth. Adam loved kissing Thomas; it sometimes seemed more erotic than having sex with him.

"Oh my God!" The voice reverberated around the room.

Adam bolted upright, Thomas falling away. His lady wife, Maude, stood in the open doorway, a handkerchief pressed to her mouth, her eyes full of disbelieving horror. Without another word, she turned and fled.

"Oh, Adam, Adam, I'm sorry." Thomas moved up behind him, his hands gripping Adam's shoulders. "What are we going to do?"

For a moment Adam could not speak. This was the day he had feared from the moment he knew that he could not let Thomas go. He had fallen hard for the younger man almost from the moment he had come to work for him, after his old valet had retired. Adam had struggled long and hard against his nature all his adult life. He tried to be a good husband to the woman his father had arranged he marry, but he had never felt as close to Maude as a man should to his life partner.

With Thomas it had never been that way. It had been useless fighting against his feelings for his manservant, even though he believed them to be pointless – not because he didn't feel the man was worthy of him, but because he had no reason to believe that Thomas could, or would, return his regard. When, almost by accident, he had discovered that Thomas did indeed share his desire for the male body, he still had no cause to expect that Thomas would *love* him. Thomas was ten years younger than Adam, and Thomas was a very attractive young man. But miracle of miracles, Thomas wanted him as much as he wanted Thomas.

The more Thomas meant to him, the more Adam feared they were living on borrowed time. Yet, still he couldn't stop. His love for Thomas would not be denied. And now their time had run out.

"It is not your fault, Thomas, never your fault. I did not believe Lady Maude would be back today. I was careless. *I* should apologise to you." He turned to face his lover. "I'm sorry I've ruined everything. We knew this might occur, my love, but knowing something in the abstract..." Adam shrugged. "It's not the same as really believing it is going to happen is it? However, now it has. I just did not expect... but we planned for this. You should leave now, go somewhere safe. We'll meet in three days at the Crook and Flail."

"You have not ruined everything. You could only do that if you no longer wanted me." Thomas managed to smile, as if he knew that day would never come. "And we can go to Italy, really? We'll be safe then?" Thomas was already pulling on his clothes.

Adam sighed. "It won't be easy, Thomas. But it will be worth it. I am sick of playing the faithful husband to a wife who detests me and for whom I have no feelings. I feel as if I am acting in a play when I am not with you. I want to be myself, Thomas. I want to share my life with you. But, now you must hurry, I want you gone before she comes back."

"But, what about you?"

"I'll be fine. I'll gather together what I need and take a circuitous route to London. After we meet up we can look into sailings for the Continent. Go, now!"

"Three days, I'll be waiting for you." With a last look at Adam, Thomas hurried from the room.

Sighing, Adam walked over to the desk by the window and opened the centre top drawer. He kept all the papers he would need in a packet at the back of the drawer. He had some money in the drawer too, and could collect more from his bank in London, and arrange for the transfer of more funds to a bank in Italy. He would leave more than enough for Maude to continue in the life to which she was accustomed. He was in the process of packing a few clothes when the door behind him banged open.

He swung around to see his wife standing there, backed by her three brothers. That he hadn't expected. He had assumed she had returned alone, there had been no plan for her brothers to accompany her, but then the plan had been for her to return the next day. He had no idea what had caused her early return, but it was his ruination.

Maude stared at him, her expression one of loathing and disgust. She stepped aside and out of his sight.

And Adam gasped. In the gap left by her leaving, Adam saw Thomas held tight in the grip of Maude's eldest brother Stephen. Thomas was limp and there were bruises on his face.

"Thomas," Adam breathed. His eyes flew to Stephen's face and the man smiled coldly at him.

Thomas was dragged into the room and the door was closed behind the brothers.

Adam made to take a step toward Thomas and Stephen gripped the younger man around the throat forcing his neck back at an awkward angle. Thomas' eyes flew open in panic.

"Let him be!" Adam demanded.

"Let him be?" Stephen replied, his fingers tightening around Thomas' neck. "I'll only let him be when he is dead. He is an abomination!" Abruptly he spun Thomas towards his brother,

Walter, who grabbed him and pulled the confused young man in a tight grip, Thomas' back against his chest.

Stephen took a step towards Adam, his arm raised, his finger pointing. "As are you, Adam Simmercy. You are a sodomite, a blasphemy against God! You bring disgrace to your name, to your wife. Your wife! What kind of man are you to engage in such disgusting debauchery with a lout like this." He glanced over at Thomas, disgust on his face. "You have forfeited everything. You understand? *Everything.*"

Adam knew in that instant that he was doomed. The Walsh brothers were all big strong men and there was no way he could free Thomas from them and allow both of them escape. The best he could hope for was to talk them out of hurting Thomas any more, though in truth he held out little hope of that either.

"Don't hurt him," Thomas croaked.

Stephen back-handed Thomas across the face. "Silence!" he commanded.

"Let him be!" Adam repeated desperately. "If you have any argument it is with me. Let the boy go, he has done you no harm."

Walter laughed. "No harm? His very existence is harmful to me. He is the devil's spawn and belongs with his master."

"No!" Adam cried.

"Robert," Stephen said calmly and he and his brother advanced on Adam. Adam set himself for a fight, but the brothers came at him from opposite sides simultaneously and there was no way he could take on both at the same time, they were too careful. Adam chose to tackle Stephen, and consequently left himself open to Robert's attack. All too soon, Adam was held tight. He was shoved into a chair and tied to it using a cord from the bed curtains.

Feeling totally helpless and fearful of what would happen next, Adam could only watch. His eyes sought out his lover, and Thomas held his gaze for a moment before he was thrust to his knees at the feet of the brothers. Thomas lifted his head.

"Don't do this, please?" Thomas said suddenly, his eyes fixed on Adam. "We have harmed no one by–" A blow from Stephen silenced Thomas.

"Don't beg, Thomas," Adam said softly. "Nothing you or I say will make any difference. They have already made up their minds." Thomas raised his chin, eyes immediately fastening on Adam again as tears spilled down his cheeks. "Remember, I love you and we will be together again soon."

"You abomination, you make me sick!" Stephen declared, cutting across Adam's words.

Adam ignored Stephen and kept his eyes on his lover. He didn't see the knife in Walter's hand until it was too late. Before Thomas could reply or Adam could call a warning, the blade was drawn swiftly across Thomas' throat. Blood spurted towards Adam, spraying the front of his doublet. Horror stricken, he heard the blood gurgling as Thomas desperately tried to drawn breath through his ruined throat, his eyes widening in fear. Walter's hand flicked again and the knife bit deeper into poor Thomas' throat. With a sudden kick to his back from Stephen, Thomas pitched face first on the rug in front of Adam's chair, his blood staining the rug in an ever increasing circle.

Adam heard screaming and didn't recognize his own voice at first. "Thomas," he gasped, his own tears dripping onto his shirt and mingling with his lover's blood as he struggled to lean forward to get closer to Thomas, but his bindings held him fast.

"Get rid of it," Stephen said harshly.

Walter grabbed the throw cover from the bed and rapidly rolled Thomas' body in it. He grabbed hold of Thomas' ankles dragging his body from the room. As Robert followed the obscene noise of Thomas' head bouncing on the floor ended and Adam had to assume they now carried Thomas' body between them.

"What will you do with him now?" asked Adam, his voice cracking. His world had ended and he just felt numb.

"What does that matter? You should have concern for yourself now," Stephen said harshly.

Adam did not reply; he knew there would be no point. He closed his eyes, trying to remember last evening with Thomas, but all he could see was Thomas' expression as he fought for life. Adam felt tears on his face again. Abruptly the door opened and Adam opened his eyes again. Robert and Walter came back in, both of them streaked in Thomas' blood.

"Send me to join him," Adam said heavily. "What are you waiting for?"

"Join him?" Stephen laughed. "Do you really expect that the Devil will allow you to see each other in Hell! You will suffer the worst torments imaginable. You both deserve every horrible thing that happens to you."

"Damn you, damn you all to Hell! God curse you for seeing only evil where you should see the purity of love. It is you who will rot in hell for the heinous crime of murder!" Adam cried. "If I do go to Hell, I'll wait for you all! *We* will be waiting. Thomas will be at my side, where he belongs. Together we will watch *you* suffer."

Stephen hit him hard across the face but Adam kept cursing them, calling on angels and demons alike as blood joined the tears on his face. Walter used his knife to cut Adam's bonds. Adam shot from the chair, his hands reaching for Stephen's throat. But he never connected. Robert and Walter grabbed and held him firmly as Stephen hit him again and again, until pain and exhaustion drove Adam to his knees.

Grabbing for Walter's knife, Stephen declared, "I think it would serve you right if I used this on your privates. They never were any good to poor Maude were they?" He wielded the knife under Adam's nose before he slowly slid it down his breastbone drawing a fine line of blood to stain Adam's shirt. A cold weight settled in Adam's stomach. He knew he was going to die, but he had hoped at least for a clean death. As he reached Adam's navel, Stephen stopped. "But, I won't soil my hands touching your foul member. You are abhorrent and only deserve to be butchered like an animal."

With that Stephen sharply drew the knife across Adam's throat. Pain such as he had never imagined flooded his body.

He gasped for breath he couldn't draw. He felt his mouth fill up with blood, the coppery smell assailing his nostrils.

He flailed, trying to fight his way free, but strong arms held him still. Seemingly from a distance he heard laughter as pain swamped him in waves. He gagged, his sight dimmed, his strength fell away. He tried to speak but it was impossible. His mind suffered a different kind of agony, as fear at what would happen to him next tore through him. *Thomas! Help me Lord!* Then he knew no more.

"When did you know you were still trapped here?" The question caught Adam by surprise and it took a moment to recall where he was – when he was. He realized the voice belonged to Hugh Preston, not one of the Walsh brothers.

"I am not sure how much time passed. Hours, days? I had no way of knowing. It was as if I simply awoke in my own bed, yet nothing was the same. The bed was stripped of all linen. There were people in the room, servants I realized, but no one could see me. They were packing things away, and cleaning. One of the maids was complaining that they would never get the rug clean. I knew in an instant that it was Thomas' blood of which she spoke and I leapt from the bed in a fury. I grabbed her shoulder and shouted something, I know not what, but the maidservant screamed. And so it began."

"Did she see you, hear you?"

"No. She said she felt a cold grip on her shoulder, and a terrifying presence." Adam laughed. "I think I was more terrified than she was. She screamed loud enough to bring the roof down and the room cleared in an instant. Over the next few days anyone who entered the room claimed they felt *something.* I admit my pain and anger made me rage at any who entered, and before long no one would go into the room. After a time I found I could materialize in certain other places. I tried to haunt my wife. That would have given me great pleasure, but she never sensed me. She always was a cold bitch."

"Did you discover what happened to Thomas?"

"No," Adam said sadly. "I have never known, and that I think, is my purgatory. I cursed them, promising I would see them in Hell with Thomas at my side. I should never have made such a promise. I condemned both myself and poor Thomas, I believe. I do not think I will be allowed to leave here unless it is with Thomas. After so many years of waiting alone, facing nothingness for so long, I can face that now, going wherever I must, as long as it is with Thomas. I had hoped for Heaven, trusting that any loving God could look down on true love between two people, even if they were of the same gender, but if we are destined for Hell, then at least let us be together."

"I don't really know what to say," Hugh said. "Or even what you expect me to be able to do for you."

"I am able to materialize in certain rooms within the Hall, this one being the easiest for me. I am also able to appear in the vegetable garden."

"The vegetable garden?"

Adam gave an odd smile. "Yes, my wife and her family covered up the *scandal* of my death by claiming I had attacked my valet and killed him. I had then bolted, and my brothers-in-law went after me to bring me back to face justice. During my flight I tried to jump a fence, but fell from my mount, and broke my neck.

"They had carried my poor broken body home to my distraught wife who proceeded to give me a quick and quiet funeral. Only my body was not in the casket that was buried in the family plot in the churchyard. I had been wrapped in a sheet from my bed and given a rough and ready burial in the vegetable garden, at the lower end of the greenhouse. No words were spoken over my graveside; no man of the cloth presided at my funeral.

"As for Thomas, I have searched every place I am able but I cannot find any trace of his last resting place. Wherever they put his body, it is beyond my reach."

"And you believe it is important to find his body? But why?"

"I believe he is waiting for me. He is as trapped wherever he is, as I am here."

Hugh stared at him, only in that moment realizing that Adam was no longer a spectre-like form. He looked completely real, alive. Cautiously, he reached out a hand to touch him and though he half-expected it, it was still a shock when his hand passed through Adam..

Adam smiled. "I was right about you," he said softly.

A thought occurred to Hugh and he glanced at Adam, not sure how, or if, he should voice it.

"What is it, Hugh? I see the quandary in your face. Do you know how expressive your face is?"

Hugh felt the heat rise in his face and was then embarrassed at such a reaction to a ghost.

Adam laughed. "Oh, you are a delight. My Thomas would like you, I know." His smile faded. "Tell me."

"I'm sorry, but it occurred to me that maybe they did not bury Thomas."

"You think that has not occurred to me? There is a large lake in the park; they could have thrown his body in there. Or even have left him in the woods bordering the park, let his sweet body rot. Damn them to Hell! They are waiting for me, I know it. I will find them!"

Ignoring Adam's angry outburst, Hugh said, "That's true, but had you also thought they might have burned him?" He hated to say it but he knew it had to be considered.

Adam stared at him with a horrified expression. "They wouldn't. Even they would not burn a body. They were very religious. They wouldn't. Dear God, they wouldn't."

Regretting causing Adam more pain, Hugh was quick to say, "I'm not saying for certain they did, but…" His voice faded; what else could he say?

"Will you help me by trying to find Thomas?" Adam asked intently.

"If I can find his body, what would you want me to do?"

"Bring him to the vegetable garden, so we can be united."

"You're suggesting that if I can find his body and bring it to where your body is buried, his spirit will come along too?" Hugh was sceptical.

Adam shrugged. "I do not know for certain if that would end my purgatory, Hugh, I can only hope. If that fails then I pray that Thomas has been in Heaven all this time. The truth is I know of no other way to free my spirit from its earthly prison."

"I will do what I can, that is all I can promise."

"I cannot ask for anything more. You have…" Adam stopped, frowning. "I was going to say you have my undying appreciation, but it is rather late for that."

"Do you have any ideas of where I might search to find out what happened to Thomas' body? It would take me far too long if I had to try and search the whole estate. I am only supposed to be visiting the family for two weeks."

Adam rubbed a hand over his mouth and Hugh was spellbound, watching as Adam then brushed the hand through his hair. The actions looked so normal. It was disconcerting to watch, and that thought struck him as odd. He found *that* disconcerting after spending almost two hours talking with a ghost?

Hugh frowned as another thought occurred. "Wait, if the family went to the trouble of covering up the murders, how did the secret leak out?"

"Salacious secrets like that never remain hidden. People talk."

"And people write things down," Hugh said thoughtfully. "Charles said something about finding out about the haunting and its history, even though his mother was annoyed that he had discovered it."

"You're right, it must be written down somewhere."

"There must be a library…"

"There is. In the west wing, on the ground floor."

"I'll begin my search there tomorrow."

Breakfast the next morning was a quiet affair, for which Hugh was grateful. Cousin Alicia, having a slight headache, had decided to stay in her room until later in the morning, and Charles seemed surprisingly silent.

By the time he was finishing his meal, Hugh was pressed to ask, "Is something wrong, Charles. Is your mother's illness not as minor as I perceived?"

"Goodness me, no," Charles smiled slightly. "Mother is prone to these early morning headaches. I think it is just an excuse to lie abed. No, I simply did not sleep very well last night. I had a most disturbing dream."

"Dream?"

Charles waved away the footman who had been serving them breakfast, and when the man had left the room, he said, "It's probably because I was speaking to you about it, but I dreamt about the ghost. He seemed to be calling to me, and I kept trying to get away from him. Most disturbing."

"Oh, then perhaps I should keep my query for another time," Hugh said diffidently.

"Your query?"

"It concerns the ghost, so perhaps now is not the best time."

"Oh, ignore my dramatics, my dear Hugh. What is that you wish to know?"

"How you found out about him? You said something about your mother being angry that you knew, so I guess it wasn't your parents who told the legend. So, how?"

Charles grinned. "Actually it was my grandfather's old cook, she's gone now. She tended to blather a lot more as she got older, and one day when we were visiting, when I was about, oh, twelve I would guess, she told me it wasn't sensible for me to play in the haunted room. Well, you can imagine how that whetted my curiosity. I had no idea until then there even *was* a haunted room, never mind which one it was."

"So you never felt anything then?"

"Lord love you, no. Anyhow, one of the maids came into the kitchen then and chased me out, but I heard her tell the cook that the master and mistress would be furious if they knew she was talking about the ghost."

"So, of course, you had to know more," Hugh said, grinning.

"Oh, you know me! I admit though that after a while I almost gave up. I had thought there would have to be something in the library, family history and all that, but I could not find anything that even suggested a haunting. Then, almost by chance a little while later I stumbled across a journal written about a hundred and forty or so years ago, and there it was. The whole sordid tale."

Hugh felt butterflies going wild in his stomach. "Can you?" his voice was hoarse. He licked his lips and swallowed. "Can you show me?"

"What, the journal? You seem very interested in all this, Hugh." Charles' eyes widened. "God, I was right wasn't I? I knew it! You did sense something in that room yesterday? I thought you looked odd, and I saw you shiver. Tell me, tell me what it felt like, and I'll show you the journal."

Before Hugh had a chance to answer there was a knock at the door, and a footman entered to inform Charles that the horses he had arranged for the stable to send around were waiting.

"Horses?" Hugh queried.

"I told you I had plans for today, the first of which was to take you for a ride around the estate. Of course, I did not know that *this* was going to come up," Charles added with a raised eyebrow. "Still, we can talk as we ride, which actually couldn't be better. Shall we?"

◈ ◈ ◈ ◈

As they cantered over the parkland, past the lake and toward the woods, Hugh's mind was full of questions, but he didn't know how to ask any of them. Charles, however, had no such qualms.

"Come on, Hugh, there must be more than just 'I had an odd feeling'. Did you feel cold, did you feel a touch, anything?"

"Please, Charles, I have told you all that I can."

"Which suggests to me that there is something you do not think you *can* tell me."

Hugh shook his head. He so wanted to talk it over with someone, and as always he felt closer to Charles than anyone else. However, he did not know how Charles would react if he told him the truth, that he had not only felt the presence of the ghost, but had seen and spoke with him – for over two hours.

They were entering the woods now, the horses all but walking. Hugh had hardly noticed, his thoughts were racing so much.

"Dismount, Hugh," Charles abruptly said.

"What? Why?" Still, Hugh pulled up his mount and began to climb off.

"Because I don't like to see you look so unhappy. Because there is more going on and I... Well, whatever is going on, we need to talk, and this is about as private as anywhere else, and I think you need privacy for your own sake, not just mine."

They tied their horses to a tree, then Charles led the way to a fallen log where they could sit in relative comfort.

"I know it's been a while since we saw each other," Charles began, "but we practically grew up together and I never felt so close, so quickly, to anyone else the way I do with you, Hugh. You're the best friend I ever had. And, I *know* something is really bothering you. Can you not talk to me, please?"

Hugh sagged a little and dropped his chin to his chest. Charles had given him the opening he wanted, but he was afraid. Afraid that Charles would think he was simple minded to believe what had happened to him. Afraid to perhaps find how much Charles was disgusted by the relationship that had existed between Adam and Thomas; still existed as far as Adam was concerned. Hugh had imagined so many times that something could take place between Charles and him, something beyond the close friendship they shared, but he was too scared to ever put himself out there for Charles to turn away from in revulsion. But, could he really go through the rest of his life in a kind of limbo, never knowing if taking the chance would have given him the prize he craved?

Lifting his head, Hugh said, "I'm not sure you will believe me. I don't want you to think me a fool, but what I am about to tell you truly happened, I swear."

Charles frowned. "If you say it happened, Hugh, I believe you."

"I hope you will still say that when I have finished," Hugh said softly, and began to explain what had happened in the haunted room the day before.

Charles listened to Hugh with ever increasing incredulity, yet as strange and amazing as each word was, he knew without doubt that Hugh believed each one to be true. And that gave Charles pause for thought. He had always trusted Hugh, and even with their recent separation he still did. Charles noted how hesitantly at first Hugh had spoken of the feelings shared between Sir Adam and his manservant, but the more Hugh spoke about it, the more clear it was that Hugh believed the relationship between the two men was not only real, it was right.

Hugh's mood changed as he spoke until the anger he obviously felt at the terrible treatment the two men had suffered resonated with each word. When Hugh finally reached the end of his tale, he was breathing heavily with emotion, eyes wide and face flushed.

Hugh met Charles' eyes squarely and said, "Thank you for hearing me out without—"

"I can see you truly believe what you are telling me, Hugh," Charles interrupted. He had no wish to hear Hugh excuse himself. "I cannot claim to believe so readily," he continued. "I admit I am incredulous at what you have said, but I know you would never lie to me."

Hugh sighed with obvious relief. "Thank you for not immediately declaring me mad." He shrugged. "I have no proof, just my word, Charles. I cannot show you Adam, for it seems you are not capable of seeing him."

"No. I have spent many hours in that room and never felt anything. But, as I said earlier, I did observe you shiver in that room when there was no cause that I witnessed. So, I will go on the assumption that what you saw and heard was real."

"Charles." Hugh put a wealth of feeling in the name.

"So, now what is it you need?"

"Information. A way to find out what happened to Thomas' body." Hugh stopped and he looked closely at Charles. "You will really help me with this?"

"Yes. Our first stop is the library. I think I might be able to remember where I found the journal and I can show you what I know. I cannot remember if there was any mention of what happened to them after they were killed, but we can start there. It is possible there were other entries in the journal, but to be honest after I found what I wanted, I never looked any further."

"Can we go there now, to the library?" Hugh was excited, and Charles felt happy that he had been able to take the uncomfortable look from Hugh's eyes.

They mounted their horses and galloped back to the stables where they left the horses with a groom, then hurried to the house. As they entered, Alicia was coming down the stairs.

"Oh, there you are. Did you have a good ride?"

"Morning, mother. Yes we did." Charles gave her a peck on the cheek.

"Is your headache better, Cousin Alicia?" Hugh asked.

"Yes, my dear. Calm and rest have always helped with my headaches. What do you have planned for the rest of the day?

Has he shown you the lake? I hope you will have a late lunch with me?"

Charles laughed. "Did you say calm, mother? You sound anything but calm. Yes, I showed him the lake. We are going to the library now, but I hope you will forgive us if we partake of a light repast in the library and we will join you later for dinner."

"The library, why–?"

"Later, mother," Charles said with a careless wave of his hand. He had no desire to explain why he was going to the library and the odds were she would forget about it by the time they met up later.

"What if she asks why again later?" Hugh asked.

"I hope she doesn't, but you're right, we should have an explanation." He thought for a moment then with a sly smile, he said, "I will tell her you asked lots of questions about the park – its design, how the lake was formed – things like that. She will like that you are interested."

Hugh could hardly believe the size of the library, when Charles showed him in. He had envisioned a small room lined with books. The room was indeed lined with books but it was most certainly not a small room. There was a large fireplace along one wall, two large windows divided another wall, but everywhere that there was free wall space, it was filled with bookshelves, floor to ceiling.

"I did not know a private library could have so many books," Hugh said as he stood in the middle of the room and turned full circle.

Charles laughed, "Oh, there are many larger libraries, believe me. My father has added greatly to the collection over the last couple of years or so. Not that he has read many; he just likes visitors to believe he has."

"How can you find anything in all of this?"

"Luckily, it has been sorted and organized and there is a catalogue in the desk." Charles pointed to a desk in one of the large alcoves either side of the fireplace. "I've never actually looked at the thing but I'm sure it can help. It better had do, because the family journals certainly aren't where they were when I found them."

Charles opened the central drawer, took out a thick book, then put it on the surface. Hugh sat behind the desk and Charles pulled up a chair beside him. He opened the library catalogue and began to scan the lines, trying to make sense of it. After a few moments, Hugh felt Charles' eyes on him and not on the book. He glanced at his friend, a question in his eyes and Charles flushed as if he had been caught doing something he shouldn't. Still, he managed a small smile.

"Hugh," Charles said carefully, "why did you stay away for so long? I know that my father's inheritance of the Hall and his decision to live here permanently made it difficult for us to spend as much time together as we used to, but you simply... stopped. You made an excuse every time you were invited, but your mother always managed a visit. I... I tried to understand. I missed you, more than I think you realize. I thought maybe I had done something, but–"

"No, no, it was never anything you did. I..." Hugh stopped abruptly, his eyes dropping to look at the book, but the words were just a jumble of images.

"I should not have asked," Charles said heavily. "It's fine, go back to looking for the journal."

"No, Charles, it's not fine. It's not been fine for a long time now." Hugh could not go on like this any longer, hiding from his best friend, hiding from himself. If he ever wanted what he really desired in this life, he had to take the chance. Maybe he was a fool, but he had been sensing... *something* from Charles almost from the moment he had arrived at the Hall. It could very easily be wishful thinking, but it was clear that Charles wanted answers. And if Hugh needed proof that Charles trusted him, he had received it today when Charles so readily believed his fantastic tale about seeing a ghost.

"You seemed to take the situation between Sir Adam and Thomas in your stride, which I admit rather surprised me after your comment in the master bedroom that first afternoon."

"My comment?" Charles asked puzzled.

"You don't remember? When you said you were not a prude, that you knew relations between men took place – but with his manservant? That, you could not accept."

"Ah, I see." Charles shrugged. "You should know me better than that Hugh. I always did tend to speak without thinking, especially when I was trying to," he paused to laugh lightly, "impress someone, but when did I ever stand on ceremony? That's the sort of thing my father would do. But, let us not get off the subject, Hugh. The situation between Adam and Thomas?"

"Very well. Yes, you hardly made any reference to their relationship when I told you about it, you were more concerned with the fact that I claimed to see and speak with a ghost."

"Well it was something of an unusual claim."

"Charles!"

"I'm sorry. Carry on. Please."

"Damn!" Hugh said. The conversation had gone off track enough for Hugh to lose the urgent need to declare himself.

"Don't stop now, please, Hugh," Charles said with an edge of disquiet.

Hugh looked up to meet Charles' eyes, and something he saw there renewed his courage. "I only stayed away because I wanted to see you so much," Hugh confessed. "Too much for the friends we were supposed to be. I could not risk… I was afraid that if you understood, you would despise me. I didn't even know for certain if you would not denounce me. I still don't."

"Yes, you do," Charles said softly. "I could never harm you. You didn't need to stay away. There was never any risk, not between you and me. I don't despise you because I know exactly how you feel. Which was why it hurt so much that you did not seem to want to see me any more. That you did not miss me the way I missed you. Or that was what I thought." He smiled, lifting a hand as if to touch Hugh's face, but he brushed it over his shoulder instead. "Did you miss me, Hugh?"

"Oh God, Charles, if only you knew how difficult these last three years have been. If only I had trusted you more."

"You weren't to know, any more than I was. I think we owe Sir Adam our grateful thanks. We might never have had the courage to confide in each other otherwise."

"Yes. Shall we return to why we came here? Talk about me and you later, somewhere more private?" Hugh's expression suggested perhaps he had something other than talking in mind.

"Yes, I think we had better," Charles agreed, his eyes raking Hugh in a most distracting fashion. "I want to touch you, and it is likely the door will open at the most inopportune moment with our lunch." Charles picked up the catalogue again and said, "Shall we?"

Charles had been right in that a couple of minutes later a footman arrived to open the door for the maid carrying the lunch tray. Hugh glanced at Charles and grinned. Hugh was surprised to discover just how hungry he was and they both quickly devoured the food, washing it down with the refreshing ale. Hugh kept glancing at Charles, not surprised that Charles seemed to find it just as difficult to stop looking in his direction too.

"Here we are," Charles said a few minutes later. "Familial Records, that has to be it. I suppose I will need to start something like this one day soon. My father already keeps one. It has become quite the family tradition." Charles did not sound too happy at the prospect.

"You don't like putting your thoughts down on paper?" Hugh asked.

"No, I like the privacy of my own thoughts," Charles replied, eminently serious for once. He looked at Hugh, and it was obvious which kind of thoughts and feelings Charles would never put on paper.

"Do you remember which journal?" Hugh asked quickly.

"Pardon?" Charles frowned.

"Which journal you read about the ghost in?"

"Afraid not. It was a dozen or so years ago. But we should be able to narrow it down. I'm pretty certain it was one from about a hundred and forty years ago or thereabouts, and they are shelved in date order. Over here."

Charles led the way to a narrow bookcase set between the two tall windows, the lower half of which was filled with leather bound books. Hugh looked over the volumes, most of them rather thin but there were a few of a sturdier size.

Studying the spines it was clear to Hugh that some members of the family had kept much more detailed journals than others. Some of them had multiple journals under one name, others merely one slim volume. Charles sat back on his haunches thinking, his teeth chewing his lower lip. Hugh stared at his mouth wishing he could be the one playing with Charles' lip. He forced himself to look away.

"I think it should be somewhere near here." Charles reached for a particular shelf, removing the end volume. Hugh noted it was rather thick and was marked 'Volume Two'.

"Whose journal is that? He seems to have been a garrulous gentleman," Hugh remarked.

Charles had been flipping through the pages, presumably trying to see if he recognised anything and he flipped back to the flyleaf. "His name was Robert Walsh. Hmm, that's strange; he's not a family member."

Hugh gasped and Charles looked at him in puzzlement. "That is the name of one of the three brothers who killed Adam and his Thomas," Hugh explained.

"Good grief! I do not understand why he should have journals here. As far as I'm aware the Walsh's had no connection with the family other than the marriage of Lady Maude. Well, marriages. As you said, she married Sir Adam's cousin, after Sir Adam died."

Hugh shook his head in confusion. "Let's read it and see if it helps clear things up."

CHAPTER FOUR

Charles flipped through the pages trying to get a feel of what Robert Walsh could possibly have written that warranted the book being kept in the Simmercy library. A word – a name – caught his eye, and he let the page fall open properly so both he and Hugh could read it.

"I wonder if allowing the rumour to spread was such a good idea," Robert had written. "When the stories first began to circulate there was nothing we could do to stop it, but we could perhaps have stifled it somewhat, but at first it was easier to keep silent, to protect ourselves. The latest version is even more scurrilous, suggesting that Adam Simmercy forced others to succumb to his evil desires."

"What date is this?" Hugh asked. Charles flipped back the page to see a date of the fifteenth of August in the year of our Lord Sixteen forty-one. "I would estimate that is probably a few years after the murders."

They continued to read a few pages where Robert described in detail the tales being spun around the death of Adam Simmercy. Everything imaginable, and some things beyond imagining were placed at his doorstep.

"Goodness," Charles said, "a lot of this wasn't in the pages I read. This is…"

"Outrageous," Hugh interjected. "You see this version? It says that Adam seduced his poor manservant and took away his innocence."

"And then in terrible remorse, the lad killed his master and then himself," Charles read over Hugh's shoulder.

"They didn't use the word but they didn't have to. If Adam were to see this it would break his heart. To be accused of raping the man he loved." Hugh shook his head in disbelief.

They turned their attention back to the beginning of the book in case that gave a clearer indication of what Robert's intention was in writing the volume, and why it was in the Simmercy library. The preface page pointed in the right direction. It stated that volume two was continuing the facts and fiction of the life and death of Sir Adam Simmercy, and that the two volumes should be read in conjunction.

"Find volume one," Hugh demanded.

Charles was already on his knees by the shelves searching for the first volume. "Where in damnation is it? It should be here."

Hugh was searching the shelves above. It had to be here somewhere, it had to. It could provide all the answers they needed. Surely the one volume they needed could not be missing.

"Here! Here it is," Charles cried.

Hugh dropped to his knees beside Charles and together they looked at the flyleaf. The writing was much neater than that in volume two, but the hand was unmistakeable.

Robert Walsh had written a kind of prologue, stating that he had begun his journal almost a year after the death of Sir Adam Simmercy. He explained that the subterfuge to explain away Sir Adam's death, and that of his valet, had not been accepted as readily as the Walsh's and Lady Maude had hoped. Before long, rumours were circulating and they were not to Sir Adam's detriment. Sir Adam had been a fair and popular master to those who had served him. There had never been a whisper of scandal about him or his treatment of his servants, and many found the story of his death difficult to believe. Now, there were whispers about the Walsh family, that it was only their word that defamed Sir Adam's reputation.

The Walsh brothers had come to the conclusion that they needed a way to take attention from them, and the increasing hysteria over the 'haunting' of the bedroom gave them the ammunition they needed. In the early days it seemed prudent to encourage the rumours. It worked, until the stories began to be more outrageous, only drawing more attention to the Hall and the family.

By this time Lady Maude was married to Sir Adam's cousin, Cecil, and they had a baby son. Lady Maude wanted her side of the story written down, clearly documenting her husband's foul behaviour, thereby protecting her son as the rightful heir.

Robert Walsh had begun his journal around this time, in part to keep a record of the various rumours thinking it easier that way for them to encourage or refute them; and in part to record the truth for the family.

"The truth," Hugh whispered. Turning to Charles, he said, "I wonder if he recorded the actual burial sites."

"No more guessing. It is either here or we will never know," Charles answered.

It was not long after they found the answer they were looking for, that Charles' mother sent word to remind them to get ready for dinner. Included in the message delivered by the footman was that she would take no excuses this time.

Reluctantly the search to confirm if Robert had been telling the truth would have to wait for the next day, but at least Hugh would have some news to impart to Adam that night.

Just as they were about to leave the library, Hugh said, "I have no doubt at all that Adam will be haunting the bedroom around midnight again."

"Has he been here while we've been searching?" Charles said, glancing around as if he half-expected to see something.

"No," Hugh said, "but he does seem aware of my emotions. I think he will know I wish to see him."

"I'm coming with you," Charles said.

Hugh glanced at him and said, "I hope you will come to see me before then."

"I had planned on it," Charles said with a grin. "Just hadn't quite worked out how to ask you."

They went their separate ways to get ready for dinner and spin a tale for Alicia.

Charles waited until he was sure his mother had retired for the night. Then he waited another half hour, just to be certain. His room was at the other end of the hall from the guest room Hugh was using, and Charles had to pass his parent's room to get to Hugh's. He knocked very carefully. The door opened immediately. Apparently Hugh had been waiting for him.

"I thought you'd never get here," Hugh whispered.

"Such enthusiasm." Charles smiled, adding, "It really is appreciated."

Without another word, Hugh pulled Charles close, his gaze flickering all over Charles' face.

"I want to kiss you, may I?" he asked softly.

"Oh, yes, please." Charles wondered if he ought to admit he had never kissed a man before. He had wanted to. He'd a most unnatural crush on a neighbour's groom a little over a year ago, but he had done no more than look and wonder. He had kissed girls, well one girl really. He had not been particularly impressed, but that had been before he'd seen the groom and had such thoughts about the lad that he had never entertained about the girl. The experience had also made him understand the attachment he had to his cousin, Hugh. Rather like being hit by the proverbial thunderbolt, he had understood why he missed Hugh so much, why he needed to see the man again. His feelings for Hugh were anything but cousinly. He was grateful that they were only cousins, twice removed.

His distracting thoughts came to a screeching halt when he felt Hugh's breath gusting over his face as Hugh closed the distance between them. Hugh hesitated a second before gently pressing his mouth against Charles'. Whatever Charles had expected it wasn't the cool softness, or the sensuous feel of another's tongue slipping inside as he opened his mouth when Hugh licked his lower lip.

Charles felt the grip on his upper arms tighten as Hugh held him closer and closer still until Charles could almost believe he was inside Hugh's skin. Feeling emboldened, Charles slipped his arms around Hugh's waist, his own erection growing as he Hugh pressed against his thigh. Hugh moved against him and

Charles gasped at the sensation that flooded his being. The kiss deepened as they explored each other, tasting all the hidden places inside, sliding over teeth and withdrawing to lick along lips.

Hugh broke the kiss, his breath coming in gasps as he dropped his head on Charles' shoulder.

"It has never been like that before," Hugh whispered.

"Before?" Charles murmured without thinking.

Hugh was shocked as he realized that Charles had never kissed a man before, the reaction quickly followed by joy that he was the first to ever claim those delicious lips.

"That makes me so happy," Hugh admitted.

"What does?" Charles asked, his face flushed, whether from his inadvertent confession or his response to the kiss, Hugh didn't know.

"That I was the first man to taste you. I am, aren't I?"

"Yes."

"I had not imagined that you were–"

"Don't say it!" Charles interrupted. "That word only fits a woman."

"Don't be ashamed of it, Charles. It is a gift I will cherish. Come here," Hugh said as he drew Charles back into his embrace. They kissed again, but this time there was more heat, more desperation and when they finally broke for air, Hugh took a step backwards.

Charles looked puzzled. "Hugh?"

"I want more, more than I think you are ready for."

"How can you say that? God, even I don't know what I'm ready for. But I want to find out, Hugh." Charles stepped forward to close the distance between them again. "Did you not feel me as we pressed together? I want to feel that again, but without clothes between us."

"God, Charles. I want that too." He reached out and caressed Charles' face. "What I want to do with you," Hugh sighed, "but, I don't want to start anything and have to stop because of Adam."

"I almost forgot," Charles said leaning into the caress. "I never truly thought this would happen you know. I hoped, I dreamed but I…"

"Hush. Let's go and let Adam find us. Then the rest of the night will be ours."

It was almost midnight as they walked to the haunted room. They walked near to each other, their hands brushing now and then. Charles opened the door and moved inside, waiting for Hugh to enter and as soon as he did Charles pushed him back against the door, closing it in the process.

"Just need a reminder," Charles whispered as he gave Hugh a quick kiss.

"You're insane," Hugh said but he rubbed up against Charles, before he moved away from him.

"Tease," Charles said, but he let Hugh go and went to sit down in one of the chairs. Hugh stood beside the bed and appeared to be listening.

"Is he here?" Charles asked.

"Not yet. He will come when he knows I have news for him."

"You have a lot of faith in him," Charles commented.

Hugh laughed. "He says it is faith well justified."

"He says? Adam is here?"

"Yes. Let me explain to him," Hugh said.

Charles watched fascinated as Hugh appeared to speak to thin air, except that the thin air apparently spoke back. It was obviously a two-way conversation. At the beginning Hugh was relaxed, smiling, but as he began to explain all they had discovered, it became clear that Adam became angry, then upset, and Hugh was vociferously trying to calm him down.

◈ ◈ ◈ ◈

"I was surprised at first when I saw you had brought that young fool with you, but perhaps I ought not to have been," Adam said.

"He is not a fool. He sometimes says things without thinking," Hugh replied. "And what do you mean, you ought to have known?"

"You were openly sympathetic to my relationship with Thomas. I did wonder if you shared our inclination but I did not think it was my place to ask. However, I watched you for a few minutes before I showed myself. And, besides, there is something different about you."

"Different?" Hugh queried, squashing his embarrassment at being seen kissing Charles.

"Yes. I do not know how to explain it, I just sense a new kind of peace surrounding you." Adam shrugged. "It matters not. I'm happy for you. Now do you have any news for me?"

"I do. We found some journals in the library, written by Robert Walsh."

Not surprisingly Adam was puzzled and listened in growing anger as Hugh explained the purpose of the journals. Hugh hadn't wanted to tell Adam some of the more salacious entries in the journal, but Adam was smart enough to know when Hugh was being evasive, and in the end Hugh told him everything. Adam was furious.

"The bastards! How could they let people believe I would treat him that way? Thomas of all people. If they were not already dead I would kill them with my bare hands!"

"Please, Adam, I know it hurts that such lies were told about you, but it is not all. You haven't let me finish. I also have good news for you."

Adam stopped pacing and stared at him. "You have found it?" he asked, disbelief in his voice.

"Yes. Robert Walsh also recorded an accurate account of your death, and he stated where both you and Thomas were really buried."

"They did bury him, thank the Lord."

"Yes. And a few days later the tree under which they buried him was struck by lightning. Stephen claimed it was a sign from Satan, that he marked his own."

"No!" Adam decried the assertion.

"Robert, however, had another opinion. He thought perhaps it was God, angry that they had dared to act as judge and executioner."

"Too late then for guilt," Adam said.

Hugh didn't think he had any right to comment on that. Instead he said, "Charles and I didn't have a chance to go and search today, we will go tomorrow."

"And you will bring him to me?"

"Yes. I'm not sure how we will accomplish that yet, but somehow we will."

"Then I am content. I trust my agony will soon be over."

Hugh bit his lip, he couldn't help but put the question. "Even if it means you are sent to Hell?"

"Even Hell would be a good place to be, if I am with Thomas," Adam replied.

CHAPTER FIVE

Charles slipped quietly into Hugh's room where he was greeted with a hug, which soon became a kiss, lingering and passionate.

"Oh, I've ached to do that," Hugh murmured as they finally broke apart. Hugh stared at him, the longing in his eyes unmistakable, making Charles' cheeks heat. "I want to see you, all of you."

"Oh, yes. I want to see you too. I want to touch you, all of you."

They began to undress each other, one piece at a time, hands exploring, caressing the skin as they touched it for the first time. Charles tentatively stretched out a hand to touch Hugh's nipple, fascinated by its warmth, and by the way it pebbled under his fingers. He lifted his eyes to see how it affected Hugh, only to find Hugh was staring at him. Obviously Hugh was enjoying watching him experiment. So, emboldened he tried something else – he licked the nipple, pleased when Hugh sucked in his breath.

"Let's take this to bed," Hugh whispered.

They lay on the bed facing each other, the only illumination coming from the moonlight as hands and lips explored new territory inch by inch. Hugh traced the shadows on Charles' chest, stopping to circle his nipples, making him moan. Hugh leaned in to capture Charles' lips and Charles held on tight, revelling in Hugh's power as he forced Charles's mouth open to taste every crevice.

Charles had imagined what it would be like to be with Hugh, but his imaginings didn't come close to the sensations flooding his body.

But then Hugh took Charles' cock in his hand and Charles knew it was only the beginning. It was his turn to suck in his breath and he gasped, "Oh God, that feels…"

"And what about this?" Hugh asked as he swirled his hand around Charles' length, moving his fingers from tip to base.

Charles gingerly attempted to reciprocate, his fingers ghosting over Hugh's cock. It was a little longer than his own, but not as thick, he thought. Charles took a firmer grip and Hugh shuddered. "That's it," Hugh muttered.

Then releasing Charles, Hugh rolled on top of him, pressing him down into the mattress. Charles gasped at the sensation of being held down, surprised by how good it made him feel. He grabbed onto Hugh as he rode out the unbelievable sensations of Hugh's body gliding over him, their cocks rubbing against each other, and all the time Hugh kissed whatever skin he could reach.

Abruptly Hugh rolled them so they were facing each other again. He ran his hand up and down Charles back, his fingers making patterns as they slid lower and lower until they brushed across the crease of his ass. Charles shivered at the amazing sensation. His cock leapt in Hugh's hand, and Hugh laughed, his eyes sparkling with joy.

Dipping his head, Hugh kissed Charles passionately and Charles held on, promising himself never to let go. He knew without a doubt that he loved Hugh, and had for longer than even he had realized.

Releasing his mouth, Hugh pushed him onto his back again, placing a hand either side of his head, staring intently into his eyes. Lowering his weight again, Hugh kissed Charles' neck as he undulated against him. Charles was writhing below Hugh now, lifting his hips in counterpoint to Hugh's movement, determined to experience all the new sensations overwhelming him. He knew he was close, he felt his climax gathering low in his belly. He had never wanted to come so much in his life, and yet he never wanted this to end.

Lifting Hugh's head from his neck, Charles took his mouth in a ravishing kiss, releasing him to nip and lick wherever he could reach, all the time lifting his hips in rhythm with Hugh's movements. Their cocks slid alongside each other, creating sparks of fire that seemed to leap from one to the other causing them to gasp and moan as their need increased.

Hugh captured one of Charles' nipples between his teeth, nibbling at the hardening nub, making Charles squirm and moan as the sensation travelled directly from his nipple to his groin. Smiling, Hugh slid his hand between their writhing bodies to grasp their cocks together in one hand. Gripping them firmly but not too tightly, Hugh worked his hand up and down, twisting a little and squeezing as he reached the heads.

Charles was gasping as he held tightly on to Hugh. "Oh God, I can't…"

"Spend for me, Charles," Hugh whispered and Charles buried his head against Hugh's neck, whimpering and shivering as his orgasm raced through him, his hot semen splashing between them.

As if that was all Hugh had been waiting for, he climaxed too, murmuring Charles' name as his seed joined that of his lover.

Hugh collapsed onto Charles, both men gasping for breath and as soon as his senses returned Charles rolled them on to their sides.

"Stay for a time?" Hugh asked softly.

"I don't want to leave you," Charles murmured, kissing Hugh and holding on tight. "Not yet." Charles wanted to say more, but knew it wasn't the right time.

Charles forced himself to stop looking at Hugh over the breakfast table. He knew he had a silly grin on his face whenever he did, and if his mother saw it she would almost certainly ask him what was so funny. He could never tell her it was not amusement that made him smile, simply the memory of the most exhilarating experience of his life, given to him by the man that he now acknowledged he loved.

He hadn't had the nerve to tell Hugh that fact yet. Though he knew that Hugh cared for him, he was not sure if the man actually loved him, and he did not have the courage to ask him.

That thought caused him to look across the table at Hugh only to find that Hugh was watching him, and as their eyes met, they smiled at each other. Charles quickly turned his attention to his breakfast plate, relieved that at that moment his mother was relaying a message to the cook via the footman. Apparently the eggs were not cooked to her satisfaction.

"You find my dissatisfaction with the eggs amusing, Charles?" she asked suddenly.

"No, mother. What I found amusing was poor Norton's face. I doubt he really wants to tell Mrs Brookes how to cook eggs."

"One would think the woman would know by now," Alicia said irritably.

"They are far more palatable than I am used to," Hugh interjected.

At the moment the sound of a carriage coming to a halt outside could be heard. "Who could that be?" Alicia wondered.

Charles got to his feet and went to the window overlooking the front entrance. "It's father."

"William? Well, that is a nice surprise," Alicia said. "I was not expecting him until tomorrow at the earliest. He said he would try and come home on Friday afternoon so he could spend the weekend with us."

Charles glanced at Hugh. They would have to talk.

As the horses moved slowly across the park, Hugh moved his mount closer. "I know you've been waiting to talk to me. I saw the concern in your eyes when your father arrived."

"He would be furious if he were to find out what you were up to, and that I was helping you. He would never understand, he would just think we were being disruptive. You know how proud he is of the family history, and he has absolutely no patience for the 'ridiculous' stories about the haunting of the Hall."

"Would it really matter? Once we find Thomas' body and take it to the vegetable garden, it will be over. He need never know."

"You think it will be that easy? We have to *find* the body first, then dig it up and take it back to the vegetable garden – right beside the house – all without being seen. But, don't forget we also have to find Adam's grave so we can re-bury Thomas with him? I'm right, aren't I?"

"Yes," Hugh sighed. He tried to think it would be a simple task. One plus two equals three; but he was only fooling himself. He was reasonably certain they could find Thomas' grave. Robert had been surprisingly detailed in describing the place where they had buried Thomas. Adam himself had roughly described where he was buried, but reuniting them in the vegetable garden would prove a lot more difficult than the simple words suggested. Hugh had always been rather in awe of Cousin William and the three years distance had not lessened his reaction.

"We can't let my father find out."

Hugh frowned at the tone of Charles' voice. He didn't sound afraid, just very determined. "What aren't you telling me, Charles?"

"Nothing, nothing," Charles said.

"You never could lie to me, Charles," Hugh said. "Tell me."

Charles smiled, "I should have known better."

"You should. Stop prevaricating."

"You remember last night, when we talked and I said I could not bear the thought of you leaving next week, not knowing when I might see you again?" Charles asked and Hugh nodded. "I couldn't sleep. I watched you. You had such a contented look on your face, and I wanted to always see you look like that, lying beside me. I know that cannot be, no matter how careful we are, but I thought perhaps it might be possible sometime. Not if you were so far away in the city, but if you were closer. Always closer."

"I don't understand. What are you trying to say, and what has this to do with your father?"

"I had not meant to speak of this yet, not until I…we…" Charles stopped, took a deep breath. "I wanted to try and find a way to keep you by my side. Here. Do not say anything," Charles said quickly. "I know this is all too soon. I never would have mentioned it if it hadn't been for my father's arrival. What I am trying to say is that we have to keep on my father's good side."

Hugh had listened to Charles in growing confusion. He had been overjoyed that Charles felt enough for him to want to find a way for Hugh to stay at the Hall. Not that he could see a way of that happening. After all, he was the sole support of his mother since his father had died, and though he hated the work he did in London he had no choice, but still he did not understand why Charles was so worried about his father.

Charles continued, "If my father knew what we were trying to do, he would forbid it. He would most likely send you home, thinking you are weak-minded or maybe just a troublemaker. Lord, Hugh, he could even forbid you ever visiting the Hall again. I cannot risk that, Hugh, I cannot. I know all my ideas, my hopes for the future, must seem impossible dreams, but please tell me you understand." Charles held his gaze as he said to Hugh, "Tell me my dreams are not so impossible."

"I do not know if the dreams are impossible, Charles, though I wish they could come true as much as you do." Hugh did not like to burst Charles' bubble but it would only hurt more in the long run. "But, Charles, I think you have your priorities confused. You are worrying about your father's reaction to my believing in ghost stories. Do you not think you should instead worry about what his reaction would be if he ever found out about our… liaison? People will accept us being close as cousins, even as best friends, but anything else?"

"You mean he might kill us, like his antecedents did?" Charles was horrified.

"Nothing so personally violent," Hugh said. "All he, or anyone else, would have to do was publicize our disgrace, and we would be taken up and mostly likely hanged."

"God, I am a fool!" Charles said. He was silent for a moment before he turned to Hugh to ask quietly, "Am I worth such a risk to you? Perhaps it should end now before it's too late."

"It has been too late for me for a long time," Hugh replied. "Do you know how long I have been in love with you?"

"Love? You love me? Truly? I wanted to tell you last night how I felt about you, but I was afraid."

"Afraid of what? Of what you were feeling?"

"I think I was afraid that it was too soon to tell you I loved you." Charles' eyes opened wide as he realized what he had said.

Grinning, Hugh said, "Thank you, I needed to hear that. It wasn't so scary, was it?"

"Terrifying," Charles grinned back. "It's probably a good thing we are riding, or I would probably have you in my arms about now."

"Keep that in mind for another time and place," Hugh said, and Charles nodded, taking a deep breath as if to get control of his feelings.

Glancing back toward the house in the distance, Hugh said, "I think perhaps we should think about why we came out here."

"You're right. So, we need to find an oak tree which has been struck by lightning in the woods east of the lake."

They broke into a canter and rode for the woods.

"Shall we split up? It will probably be quicker to find the spot that way," Charles queried.

"Maybe, but I prefer we stay together. Don't ask me to explain, it is just a feeling I have."

CHAPTER SIX

"Damn, but you would think it would be simple to find a tree that had been blasted by lightning," Charles complained.

They had been searching for almost an hour, and hadn't found anything that looked the way Robert had described.

"It's been over a hundred and fifty years since it happened," Hugh said. "Living things heal, trees too. After all this time the damage would not be so obvious, especially with the amount of growth that will have taken place. We will just have to be methodical so we don't miss it."

They were getting nearer to the lake which Charles didn't think seemed right, and meaning to say so, he glanced over to Hugh – and froze.

"Oh my Lord!" he breathed.

"What is it?" Hugh said, turning to follow Charles' gaze.

"It never occurred to me," Charles said, as much to himself as to Hugh. "The old oak. It was just about my favourite place to play as a child when we came to visit grandfather. I often thought it could have been created just for a boy to clamber all over. You see the way that side of the tree grows almost horizontal? Now, of course, I understand. It was made that way when the lightning blasted the tree so many years earlier." Charles ran his hand over one of the thick branches running almost parallel to the ground. "I played over Thomas' grave and never even knew it," he added in a much more serious tone.

"No reason you should," Hugh told him. "Any more than I think I would have ever have known this tree had been struck by lightning. Time and the clinging ivy have all but covered up any evidence of damage."

They had not wanted to risk carrying a spade; it could easily have caused questions they didn't want to answer. Charles had been able to secret a couple of garden trowels into his saddlebags and they each took one as they began to search for any signs of Thomas' grave. Other than describing the tree, Robert had only said that the body was buried among the roots of the huge tree on the opposite side of the tree from the lake. The tree was even larger now, the canopy of the oak covered a large area, shading the ground beneath for quite a distance. Also, other old tree growth encroached on the area, so most of the earth was only covered in low ground cover. Robert had also written that the body had not been given a proper burial in that it had not been planted anywhere near six feet deep.

"Shouldn't say this, I know," Hugh commented, "but their disrespect will probably make our job easier."

"True," Charles agreed. Unfortunately, that did not prove quite true. It had taken them so long to find the tree that they had little time left for searching. They couldn't find the burial site that day, the failing light warning them when the time came to return home for dinner.

Hugh felt unsettled during dinner, the situation not being helped by his host. William seemed to be concentrating his attention on Hugh and seeing as Hugh's mind was a hundred and fifty years in the past, or across the park by a blasted oak tree, he was having difficulty paying attention.

"Are you unwell, Hugh?" William suddenly queried.

"Er, no, sir, not unwell. A little distracted, I confess. Charles had been an excellent guide, showing me your estate, Cousin William. I had no idea until I arrived how large the estate was."

"Indeed, and where did you explore today?" William asked.

It was entirely possible, probable even, that Hugh was seeing more than was actually there, but it seemed to him that William was being particularly probing. It bothered him. "We rode across the park to the woods bordering the east end of the lake, and then circled the lake and returned from the west." It seemed best to stick to the truth as far as possible.

"You were gone for quite a long time even so," William said; an unspoken question evident from his tone and his expression.

"We took a dip in the lake too, father. Hugh didn't believe me that the water is surprisingly warm."

Hugh laughed, taking the lead Charles had provided. "I suppose it all depends on one's definition of warm. I still found it too cool for comfort."

"Really, Charles, you are no longer a child to indulge yourself so."

"Mother, Hugh and I have been indulging ourselves since we were youngsters."

"That maybe so, Charles," Alicia said, "but you are no longer children, and such antics are not in keeping with your position."

"As you wish, mother," Charles said, but there was a twinkle in his eye as he looked at Hugh and Hugh wished they had indeed been swimming in the lake. He would have liked to see Charles with water sliding over his smooth skin. He closed his eyes for a moment trying to banish the gratuitous thought. He failed.

They left the house the next morning as soon as feasible without arousing any suspicion. At one point, Charles had feared that his father might volunteer to join them on their ride but William demurred, saying he had not slept well the night before and planned to have a quiet day.

They rode directly to the blasted oak and continued their search from where they had left off the day before. Charles complained about the lack of a spade, bemoaning the fact that he did not have the nerve to tell his father the truth.

"It doesn't matter, Charles, we'll manage, and you know this is a safer course."

"I know. It's just… frustrating!"

"Stop complaining and dig!" Hugh demanded.

It was Charles who, fifteen minutes later, exclaimed, "I've found something!"

Hugh hurried over from where he had been digging, a mixture of disquiet and exhilaration filling him. "What, what is it?"

"Well, I'm not positive, you understand," Charles prevaricated, "but my trowel hit something hard but it wasn't a rock." He continued to dig and scrape away the dirt as he spoke.

"It's him," Hugh murmured as a sense of rightness filled him.

"Look," Charles said, pulling out a scrap of dirty material.

Hugh began to dig too, and it was not very long before they were pulling out more, larger, scraps of decaying material. "I think it might have been the sheet they wrapped him in," Hugh said quietly. He dropped his trowel and began to dig with his bare hands, Charles immediately copying him.

Clawing dirt aside they uncovered Thomas' remains. There was nothing more than bones covered in scraps of what must have been his clothes, with the remnants of the sheet disintegrating even as they tried to pull it away. Staring at the pitiful remains of what had once been a young man full of life and love strongly affected Hugh. He looked at Charles to see he was as disturbed. At first unable to take their eyes from the corpse, they soon found themselves unable to tear their gaze from each other. They were as guilty – and as innocent – as the victim they had unearthed.

"Now we have found him, what are we going to do with him?" Charles suddenly asked.

"Get him to the vegetable garden," Hugh answered, frowning.

"I know," Charles said, "but how exactly?"

"I brought the coverlet from my bed, we can wrap him in that," Hugh said. "I will lay him in front of me across my horse–" Hugh stopped as he realized what Charles meant. "Damn, I can't just ride to the vegetable garden and..." He looked at Charles, hoping for inspiration. He knew the Hall an awful lot better than Hugh did.

"Right, let me think."

Charles' teeth gnawed at his lower lip as he pondered and Hugh had the ungodly desire to nibble the exact same spot.

A slow smile spread over Charles' face. "I think I have it. It will mean leaving Thomas' body on the wrong side of the vegetable garden wall for a time but I think it is the only way. This time we really will circle the lake and, coming back to the house from that side, we would have to pass the vegetable garden wall to get to the stables, so if we were seen riding in that way it would be perfectly normal. You drape your cloak across the front of your horse disguising the body, and then when we are hidden from the house and the stables by the garden wall, we can hide the body at the base of the wall. Then tonight, we can get the body, bring it inside through the side gate, and bury it with Adam."

"That should work," Hugh said thoughtfully. "We just have to be sure where Adam is buried, we can't go digging around the vegetable garden in the dark, it will be difficult enough re-burying Thomas. After dinner, you're going to show me around the vegetable garden. I have absolutely adored the home grown vegetables Mrs Brookes has served up," Hugh grinned.

"Father will think I've gone soft," Charles groaned.

"You are a good host, and a better cousin," Hugh stated. His voice lowered, "Not to mention the love of my life."

"Hugh," Charles breathed, a flush colouring his face, his eyes wide and full of joy. "Perhaps you can show me later."

Keeping any further thoughts internal, they prepared to wrap the body in the cloth that Hugh had brought. They laid it out beside the makeshift grave, then carefully lifted the remains and laid them on the cloth, wrapping it around the body and tucking the ends in securely so it would not come loose as Hugh rode back to the house.

Hugh was in the process of changing for dinner when Adam appeared in his room. It was the first time Adam had done so, and Hugh was taken aback.

"Tell me," Adam demanded the instant he appeared, seeming irritated at Hugh's discomfort.

"Something happened, I can sense it. Thomas? You found him?"

Hugh finished dressing as he said, "We did. We found his body by the blasted oak just as Robert had written."

Adam's appearance instantly changed, he became infinitely more insubstantial and for a second Hugh thought he was leaving, but slowly he reconstituted until he looked solid again. When he spoke his voice was so low Hugh could hardly hear him. "I prayed you would find him, but I had no cause to expect God would answer me."

"We brought him as far as we dare during daylight hours. We hope to—"

"He is here?" Adam interrupted, his form suffused with a soft glow that Hugh had never seen before.

"Yes, and no. We hid his body on the other side of the vegetable garden wall. We intended to bring his body inside tonight, but first we need to know the exact location of your grave."

"Tonight," Adam said softly. "Perhaps it will all be over tonight." He walked to the window and looked up at the lowering sky. Abruptly he turned to Hugh. "Did you see anything? Sense anything, anything at all?"

Hugh frowned, unsure what to say. How to say it. "I'm not certain," he admitted. "Look we'll have to talk about this later. I have to go downstairs. Can you show us where your grave is? It would be a lot easier and less difficult to explain than if we were seen digging up bits of the garden."

"Now?" Adam asked, clearly distracted by his own thoughts.

"No, we have to attend the family dinner now. Later, Charles and I will go out to the garden, meet us there then."

Without another word, Adam vanished. Hugh looked at the spot he had occupied moments ago, and wondered if everything was going to go terribly wrong at the last moment.

CHAPTER SEVEN

Dinner was less of a drawn out affair that evening, and Hugh's laboured attempts to praise the vegetables served at table to give them an excuse to visit the vegetable garden proved unnecessary. It transpired that cousin William had arranged to go out for the evening immediately after the meal was finished to play cards with a friend and neighbour. Alicia was accompanying him to spend some time in the company of the man's wife, a lady friend whom Alicia saw all too infrequently.

"Well, that was a lot easier than I expected," Charles said as he and Hugh stood on the steps waving as his parents' coach drove off.

"Indeed," Hugh smiled. "Finding the grave should be considerably easier too. Adam visited my room earlier and has agreed to meet us in the vegetable garden to show the precise location of his gravesite."

"In your room?" Charles frowned. "He has never been there before, has he?"

"No, and once was enough, particularly as I was dressing at the time."

"And here I thought only I was treated to that vision," Charles said.

"You are; he wasn't invited. You have a standing invitation."

"Come, let's get this done with," Charles said tugging at Hugh's sleeve and Hugh laughed at his sudden enthusiasm.

Charles walked around the vegetable garden with Hugh, ostensibly pointing things out to him, just in case anyone was watching from the windows.

"The light is beginning to fade," Hugh commented, "We should be able to bring Thomas inside shortly.

"Now would be a good time for Adam to appear so he can show you where he is buried."

"Perhaps he is waiting until Thomas is here. He knew something had occurred today, but not what," Hugh explained.

Adam appeared behind Charles and said to Hugh without preamble, "It's over here."

"Come on, Charles, this way."

"He's here?"

"Yes. He says the grave is over here."

Adam led them to the greenhouse on the far side of the garden, parallel to the outer wall, walking to the end farthest from the house. He stopped at a point about half way along the short side. "You will find me in there," he said dispassionately.

"Where are the tools stored?" Hugh asked turning back to Charles but he wasn't there. Hugh saw him hurrying towards them carrying a spade. "Good thinking," Hugh said with a smile.

"You want to start there," he added, pointing to the spot Adam had shown him.

"Sneaky," Charles retorted, but he began to dig, being careful not to be too rough.

"I'm going to recover Thomas," Hugh said, speaking as much to Adam as to Charles. He hurried away, the need to bring this to a close suddenly urgent. The body was precisely where they had hidden it, in the long undergrowth at the base of the wall. Hugh picked up the wrapped form and carefully carried it back to the gate and inside the garden.

Adam met him at the gate, staring at the wrapped form. "Thomas," he whispered. Eyes never leaving Hugh's burden, Adam walked alongside Hugh as he took the body to Adam's graveside.

"I asked you before," Adam said, "if you had seen or felt anything when you found the body and you seemed reluctant to tell me. Please, I need to know."

Hugh nodded. "I know." He took a breath. "Charles found the grave first and when I walked towards it I felt unaccountably sad. My own emotions I thought at first, then almost at the same time I felt a flash of anger that surged into what I can only describe as rage. But it disappeared as quickly as it had come, and I still can't be certain if I didn't just imagine it. I never saw or heard anything. We had spent hours searching for the grave and I..." Hugh didn't know what to say. He had no right to tell Adam how difficult that was.

They had by now reached the burial place to find that Charles had uncovered the remains inside the shallow grave. Hugh laid Thomas down alongside the grave and unwrapped him, glancing up at Adam as he did so.

"It is so hard to see him like that. He was so beautiful." Adam turned away from the decaying remains. "He's not here, Hugh. I hoped..." Adam paused, sighed and turned back to Hugh. "My greatest fear is that Thomas blamed me for his untimely death, that he regretted the relationship we shared. I was smitten almost the moment I saw him and I ...enticed him I think would be a fair description. All I brought to him was pain and destruction."

"No," a hoarse voice spoke but there was no one else to be seen except Hugh, Charles and the ghost of Adam. "I never blamed you, and I never, ever, regretted what we shared. You brought me love and happiness, Adam. *They* brought me pain and destruction. For no more than the crime of loving you they tore me from you, destroyed me and left me alone, not even knowing for certain what had happened to you. I spent many lonely years imagining all kinds of terrible things being done to you. And, as if that was not enough, I was so afraid I would be trapped for eternity in the roots of that tree under which they buried me, forever kept from the only chance of peace I would ever know. With you." As the final words were spoken, Thomas took form, ethereal and insubstantial.

"Oh God, Thomas," Adam declared, reaching for him but afraid to touch. "I was so afraid you would have passed on long ago without me. Is it evil of me to be grateful you are still here? It was my fault your spirit was trapped with your body. I was so angry when they... when they murdered you, gloating that you would suffer all the torments of Hell, that I invoked God's name and cursed the brothers to Hell, saying you and I would be waiting for them and would watch them suffer. I swore you would be by my side. Forgive me, Thomas." Adam was barely holding back his tears.

"There is nothing to forgive. I would have joined you in that curse if I had been able. I would join you anywhere in life or death, do you not know that? Heaven would be as Hell to me if you were not there with me." Thomas' hand reached for Adam and it was now more substantial.

Hugh could see that Adam could feel the caress as he leaned into the touch. Charles leaned closer and asked Hugh to tell him what was happening and Hugh explained as quickly as he could.

Thomas turned to Hugh, giving him a bow. "I cannot tell you how grateful I am to you, and your friend, for the service you have given to Sir Adam and myself. It is a debt we will never be able to repay."

"There is no debt, Thomas. My – our – reward is in knowing you two are reunited, at least in spirit."

"Should we not finish the job?" Charles interjected; only aware of Hugh's portion of the conversation taking place.

"Charles is right," Hugh agreed. "We need to finish burying you together as you requested, Adam."

"Burying us together," Thomas said. "A nice gesture, Adam."

Thomas stood closer to Adam and Adam took the younger man in his arms. "More than just a gesture, Thomas. I believe it will cause our final release, though whether to Heaven or Hell, I cannot say. Do you want us to be buried together? Even if it is likely to invoke my curse?"

"It could be no more of a curse than what I have suffered since my death. All I want is for us to be together. Bury me with you. If we stay here we can haunt the family together, or perhaps we'll be sent to Hell to haunt the brothers there," Thomas said with a cold smile. "But, maybe, just maybe, God knows better than man gives him credit for, and will take us up into Heaven."

Adam smiled, "I do not know how I earned your trust, but I'll always be grateful for it." He glanced at Hugh, "Yes, Hugh, bury him beside me, where he belongs."

"What's going on Hugh?" Charles queried.

"Come on," Hugh said, "let's finish burying Thomas in Adam's grave."

It was odd burying a body while its ghost stood at the head of the grave and watched. Hugh wished at that moment he could be as oblivious as Charles to the presence of the ghosts. That was until he happened to glance up and catch a look passing between the two spirits, a look of such contentment and peace that he was glad to have seen it.

With Charles' diligent help it did not take long before the two men were throwing the last of the dirt back onto the grave, and Hugh gave a final pat with the back of the spade on the burial site.

Hugh glanced at Charles who said quietly, "What next?" but Hugh shrugged and turned to look at the ghost couple. Adam and Thomas were looking at each apparently as confused and uncertain as Hugh and Charles were. Abruptly Adam tensed and reached out to grip Thomas' hand.

"Something is happening," Adam declared sharply. "I feel strange, as if …as if…"

"I feel it too," Thomas agreed, "As if I were being stretched, pulled…"

Hugh watched not knowing if he should be alarmed, or rejoicing for them.

"Don't let go, Thomas," Adam cried.

From Hugh's point of view Adam's voice was fading, even as the ghostly forms of both men were becoming more and more insubstantial. "Lord, it's happening, Charles," he breathed. Even as he spoke Adam and Thomas disappeared from his sight. Next, as if from a long way away Adam's voice drifted toward Hugh, "Thank you, Hugh, for everything."

Then there was only silence and a warm breeze arose, wafting around Hugh ruffling his hair and lightly brushing his cheek before dropping as swiftly as it had arisen.

"Did you feel that?" he asked Charles bemused.

"Feel what?" Charles queried.

CHAPTER EIGHT

"Please Hugh, I'm feeling really left out of things here. Hearing one side of the conversation can be confusing, you know. What exactly happened?"

"Oh, I'm sorry, Charles, it's difficult to remember on occasion that you're unaware of all that is taking place." Hugh explained precisely what he had seen and heard happen to Adam and Thomas.

"So, it really is finally over," Charles said with a relieved smile. "I do hope they received what they deserved, what they hoped for."

"That's the worse part," Hugh confessed, "not knowing what's happened to them now. I can only hope that Thomas was right and that God judged them more fairly than man did."

"We have to let go now, Hugh. It will only trouble you if you don't put it behind you." Charles took Hugh's hands in his and to emphasise his point, he added, "I'm in need of your help now, Hugh."

"Oh yes?" Hugh asked with a twinkle in his eye.

Charles was pleased to have redirected Hugh's thoughts. "Indeed, I require reassurance and comfort. In short, I need you, *now.*"

"I have washing facilities in my room," Hugh said, tightening his own hold on Charles' hands. "You are very welcome to share with me," he added enticingly.

Looking at their grubby hands, Charles grinned as he said, "Just the washing facilities?"

Hugh stripped down and washed himself, vitally aware that Charles was watching him as Charles slowly divested his own attire. When he had finished, instead of reaching for a towel, Hugh turned to Charles and said, "Come here."

Charles raised an eyebrow but stepped closer.

"Nearer," Hugh encouraged. "I want to wash you," he added, making sure that his lascivious intent was clear, and Charles sucked in a breath obviously aroused at the thought.

Hugh first washed Charles' hands before slowly passing the wet cloth up Charles' right arm and across the front of his chest, then down his left arm. Hugh's eyes never left Charles' face as he continued to work the cloth over his chest and belly. Hugh was fascinated by the narrowing of Charles' eyes and the tension of his mouth as he reacted to the sensations created by the movements of the damp cloth as it caressed his body. Finally, when Hugh reached his privates, Charles' eyes closed and his head tipped back.

"That's it, Charles," Hugh whispered. "Feel it, feel everything and know I love you. Every caress, every kiss is a testament to how much I love you."

"Oh, God, Hugh. What you do to me."

"I want to do so much more, if you will let me," Hugh murmured. "I want to join my body to yours."

"The way our hearts are joined?"

Putting a hand either side of Charles' face, Hugh pulled him in close and took his mouth. Charles immediately opened up to let him in, to share a lingering kiss. When they separated, Charles led Hugh over to the bed. Standing with his back to the bed, facing Hugh, Charles said, "Take my body, Hugh. Then we will be joined body, heart and soul."

If Hugh wasn't already head over heels in love with Charles, he would have fallen for him in that moment. Holding him tightly, Hugh kissed him again and felt Charles' heart pounding in his chest, echoing the racing of Hugh's own heart.

Pressing Charles back to lie on the bed, Hugh joined him immediately, never losing contact. They caressed each other, their kisses constant, lingering and passionate. Rolling over and lying half across Charles, Hugh ran his fingers over Charles' chest. Charles pulled his head down for a kiss, one hand caressing the nape of Hugh's neck, the other drifting down Hugh's spine.

Breaking the kiss, Hugh slid down Charles' body, licking and kissing his way, playing with his nipples for few moments, teasing the hard nubs, until Charles was squirming and panting.

Settling comfortably between Charles' legs, Hugh licked around Charles' navel, plunging his tongue in and out, swirling it around again.

"You are a tease!" Charles protested.

"Oh, you have no idea," Hugh grinned, his hands caressing Charles' flanks while his tongue continued to taste his body. Finally reaching his goal, Hugh licked the rosy tip of Charles' cock and he had to hold Charles down as his lover almost arched from the bed. "Easy," Hugh murmured. Eyes watching Charles' reaction, Hugh licked him again, this time along the underside of his length.

Charles was incapable of speech now, murmuring nonsense as he tossed his head on the pillow.

Hugh licked the white pearls of pre-come from Charles' cock before he surged up quickly and kissed Charles, wanting to let his lover have a little taste of himself. Eyes widening at the unexpected taste, Charles moaned low in his throat, the sound travelling straight to Hugh's groin, and he wanted Charles more than ever. Breaking the kiss with a final nip to Charles's lower lip, Hugh slipped down again and swallowed Charles whole.

"Hugh! Hugh, oh my, oh God!" Charles cried, his hands blindly searching for his lover.

Hugh slipped a hand behind Charles' balls teasing his virgin hole as he sucked and licked at his cock, feeling its hard length shudder against his tongue as he pressed one finger against Charles' opening. Keeping one hand firmly on Charles' hip, Hugh pulled back, almost releasing him before suddenly swallowing him whole again. Working his tongue firmly along the length, Hugh sucked, feeling the quivers run through Charles' body and knowing he was very close now.

Charles curled up, hands gripping Hugh's hair tightly, gasping as he climaxed and poured himself down his lover's throat. Hugh swallowed every drop, finally releasing Charles with a final lick to the tip.

Charles lay panting as he recovered, opening his eyes to see Hugh lying alongside him, watching, with one hand still lying gently on Charles' hip. He also felt something rather hard digging into him and glanced down to see Hugh's erection. Charles rolled over slightly to face him, smiling as he leaned in to kiss him. Charles sought out Hugh's cock and gently caressed him.

Hugh sucked his breath in and put his hand over Charles' stilling him. "Thank you for the thought, but if you keep doing that I will come too soon. I want to be inside you when I do that."

Smiling, Charles asked, "Then what must I do?"

"Simply let me make you ready first. You trust me?" Hugh asked.

"Of course." That did not mean he wasn't nervous at what was to happen, but neither did it mean he didn't want it to happen. He trusted Hugh in all things.

"I know you are new to this," Hugh began as he gently urged Charles to roll over, "Let me–"

"I need to see your face," Charles quickly interrupted.

Hugh smiled, "It isn't the easiest way, but I want to watch you too." Hugh reached for the small dresser by the bed and took a small bottle of oil from the top drawer. He removed the stopper and dribbled a little over his fingers, glancing up as if he sensed Charles watching him. "Roll on your front while I get you ready."

Charles settled himself comfortably, his face resting on his folded arms so he could watch. Hugh knelt between his spread legs and began to circle his opening. Charles gave himself over to the unusual sensations, hissing in surprise when Hugh slipped a finger inside. Charles forced himself to relax as Hugh continued to stretch him, getting him ready to accept a second finger.

"How does that feel?" Hugh asked.

"Surprisingly good," Charles replied.

"Just wait," Hugh said and something in his tone made Charles open eyes he hadn't realized he had closed. Suddenly a jolt of pleasure shot through Charles and he bucked.

"What...?" Charles floundered.

"More?" Hugh asked, a pleased smile gracing his features.

"Yes, yes." He had hardly got the words out when Hugh touched him inside again and Charles gasped, "Hugh!"

"I think you're about ready," Hugh said grinning.

When Hugh removed his fingers, Charles immediately missed the warmth and rolled onto his back, watching as Hugh oiled himself.

"Ready?" Hugh asked as he moved himself forward. When Charles nodded, Hugh pulled Charles' legs over his thighs and positioned himself to enter. Hugh watched as Charles took a calming breath, then Hugh pushed himself slowly inside, an inch at a time, carefully watching Charles' face.

When he was all the way in, his balls touching Charles' ass, Hugh waited for a moment, allowing Charles to adjust to yet another new sensation. Then he slowly pulled out before thrusting back inside.

He began a slow steady rhythm, building with each stroke until Charles murmured, "I never expected it to... More, Hugh, more."

Hugh lifted Charles' legs over his shoulders so he could achieve a better angle, then he increased the pace, searching out the perfect spot over and over. He wanted to give Charles the most ecstatic experience of his life. Charles' mutterings were unintelligible now except for when Hugh heard his name. Each time Charles called his name, Hugh thrust harder until he was pounding so deep that he was pushing the young man up the bed with each thrust. Hugh felt he could touch Charles' heart and soul.

Feeling his orgasm begin in his toes, it raced up Hugh's legs into his groin to explode inside the man who had come to mean everything to him. He felt Charles' muscles tense around him, holding him tight inside as his cock pulsed and he threw back his head, crying out his lover's name as he came.

Charles had never felt such all encompassing sensations before. Everything was intensified, each feeling was multiplied by the knowledge of the deep love Hugh had for him. He felt as if tendrils of fire were leaping along his nerves beginning deep inside and spreading throughout his body.

Charles heard Hugh cry out his name with such passion that it brought tears to his eyes and he was waiting to catch Hugh when he finally collapsed onto him, sliding out of his body as he did so. Feeling the loss of Hugh from inside him, Charles held Hugh tightly in his arms, murmuring words of love and need into his ear.

After a few moments, Hugh whispered, "I love you too."

Charles squirmed back against Hugh, making himself more comfortable. He liked the feel of Hugh's heart beating against his back. He tightened his grip on Hugh's arms which were wrapped around him. He couldn't remember ever feeling so comfortable, relaxed – and whole.

"I can't stop thinking about Adam and Thomas," Hugh commented in a low voice interrupting Charles' drifting thoughts.

"Hmmm," Charles murmured. "You can let go now, Hugh, they're finally at peace."

"Are they? That's what I can't stop wondering. Does it make you afraid, Charles that perhaps they are in Hell?"

"Make me afraid?" Charles queried, disturbed by the turn the conversation was taking. "What do you mean?" he added, as he rolled over to face his lover.

Hugh caressed his face, smiling gently as he asked, "I'm asking if you are afraid that we are consigning ourselves to damnation."

Charles placed his hand over Hugh's on his face, stilling the movement. He turned into the hand and kissed Hugh's palm, before turning his cheek to rest against the warm skin again. "I cannot deny that the thought has occurred, but neither can I deny the love I feel for you. It feels so good, so perfect, that I cannot reconcile my emotions with the evil that men assign to it." Charles dropped his eyes and stared at their entwined legs, smiling at how close they were, how right it felt. Looking up at Hugh again, he continued, "Maybe it is blasphemous, but I often think the hand that wrote the words decrying the love shared between men was man's and not God's." Charles searched Hugh's eyes, finding only confusion. "Are you afraid of what loving me might bring you, Hugh?"

"I would rephrase Thomas' words, Charles. Life without you would be as if I were already in Hell. The fear exists, but it is outweighed by my need of you. I saw nothing but contentment in their faces before Adam and Thomas faded from my view, Charles, even knowing what they may be facing. If they still felt like that after all they had been through," Hugh paused, smiled and concluded, "Can we dishonour their memories by loving each other any less completely?"

"No, by Heaven, no. Show me again, Hugh, just how much you love me."

THE SHADE ON A FINE DAY

CHARLIE COCHRANE

CHAPTER ONE

The church bells rang out into the December night - they'd been pealing for an hour now, working through one of the intricate set of changes so beloved of the curate. William Church may have only come to St. Archibald's at midsummer, but he'd already inspired his flock with his love of campanology, so much so that the dormant art of change ringing had been reintroduced, and the old set of bells had sprung into new and glorious life. They quivered with joy, sending a sweet sound into the frosty air that said, 'Come and worship.' His intention was for God to be venerated, but the ladies of Blaydon, tucked away in the recesses of Hampshire, had other ideas in mind when it came to the object of adoration.

It was just as well that the incumbent, Canon Newington, wasn't a jealous man, or else he might have been envious of the number of enraptured faces filling the congregation when his young curate preached at evensong. The rector was pragmatic about the favourable ambience a late summer's evening could produce, and amused that many of the congregation, the ones who showed most delight, were the spinsters among his flock. Girls of no more than fifteen through to old maids of seventy, who should have known better. He supposed it was the effect of the setting sun on Mr. Church's golden locks, or the mellifluous sound of his voice against a background of birdsong and the lowing of the cattle in the water meadows, which enhanced the man's already numerous attractions.

"Just you wait until the days shorten, my dear," he told his wife after one particular sermon had been punctuated with sighs and simpering from the pews. "The cattle will all be milked when the time comes for evensong, there'll be no rooks cawing in the elms, then the audience for Mr. Church's monthly homily will diminish."

"If I were the sort of woman who lays bets, I'd wager you that you're wrong. Hopelessly so." Mrs. Newington produced her wide, handsome grin. "His attraction for the ladies of your parish won't wane with the daylight. The same string of eligible young women will continue to tread a path, deep and wide, to the door of Mr. Church's lodgings." If she'd stooped low enough to be a betting woman, she'd have won her wager fair and square. The hay was gathered in, the equinox passed and young women still arrived bearing cakes and comforters, and other delights for the curate's delectation.

It was the sort of burden that any passably good-looking, unmarried priest had to endure but at least it meant, by devious means, that the poor of St. Archibald's were better looked after than usual. By October it had become the norm for all the spinsters of a marrying age to be vying with each other to impress William Church with their acts of charity or piety. The curate was handsome, well bred and unattached, any of which would have made him a target for the matchmakers of the parish and which, in combination, made his stock almost as valuable as Mr. Swann's, the previous holder of the title 'most eligible bachelor in the parish'.

Some of the ladies in the congregation at St. Archibald's found it hard to decide whether to rest their gaze on the man in the pulpit - when the curate was preaching - or the equally lovely one in the third pew from the front. Benjamin Swann scored equally highly in the matter of looks, breeding and availability, although his hair was a shade darker than Mr. Church's and he smiled less readily. But when his pleasing baritone rang through the air at matins it was enough to make any young woman of sensibility swoon. Except Benjamin's sister, of course, who only had eyes for the spinsters' delight delivering the sermon or reading the lesson.

"Did you hear the bells last night?" Madeleine Ardleigh sipped her tea, eyes shining in remembrance of the previous evening's peal.

"I did. The tenor was particularly lovely." Beatrice Swann smiled as if she had some secret knowledge of what had gone on in the bell tower to make the sound so heavenly.

"Was that Mr. Church's bell?" Madeleine always listened to a peal with pleasure, not least because it made her think of the curate's strong arms caressing the sallies. She was among those spinsters who were smitten; when she came for tea up at the big house, which was frequently, she always hoped that Mr. Swann might be there to favour her with a smile.

"I believe so. My brother says it takes a deft hand to make it sound so sweet."

"Is your brother to join us?" Madeleine felt the flush rise on her cheeks and wished she could restrain it.

"He said he intended to. I have no idea what could have kept him. Too fond of…ah."

The door of the drawing room opened, Benjamin Swann appearing full of apologies. "I'm sorry, Beatrice. Miss Ardleigh, forgive me, but my favourite hound decided to pup at the most inopportune of moments."

"Can't you leave that to the gamekeeper to attend to?" Beatrice rolled her eyes in an eloquent gesture signifying *Brothers, what can you do with them?* Madeleine, who had no siblings, tried to return the look knowingly.

"I have now, but I wanted to be there for a while. I've had her a long time." He took the cup which his sister offered.

"We were discussing the church bells." Beatrice turned the talk away from such mundane matters as hounds.

Benjamin took the hint. "Did you hear them last evening, Miss Ardleigh? They seem to be getting better and better."

"Mr. Church has certainly enthused the verger and his team." Beatrice offered her brother a small, sugary biscuit.

"They excelled themselves last night. Wild and dangerous I'd have called it if I were a poetic man."

"I don't follow you, Mr. Swann." Madeleine felt herself flushing once more, at the brief association of the word 'wild' with the handsome curate.

"Don't you find there's something unconstrained about the tolling of the different bells? I have a fancy they might leap out from their well ordered courses, break the pattern and infect the English night with anarchy." Benjamin's eyes shone. "A glorious chaos."

"Nonsense, dear." Beatrice rolled her eyes again.

"I must agree with Miss Swann." Madeleine hated to gainsay her host, but it was safer than crossing his sister. "They're the least chaotic things I can think of." The bells spoke to her strength restrained and controlled, just as Mr. Church's bulging black jacket did.

"Quite right, my dear. Now, have you been invited to the Newington's for dinner?" Beatrice pointed vaguely in the direction of the mantelpiece, where invitations, old or new, sat in a neat row.

"Oh yes." Madeleine almost squealed with delight. It may not have been an invitation from the curate himself but the next best thing. *Canon and Mrs. Newington request the pleasure of your company at dinner, Friday next.* The Ardleigh and Swann households were awash with excitement, much more than should have been warranted by just a summons from the manse to take a meal with the rector and his wife. Ever since the invitations had arrived, dresses had been fetched out, put away, fussed and fretted over, swatches of material looked at and colours compared.

Madeleine had heard the curate was said to favour blue as a colour appropriate to pretty girls with blonde hair but whether he would approve of the same on a rather plain brunette was a moot point. She was veering towards wearing green as it suited her eyes, but had decided not to make a decision until the last moment. Rumour had it Beatrice had been seen with yards of sprigged muslin and some rather overstated ribbons, all of a rather bold hue, although one which remained unspecified by the informant. Madeleine had been trying to drop subtle hints on the subject but had met a stone wall, much to her annoyance. No decision could be made on an outfit until one knew the colours the enemy would be decked in.

"I did find the invitation rather puzzling. The canon has a rather unusual way of putting things." Madeleine stuck out her bottom lip in what she hoped was an attractive pout, although she regretted wasting time on such fripperies when she needed to execute her plan of campaign in terms of dresses.

"That'll be his wife. Benjamin, oh…" If Beatrice was about to ask her brother to fetch the invitation, he'd pre-empted her.

"The Canon merely has an impish sense of humour, my dear, as appropriate for someone who spent four years as a missionary on the Pacific islands." Benjamin pointed to the elegantly sloped handwriting. "*It will be an interesting evening.* Is that the part you refer to, Miss Ardleigh?"

"Yes." It was going to be interesting whatever occurred. Madeline's parents were perplexed at what all the fuss was about, why she'd not expended half the effort on her clothes for the midsummer ball up at the Swann's house. If they'd bothered to ask in the right quarters, anyone could have told them that Mr. Church had been away visiting his family at the time of the ball, so all extra feminine effort would have been wasted. "I wonder what Mr. Newington thinks might be in store?"

"Apart from my sister making eyes at the curate? I can't guess." Benjamin's words were drowned under howls of feminine protest.

William Church walked down the Hatton's path, stopped a moment to admire an early hellebore, then made his way to the church. There were worse places he could lodge until he found a suitable place of his own. Mrs. Hatton came from impeccable stock, with only one thing which could be held to her discredit - she had married slightly below her station. It was a lodging convenient for visiting the heart of the village and had stabling for his horse, so he could easily reach the more far flung parts of the parish. It would be no more than a gentle stroll over to the rectory for dinner tomorrow evening so even if the threatened snow arrived he would still get his entertainment. He'd been careful which invitations he'd accepted these last few months, well aware of the machinations of mothers with eligible daughters. Luckily the Newingtons didn't possess any of those, even if there'd been some invited to their table. He swung open the lych gate then set it lightly on its latch.

"Mr. Church!" The verger struggled up the path, laden with greenery.

"Let me help you with that, Mr. Hawthorne." The curate took some of the burden. "Are we creating booths for the feast of Tabernacles?"

"We'll have none of that nonsense here, sir. This is for Lady O'Neill." It needed no further explanation. Sir Roger O'Neill had been very fond of evergreens and the anniversary of his death was always marked by a simple, moving service of remembrance, the church decked out like a woodland glade. It was possibly the only thing her ladyship did which had subtlety and good taste about it. "Mr. Swann was looking for you, sir."

"Was he?" William struggled to manoeuvre a large piece of holly into the porch without impaling himself.

"Aye. Makes a change from Miss Swann looking for you. With an apple pudding or something."

"It does indeed. At least I don't have to hide in the bell tower this time. I wonder what he can want." Church deposited his load of greenery at the feet of Mrs. Hawthorne for her to work marvels with, then sauntered into the graveyard. "Mr. Swann." He spotted a familiar shape lurking by the imposing memorial which dominated the east side of the churchyard. "I believe you were…oh, I'm sorry." There was more than a hint of sadness on Benjamin's face as he lifted it. "I had quite forgotten. Unforgivable, I know."

"Please don't worry. They've been gone so long now that I don't feel any pain of grief. But I can't help missing them."

Benjamin stood with head bowed, lips tightly pressed as if preventing himself speaking his thoughts aloud.

"I can appreciate that." They stood for a moment, looking over the impressive, well maintained plot; the last two generations of the Swann family lay here and the next few would join them when their time came. "You wished to see me?"

Benjamin nodded. "I wanted to enquire whether I had in some way offended you." He kept his eyes fixed on the memorial. A robin sang from the yew hedge, the faint sound of organ music came from the church – the answer seemed to take forever to come.

"Mr. Swann, if I have in any way given you that impression, then I apologise unreservedly. I'm racking my brains to think of what I could have done…"

"My father's walking stick. I was in Harmington yesterday, visiting a friend near the almshouses by St. Benedict's. One of the residents was out in the lane, using that stick. It is quite unmistakable."

William took a long look at the man beside him. Benjamin had a fine profile, featuring an elegant nose which was clearly a family trait. On his sister it looked too forceful – on him it gave an air of gravitas. "I didn't realise it was your father's. If I'd been aware of what it meant I wouldn't have been so insensitive. I'm sorry if your sister was offended."

"My sister? I'm not sure she even knows it's gone."

"But she gave it to me, last Saturday, or I thought she did." William ran his hands through his fair hair, leaving a trail of little green leaf fragments. "I've made an awful mistake somewhere, but I can't work out what."

"How did this man end up with my father's cane?" Benjamin turned his gaze on the curate for the first time. His grey eyes were awash with pain, the grief of bereavement remembered combining with a sense of betrayal.

"Come, it's cold standing here. Let's walk awhile and I'll explain." William indicated the path down to the village green.

"Mr. Swann, I'm not sure how it is for you up at the big house, but for a bachelor in holy orders although out of wedlock, life can be difficult. I find myself having continually to walk a thin line. Hardly a day goes by when I don't receive a basket of cakes, a jar of jam or a scarf. If I kept them all, it would be the height of greed."

"So you give them away?"

"I do. Every one of them, although I'm not stupid enough to do it in this parish. And I wouldn't have done it in this instance, had I known." William cast a sidelong glance at his companion – a slight thawing was evident. "The only thing that stops me becoming obese or overwrapped is the reciprocal arrangement I have with Mr. Regan. He's the curate of St Benedict's in Harmington."

"Is he regarded as highly eligible, too?" There was a sudden release of tension, and an unexpected hint of amusement, in Benjamin's voice.

"Exasperatingly so, at least that's what he tells me. I think he might have an even harder time of it. There's a greater concentration of young ladies within the town. This way, our respective parishioners can fill their stomachs, clothe their necks, and be duly grateful to benefactors unknown."

"You don't tell them where the gifts come from?"

"Not specifically. The poor of the country are grateful for the generosity of the young ladies of the town and vice versa. No-one is any the wiser."

"Does the canon approve? Doesn't he shudder at his curate flying false colours?"

William took another glance at the man beside him. There'd been a certain inflexion in the last remark he couldn't quite put his finger on. "It was Canon Newington's idea in the first place. He doesn't want any unpleasantness among the ladies of his flock – no favouritism to be shown. That's why I don't retain anything I'm sent. That's why I passed on that excellent cane, much as I would have liked to keep it."

"You'd mentioned your need of one, just the Sunday before, when my sister and I met you out by the lych gate."

"I remember." The curate smiled. "I'd been admiring your silver topped walking stick." He stopped, suddenly distressed. "You didn't think I was hinting, did you? I mean to go up to London and get one of my own in a fortnight. I didn't want charity."

"It wasn't charity. I wanted it to have a good home."

"I'm sorry, I really did think it came from your sister – I couldn't have kept it." William gently touched the other man's sleeve. "I can't have favourites among the ladies, you see."

"Why on earth did you think my sister had sent it?" Benjamin didn't pull his arm out of the contact.

"Because it arrived with a pot of bramble jelly, borne by your footman, and a note in Miss Swann's fair hand. It never occurred to me the two items had different provenances." William took his hand away at last. "I wish I could get it back. If I had known, I wouldn't have been so callous."

"Too late now." Benjamin clapped the curate's back. "Your intentions were honourable, that's all I needed to be assured of. And my father would have been pleased to see some poor old codger getting the benefit of it, rather than a healthy young man."

"Then I'm pleased, too. Only, promise me you won't tell your sister about my 'arrangement'. If it became common knowledge I'm not sure the scandal could be borne, not in either parish."

"I won't tell a word. But only if you promise in return that you'll let me give you another silver topped cane. There are far too many in the house for me to make good use of, my father had a passion for collecting them and I keep finding them stashed away." Benjamin smiled, his handsome face even more striking in its animation.

"You have my word." William held out his hand to be shaken before they parted ways. "And this time I'll be happy to keep the gift. No favouritism among the *ladies*, that's the rule."

CHAPTER TWO

"Will this muslin work this evening or should I wear my dark blue?" Beatrice Swann swooped around the drawing room like a bird, her long and full dress billowing into elegant wings.

"The blue makes you look like a post-captain." Her brother spoke from behind the newspaper. "They'd think it amusing at a ball in Portsmouth, but they're not quite so modern here. Wear the muslin, it looks nice."

"You're not even looking at it, are you?" The newspaper was snatched away and slammed onto the table with emphasis. "I can understand why no woman seems to have patience with you."

"Perhaps I don't want to have patience with them." Benjamin tried to retrieve his paper, but was foiled.

"Nonsense. You need a wife to sort you out. Otherwise you'll spend all your life just mouldering away here in the middle of nowhere." Beatrice smoothed out the skirts of her dress, emphasising her slim waist and trim figure.

"I like mouldering away. And won't that dress be a bit cold for November? How you girls don't catch your death of cold with those new necklines is beyond my comprehension."

"I shall wear my fox fur wrap. And the Newingtons always keep their house warm, probably to remind them of tropical climes." She saw the look of disapproval cross her brother's face and neatly changed the subject. "The muslin it is, then. I don't suppose you'll be making any special effort? Miss Ardleigh will be there and she does so admire you when you turn yourself out well."

"I bet Miss Ardleigh won't be wearing anything as summery as this." Benjamin jabbed his finger at his sister's gown, sat back and waited for the tirade of comments on Miss Ardleigh's dress sense to begin. After two minutes he was able to retrieve the newspaper and find his place once more. His attention went back to the one-sided conversation when a familiar name came up.

"Of course, Mr. Church is said to favour dark shades like cobalt, which is why I wondered about my blue, but if you think it makes me look like Admiral Collingwood I don't think I'll ever wear it again. I'll give it to my maid." Beatrice was admiring herself in the mirror, a blue cushion she'd snatched from a chair, being held to her bodice, taken away and brought back again.

"If Mr. Church likes the colour then you should wear it for him and hang what other people think. I sometimes think you girls only dress to impress each other and have no regard for male sensibilities. Maybe I should put on my blue waistcoat just to show you what style really is."

"Miss Ardleigh would be impressed." Beatrice grinned, settling herself on the couch and fiddling with her brother's stock. "You do scrub up nicely when you try. Promise me you'll look your best this evening. Please."

"I will, just for you. Blue waistcoat and all."

Canon Stephen Newington attended to his cravat, twitching the fine linen into an attractive yet understated knot. His guests would be arriving within the half hour and he wanted everything to be ready in time, himself included.

"I wonder if the young ladies will be late or early?" He allowed his wife to make a small, necessary adjustment to his collar.

"It depends on whether they've changed their dresses a dozen times, set and re-set their hair, and generally done everything possible to keep their carriages waiting." Jane Newington grinned, then planted a kiss on her husband's nose.

"Maybe they've been so eager to enter the fray they've have had to send their drivers by the longest possible route to avoid the embarrassment of being twenty minutes too early." The canon smiled.

"Well, what do you expect when you made such a point of advertising your curate's presence at the meal?" Jane picked a miniscule speck of dust from her husband's shoulder.

"Allow me my little pleasures, my dear. Nothing makes for innocent amusement quite as much as two women fawning over one man."

"Doesn't Mr. Swann get a look in? Or doesn't he count because only Miss Ardleigh will be fluttering her eyelashes at him?"

"Mr. Swann can take care of himself. It's the pressure on my curate which concerns me." The Canon took a last look in the glass, admiring the firm set of a jaw which hadn't lessened in determination or spirit these last twenty years since he'd caused a sensation among his fellow doctors of divinity. Not that it had created a particular stir when he announced he felt the call to preach in the nether regions of the world. He was young, he had few commitments and, if successful, it might speed his route to a bishopric. It was the outcome which had been so shocking. "You look lovely as usual, my dear." He admired his wife's dusky complexion, still as clear as a girl's.

"Thank you; I hope our guests will think burgundy velvet is acceptable." Her nimble fingers smoothed out her skirt, picking off little wisps which spoiled the fabric.

"It's what we think that matters." Mr. Newington had come back victorious four years after leaving English soil, having founded churches which successfully survived his leaving the islands he'd planted them on. His sojourn ended up producing a lot of goodwill for both Christianity and cricket, two points of merit to be displayed on his return to England, and a wife whose dusky complexion and strange name were going to be rather out of place in Hampshire. "We've always said that, Jonhonto."

"It makes me so happy when you call me that, my British boy." Jonhonto, a name which had metamorphosed into Jane as its owner passed over the oceans to tread the exotic shores of Hampshire, spoke excellent English. Her husband had taught her to read and she'd developed a fine taste in books, alongside a relish for Shakespeare. Despite all the rumours, she didn't eat human flesh, nor had her family for the last two generations, but she wasn't white, and therefore all chance of Newington being given a bishopric went out of the window. It didn't seem to matter any more.

Jane had made an admirable vicar's wife, bearing him a son and daughter, and was as generous as anyone could wish in her time and energies towards the people of the parish. The poorer families had ceased to notice her skin colour, welcoming her, and her deep, chuckling laugh, into their homes with affection. If she was still not welcome in the homes where folk believed they were of a higher quality, that was their loss – invitations not received were invitations which didn't need to be returned.

"And are you worried about tonight? Eight at dinner and all?" Canon Newington held his wife's delicate hands in his own, as much in love as he'd been twenty five years previously.

"Does that mean do I think *he* will visit?" Jane shrugged her shoulders, a beautifully eloquent gesture. "Maybe. If he has messages to bring."

The sound of hooves clipping along the gravelled drive brought speculation to an end and sent host and hostess scuttling down the stairs to welcome the first of the combatants.

Jane Newington looked around her large, well laid out table with much interest and a keen eye for anyone who seemed nervous. The curate was charming all and sundry as ever, Madeleine Ardleigh on one side of him looking flushed and excited, Beatrice Swann on the other riveted to every word he spoke. Jane noticed that Mr. Swann, whom she'd placed between herself and her husband's aunt, was also gazing over at the other young people with curiosity, an intensity in his gaze suggesting he was perhaps willing the pair to an even more intimate conversation. There were going to be many sisters' hearts broken, and perhaps a few brothers' noses bloodied, before the lovely Mr. Church settled down.

"Do you believe in ghosts, Mr. Church?" Madeleine's fine, alto tones floated along the table.

"I do, although I've never seen one. My father has — it was his own grandfather, walking along the riverbank with his favourite fly fishing gear in his hand, not an hour after the man's funeral."

"Ooh." Beatrice shivered. "If that had happened to me, I'd have fainted."

"I've never known you faint at anything, my dear," her brother chided. "Mr. Church, I find this fascinating. I too have never seen a ghost, although I value the testimony of two other people who've told me they have. I will add your father as a third. In all cases the experience has been benign, less frightening than expected. Was that true of his case?"

"It was. He felt no fear at the sight, just a deep contentment, like he'd felt as a boy when grandfather took him fishing. That's not to say the spirit world can't be frightening and at times downright malignant - exorcism is still a rite we have to perform when the occasion demands. But there must be good and bad among phantoms as there is among men. Do I speak out of turn, Canon?"

"Not at all." Newington drew his hands together over his plate as if he was about to pray. "My belief is that benevolent ghosts are varieties of angels, just as evil ones are a variety of demons."

"You'll have them in your culture, my dear." Sir Clarence Raleigh's stentorian tones cut across his host.

Jane turned to regard her extremely loud and slightly annoying guest. If she was regarded as not quite the thing, then the squire of Raleigh manor had an equal reputation, if not a far worse one. Jane's skin may have been black, but Sir Clarence's heart was said to be blacker by far and he was only a regular guest at the vicarage because he had the living in his control. He had chosen Newington to come to St. Archibald's because the man had been up at The House, as Sir Clarence had before him. He also admired the way the priest had cocked a snook at convention by marrying a dusky beauty. If Sir Clarence on occasions attempted to be a little too forward, for example nestling his leg next to his hostess', she knew well enough how to deal with him and wasn't afraid to dig any item of cutlery she happened to find handy into the gentleman's thigh. Nice and deep with it.

"We do, Sir Clarence, although I hope you're not implying that's because we are in any way primitive. My ancestors would be horrified at some of the goings on they might read about in the Old Testament."

"I meant no such…"

"Good." Jane smiled. "Then I will tell you about a particular spirit, Toomhai Gamali, who is said to turn up at feasts and communicate with those present. I have heard of one instance from our family and many others from around the islands."

"It'll all be superstition of course." Sir Clarence gestured dismissively with his hand.

"I think not," Canon Newington wouldn't make such a sweeping judgement. Over the years his faith had increased although his certainties had diminished. "I heard of a case where several witnesses testified to a visitation."

"And I certainly wouldn't be so ready to dismiss it." Mr. Church was, by nature, quick to chip in when he believed he'd a valid point to make. "We know that angels are used by our maker to send messages and to help people in need. Why shouldn't this happen in Mrs. Newington's homeland?"

"Why not indeed? England can't claim a monopoly on divine inspiration." Lady Finsbury, the Canon's aunt, completed the guests at dinner. She was the person from whom the family alleged he got his wayward tendencies. Rumour had it she'd been quite a gal in her youth, disgracing herself by taking up cigars - something not a single one of the Newington females had ever done - and then running off to join a theatrical company. She'd compounded the disgrace by being wooed and wed by a Lord, albeit an impoverished one, and acquiring herself a title, something else no-one in the family, except a distant cousin, had. Her nephew and his wife had taken her in to help raise the children, Jane preferring the tradition of her own country where the older generation had much to offer in the way of bringing up the young. She was loathe to commit her children to the care of some wet behind the ears nursery maid.

"I wish you'd tell that to Lady O'Neill when she's giving me one of her sermons." Newington speared a potato as he might have hoped to spear annoying females in his parish. "She can't quite grasp that Our Lord was born in a stable in Bethlehem rather than the cathedral close in Salisbury." Making Lady O'Neill see sense was far more difficult than the proverbial camel passing through the eye of the needle.

"This Toomhai..." Benjamin turned a winning smile on his hostess. "What prompts him to come? Is it when he has a particular message?"

"So they say." Jane looked around her table again, taking a deep breath. "Although there is more. He first comes when there is something significant to communicate, but only when there is also a certain number gathered."

"Thirteen, it must be that." Beatrice's high pitched, girlish voice sounded rather vapid after Jane's rich tones.

"No, Miss Swann. The significant number is eight, although I couldn't tell you why. I suppose there were eight people eating together the first time he came, and then perhaps the second. Every subsequent visit was when eight were gathered, and always at a meal. After a while my people ensured that extra guests would make the numbers higher."

"But there are eight of us." Madeleine spoke what everyone had realised a minute ago, yet kept to themselves.

"I think that has just become a significant factor." It always seemed an unbelievable cliché when an author described a sudden chill coming over a room and everyone being aware of it, or so it struck Benjamin Swann. But now he was witness to that very occurrence - it was as if the temperature had dropped a good twenty degrees and both of the young ladies present shivered, the roaring fire notwithstanding. A silence fell on the company, even though the evening had so far been lively and garrulous. They looked around, anticipating some momentous and outlandish occurrence.

"Toomhai Gamali," Jane Newington muttered, crossing herself.

"And do you think we're going to be visited by your ghost chappie now?" Sir Clarence's tone made it clear he'd never heard such stuff and nonsense, although he too had begun to shiver.

"I think we should wait and see." Canon Newington took the opportunity to surreptitiously cross himself, as well.

"I think if something happens it will turn out to be a manifestation of our own consciousness, combining to a metaphysical effect." Beatrice read many an 'advanced' book although she didn't really understand any of them. She felt the strange, tangible presence in the air, though – they all did.

"It might make itself plain in a mass hallucination." Madeleine wasn't to be left out of a discussion, especially one which might make her sound clever. Mr. Church was said to like bookish girls. "We'll see what we expect to see. Something like Banquo's ghost or Hamlet's father or..."

She was stopped short by something manifesting itself, although it didn't resemble either of the characters the girl had suggested, or indeed anything it was expected to. This was no strange Polynesian spirit, daubed with tattoos and wearing just some beads and a rush skirt, nor was it a good old fashioned English ghost in doublet and hose with his head tucked under his arm. Instead, the visitor who suddenly appeared by the fireplace looked remarkably like a solicitor, his neat suit, shining shoes and trim little spectacles adding to the impression.

Those present couldn't have been more astonished if a fully grown cherub had made itself visible, wings and all. Both the young ladies screamed, Sir Clarence leapt up then sat straight down again, and most of the others around the table turned deathly pale. Alone of all those present, Lady Finsbury acted as if nothing out of the ordinary had occurred. "We are eight gathered at dinner. Are you here to give us a salutary communication?" Her ladyship, breaking their stunned silence, expressed what was on everyone's mind.

"I am indeed. As you might have guessed, from Mrs. Newington's excellent introduction, I am someone who no longer walks this earth in carnal form. Several of us have been given employ as ethereal messengers. Some of us have specific names, such as your Toomhai Gamali, although I must admit we interchange our roles. It might become rather tedious only to be allowed to travel to the islands or be confined to the castles of Scotland." The thing polished its spectral spectacles. "I am here because it is felt that several of you should be beneficiaries of some prudent advice." He even spoke like a solicitor.

"And how," Canon Newington wished to assert his rightful place as master of the house and the situation, "is this to be done?" The last thing he wanted was for anyone's dirty linen to be washed at his dinner table. He knew Toomhai's reputation for bluntness; even if this wasn't actually him, perhaps all spectral messengers would be just as forthright.

"I thought I would take as my model one of your excellent sermons, Mr. Newington. It has been noted that you have a most effective way of taking the particular faults of members of your congregation and making them the subject of one of your homilies, then relying on their consciences and the influence of my master to do the rest. It has proved surprisingly and most subtly effective." The ghost, if ghost it really was and not someone playing an impressive practical joke, found a spare chair, placed it in the position he required to best address the company, then sat primly, hands folded in his lap.

Hardly a breath could be heard around the table. Eventually Lady Finsbury could bear it no longer. "Well, can we be getting on with it?"

"I'm sorry, at this point people usually bombard me with questions. I did not realise you would all be so polite and patient." The ghost beamed. "Now, I have some general things to say to start." He produced a document from his pocket and looked rather like he was about to read a will. "Several of you have secrets but I will not be referring to them, please be assured of that. It is not within my remit."

There were sighs from various parts of the table, although no-one afterwards could quite say who had displayed such audible relief.

"I am to congratulate three of you, however, on having made a brave decision - the correct decision - in the past, one that set you at odds with your family and society. It is not always wrong to follow one's heart; what pleases God is not always what pleases Lady O'Neill of Jarosite Mansion."

Benjamin, who'd heard her ladyship lauded often at his own hearth, stifled a snigger.

"I hasten to add," the ghost briefly fixed Sir Clarence with a lancet glance, "that not all rebellions against what is considered correct behaviour are legitimate. The abuse of power or privilege, the ruining of other people's lives, whether at the gaming tables or in the bedroom, is abhorrent. When I applaud the courage of this trio, I refer simply to swimming against a tide of mores that have been built up by men, and made to resemble holy writ. Society is to serve man, not man to serve society."

Lady Finsbury smiled and whispered under her breath. "Well said, old Mole."

The ghost tipped its head in acknowledgement. "There are others around this table who would benefit by taking their example from the valiant characters who have sought to find the true course for their lives. Several of you have decisions to make, and you should not always choose the easiest option. Or that of which the world at large will approve."

"And where will we best find guidance? If we have choices to make?" Mr. Church's voice was little more than a whisper, and the two women at his side felt tingles up their spines. The curate's voice was magnificent orating from the pulpit. What must it be like murmuring words of love in a bower or - the thought made them both blush - a bedroom?

"There are four excellent books - you know which they are - and a man could do no better than study them. If the answer can't be found there then perhaps it is unknowable." The ghost rose, returned his chair to whence he'd found it. "I shall return in due course to see whether you have heeded my message. If you haven't, then you must live with the consequences. But at least I can tell you categorically whether you chose right or wrong; not many people have that luxury." The ghost bowed and disappeared to a collective gasp from the company.

Silence fell, one that lasted a good two minutes until Jane Newington sighed, smiled and said, "If that is Toomhai Gamali, then he is welcome at my table at any time."

CHAPTER THREE

Beatrice Swann had been plying her brother with questions all the way home, to the point he'd contemplated getting out and walking the rest of the way, easterly wind and flurries of sleet notwithstanding.

"But which of us there tonight could have such terrible secrets that the ghost, or whoever he was, said they were not to be referred to directly?" Beatrice's fingers tapped impatiently on the carriage door. "Do you think he might have meant the vicar's wife? Perhaps she really is a cannibal as I've heard said up at Lady O'Neill's."

Benjamin snorted. "The rubbish spoken around that woman's drawing room would put a tavern full of superstitious sailors to shame. I'm surprised you pay any heed to it."

"I can't refuse her invitations. She's the heart of what passes for society here." Beatrice tossed her head, frustrated that her friends always seemed to be meeting eligible young men on promenades in elegant towns, while she was being stifled in the countryside.

"I suspect that ghost spoke a lot of sense, more than you'd hear at her ladyship's fireside. It isn't hard to work out who he congratulated on following their hearts rather than convention. Your Lady O'Neill would have a fit if she'd heard him." Benjamin drew his greatcoat around him. "I'd like to see a meeting between them. Toomhai Gamali wouldn't stand for any of her nonsense."

"You have no appreciation of the finer things in life. Or the finer people. I swear you'd rather be out with the beaters than the guns."

"What I appreciate is my own business, as what you appreciate is yours. Neither is any business of Lady O'Neill's."

Beatrice narrowed her eyes, but let pass the insults to she who set Blaydon standards. "Didn't you even wonder who that fellow meant when he said someone had to decide whether to follow their heart? I refuse to believe he had either of us in mind."

"I really can't be bothered to worry about it. Conjecture is pointless, and I'm tired." Benjamin rubbed his eyes. He looked weary, unusually troubled.

"Have you no curiosity? We meet a ghost - a bit of a disappointing ghost, I have to admit. I'd always hoped they'd be dressed in white with an accoutrement of dusty chains. And you seem to have no interest in what he had to say." His sister rapped her hand on the side of the carriage.

"If I say that I'm fairly sure it was Sir Clarence given the spectral wigging, is that enough for you?" Benjamin refused to be drawn into further conversation.

"No, but it will have to be, I suppose." Beatrice looked out at the stars. "Miss Ardleigh looked rather nice in that bottle green." If she'd been with her female friends she'd have been less generous. *Such an unfortunate choice of colour – it made her look quite drained. She suffers from a sallow skin, of course.* But now she had to be charitable; nudging her brother in Madeleine's direction, and vice versa, would leave her own path clear, the one which headed in the direction of Mr. Church.

"I think it suited her well enough." For Benjamin that was almost fawning praise. He never spoke poetically about any of the women he came across, not as poetically or passionately as he spoke about his hounds or horses. Or how fine the church bells were sounding now, compared to a year ago.

His sister took it as a positive sign. She was certain Mr. Church was the person the ghost had been talking about – hadn't the curate's reaction suggested as much? The spectre must have been referring to a decision concerning the lady to whom Mr. Church was to offer his heart; that was the only sensible explanation. Beatrice had tried to keep a tally of time the curate had spent talking to *her,* compared to the time lavished on his neighbour on the other side. It had been, disappointingly, about the same allocation to each. She hoped that the words of the spectre – or manifestation of subconscious feelings or whatever it was – would work in Mr. Church's heart, and make him realise that *she* would be the best possible option for the wife of a handsome clergyman with excellent prospects. And perhaps her brother might consider those same words and think about offering Madeleine his hand. "That would be very tidy all round." Beatrice's thoughts came uninvited into her spoken words.

"What would?"

"I was just thinking how neat it would be, for the convenience of the parish, to see a union between the Swann and Ardleigh families. Everyone would welcome it." Her thoughts drifted off into double ceremonies, joint celebrations held out on the lawns of their house. "The Church and Swann households, too, perhaps…"

"Ah." Benjamin's voice softened. He patted his sister's arm with brotherly affection. "An excellent idea."

Beatrice couldn't help wonder all the rest of the journey why that answer, ostensibly just what she wanted, was vaguely unsettling.

Canon Newington said his prayers with renewed enthusiasm, then slipped between the sheets of his comfortable old bed.

"It did turn out to be an interesting evening. Perhaps you're a prophet, dear." Jane snuggled against her husband's back.

"I doubt it. A coincidence." He sighed. "I understand that members of my profession would frown on communing with ghosts, although the same men might not object to communing with the bookmakers on Epsom Downs. But how could anyone make a protestation against such a well behaved, articulate, and clearly spiritual spirit as visited us tonight?"

"You were right, you know. I'd suspected Toomhai Gamali would come, ever since Mr. and Mrs. Hawthorne came down with colds and sent their apologies. Yet I was surprised that, rather than terror and strife, he should bring peace and compassion. Remember the tales of when he came to my great grandfather's family feast?"

"When he made his proclamations 'with a voice like an earthquake'? Your father made me have nightmares when he told that story." It had caused the death of three men from sheer terror, and led to the abandonment of cannibalism, it being man's flesh gracing the banquet that night.

"He has taste and wit, though, that ghost. To have your sermonising lauded in the process would make even the humblest of men proud." Jane put her arms around her husband's lean frame.

"It wasn't that which pleased me the most." Newington turned round, into his wife's embrace. "I'm sure it was the three of us he singled out for commendation in having followed our hearts and ploughed our own furrows."

"Ah, I knew you'd spot that. You aunt was delighted, too."

"I wonder why she'd wished to speak to you when our guests went home. I should have known – I've not seen her smile like that since her husband was alive."

"She was the least perturbed of all of us at seeing a ghost. She even called him 'the funny little man who entertained us at dinner'. Said he looked the image of the vestry clerk at St Martin's in the Fields, where she'd been married."

"I remember the story." It was another part of Newington folklore. A peculiar little chap, precise and almost matronly, who'd been run down by a bolting horse only two days after the marriage.

"Your aunt swears there was a knowing look in his eye every time he'd spoken to the company, as if he had at least one old friend around the table. She said she almost asked him if he still had the hoof marks in the back of his head, but felt that too impolite a question even for so obliging a spectre."

"Then he can't be your Toomhai Gamali. The times won't work."

"For an intelligent man you aren't very bright at times." Jane pinched her husband's cheek. "I have seen three different actors play Hamlet, and two play Lear. The answer seems so obvious I shan't explain further. And as far as the females of this household are concerned, the whole episode makes perfect sense. Wouldn't you rather speculate on who it is has secrets to hide and decisions to make?"

"Who might themselves have to swim against the tide? I've decided it would be neither godly nor profitable to do so. We'll find out soon enough if we're meant to." The canon kissed his wife with great passion and settled down to sleep.

Jane stroked his head as he slumbered, as she'd done since first they shared a bed. Toomhai had come, and would return. No turmoil would follow his visit, and if she'd ever been in doubt, she now felt entirely vindicated in her choice of husband and faith. An even happier smile than normal would be seen around the parish over the next few days.

Madeleine Ardleigh studied her face in the mirror as the maid helped her prepare for bed. One hundred strokes through the hair were absolutely necessary, or so she'd been told since childhood.

"It must have been a lovely evening, miss." A lady's maid could only dream of having dinner with young men of such quality.

"It was." Madeleine bit her lip. Normally she'd share all the details – who danced with who, which couple lingered a little too long when the music stopped – but tonight she had to hold her tongue. "Mr. Church was very amusing. And Mr. Swann told such a story about his favourite hunter." Those at table had taken an oath of silence as they'd left. Tonight's proceedings, or at least those concerning the ghost, must remain a secret until they'd all had time to consider them. It had seemed a sensible approach, especially as dear Mr. Church had been so adamant in supporting the idea, but it was a nuisance. To have such a colourful tale to tell and no outlet…

"What was Miss Swann wearing?"

"Muslin, far too pale for her complexion and not at all suited for such a night." Madeleine went on to describe all the outfits in great detail, all the time her mind worrying at what had been said, like a dog with a bone it can't put down. Working out who was being praised and who'd been castigated was hard enough, although when it came to the matter of 'making decisions' she had a name which fitted. Long before the ghost had come, poor Mr. Church had been embarrassed, turning a fetching shade of red, when the conversation turned to marriage.

"And was it an interesting evening, like your invitation said?" The maid might have been regarded as forward in any other household, but Madeleine lacked a suitably close female companion, so she'd taken up the role. "Oh yes. Canon Newington was rather mischievous, referring to the matter of young curates and the problems they had finding a suitable spouse. Poor Mr. Church didn't know where to look." He hadn't been able to face her, or Miss Swann the other side, for several minutes, crumbling his bread and pretending to eat it. "Mr. Swann had to come to his rescue, changing the subject to whether Mr. Newington's horse had recovered from a strained fetlock."

"Mr. Swann is a real gentleman, although the maids up at the big house do say he's no great one for the ladies."

"I wouldn't be too sure they're telling you the truth." Madeleine was confident she knew better. She'd seen how affected he'd been by the matrimonial discussion. He'd looked in her direction often and often, especially when she had been tête-à-tête with Mr. Church - a little thrill coursed up Madeleine's spine at the thought that Swann might have been jealous. "He looked at me particularly closely after…" She was going to say *after the spectre's visit* but stopped herself. "After some remarks about marriage." He too must have been wondering what the curate's choice would be, and how it would affect them all.

"You do break some hearts, miss." The maid finished her brushing, then helped her mistress complete her toilette. Madeleine prepared for sleep, expecting nothing but sweet dreams, not really caring if they concerned short, fair curates with strong arms or tall, sinewy, dark haired men with annoying sisters. To have one handsome man play court to you was fine enough – to have another in the offing was absolute heaven.

Benjamin Swann couldn't sleep at all. Dinner, excellent as it had been, lay heavily on his stomach, while thoughts oppressed his mind. He looked out over the fields, their thick coating of frost resembling snow in the moonlight. He loved winter, the white and grey tones, the clear light and sharp air all helping to bring his life into a clearer focus. Not that it needed to be brought much further into focus after tonight. He wandered down to the library, where a fire was always kept burning low on cold nights. He coaxed it into life, laying another log on, then found his favourite pack of cards, dealing out hands without thinking.

Queen of Hearts. He considered the ladies sleeping in houses and cottages all over the parish, lost in dreams of suitors and admirers, then held the pack to his head in an attempt to cool his restless, guilty thoughts.

Queen of Clubs. His sister too, not thirty yards up the stairs, along the corridor of the big house, asleep, and no doubt dreaming, like all the other maids who frequented St. Archibald's, of a pair of blue eyes and a flashing smile.

Jack of Hearts. The only decision William Church could make which wouldn't disappoint any of them, would be the offer of his hand.

Jack of Spades. Well, whatever the man chose to do, there would be many a long face in the parish. Everyone with any sense had seen the risk of that eventuality. From the moment the curate had arrived and swept the spinsters off their feet, the likely number of potentially broken hearts seemed to increase weekly.

King of Hearts. Only one person could win the man's lasting affection. Benjamin was sure William was no cad and wouldn't seek to play the field. Whether he'd be brave enough to go where Benjamin felt his conscience might lead him, was another thing.

Nine of Diamonds. Why did life have to be so ridiculously complicated?

William Church, watched the same moonlight playing on the water meadows while he contemplated the same ghostly message, had the same run of thoughts go through his head. Whatever he did, somebody would hate him; it seemed inevitable, whichever path he decided to tread. "I never asked young women to fawn on me." He poured an inch or two of water from the ewer, then swept it up to cool his face.

"We are well aware that you didn't but, alas, that is what they do."

William recognised the voice. Prim, proper, and last heard at the canon's fireside not more than a few hours previously. He turned, to find Toomhai Gamali, or whoever he was, sitting on the old chair by the hearth, glasses laid neatly in his lap. Maybe ghosts found the earth rather cold, given the affection they seemed to display for the fire's warmth. "You're back."

"I am. I couldn't be entirely frank earlier, so I have asked leave to return and clarify matters." The spectre seemed eminently reasonable, even if he took his habit of butting into people's lives a step too far.

"Starting with girls bearing gifts? The gifts I haven't asked for?"

"They make cakes and knit mufflers." The ghost appeared to have a list in his notebook of all the things the curate had received, referring to it with a sad shake of his head. "They seem driven to do it, as a water bird might present a juicy piece of weed to a female he is trying to impress."

"They don't impress me." William sat wearily on the bed. "I just want to ring the bells and take services, make my visits, and enjoy such leisure as I have time for in my own way."

"Indeed." The ghost polished his glasses again. "Life for a handsome curate in a small country parish appears to be as perilous as being a clergyman on a frigate blockading Brest. I don't envy you. Particularly in your position." They sat a while in silence, contemplating which was more dangerous, cannons or spinsters.

The curate ran his hands through his hair, words spinning around his head as they'd done all evening. "You meant me, didn't you? Tonight, at dinner. *Follow your heart. Some of you have secrets. Decisions to make.* That's why you're here now."

"Very perceptive. I didn't just refer to you, but you were one of my intended recipients. Some people spend too long not being able to follow their hearts, hiding all their secret thoughts for fear of hurting or offending other people. You have shied away from the really important decisions." There was no harshness in the spectre's words, his tone suited to a kindly uncle with a favourite nephew.

"I have cause to hide. You must know that, as you seem to know everything else. Whatever I choose to do, people will be hurt."

"That applies to almost every decision one makes. The pig farmer is hurt if you choose to buy a side of beef, and the fisherman offended if you choose bacon over sole."

William couldn't help laughing, frustration at his lot dissipating in the absurdity of discussing the lot of a bacon farmer with a ghost. "If I considered those sorts of things, I'd make no decisions at all. Forgive me if I say they're just trivial examples."

"Ah, but life is made up of small choices. Miss Ardleigh was hurt every time you spoke to Miss Swann at dinner. Miss Swann was in agony every time you granted Miss Ardleigh a smile." The ghost laid his hands in his lap, looking as serious as the bishop delivering a threat of excommunication. "I could name someone else who suffers because of your lack of decision – someone who might matter more in the greater scheme than either of the young ladies I've mentioned. Someone who would value a little clarity of mind."

"And that's exactly what I want as well." William slouched, put his aching head into tired hands. "I don't have the heart for any of this."

"On the contrary, you have exactly the heart for it. A magnificent heart, more suited to the battlefield than fighting sin in a genteel parish. You don't lack bravery." The ghost leaned forward, his eyes bright with some burning emotion, if spirits felt such things. "I don't think you can't make up your mind. You know precisely what you would do if you had free choice, don't you?"

"Of course. And you know that my hands are effectively tied." Those hands felt hot against his eyes, the sweaty palms offering no sort of solace. "It would be hard enough in any profession to feel how I do. Your poor sailors blockading Brest would risk their very lives – a piece of rope from the yardarm is every bit as fatal as a French cannonball. But to be a clergyman, to preach about sin and redemption…it's agony." William's face stayed buried in his hands. "It breaks my heart every time I read Leviticus."

"Yet you didn't enter the church as many of your contemporaries do, for a career, the tradition of the third son." The ghost's voice was full of compassion. "You felt called and you struggle to reconcile the two warring factions."

"You understand me too well, whoever you are." Somewhere over the fields a fox gave its unearthly cry. "Is there nothing you can say to help me?"

The spectre tilted his head to one side like a robin, then produced a disarming smile. "Of course. Your bishop. He wears spectacles, and has one eye slightly clouded over. And Lady O'Neill invests with a firm who lend money." He sat back as if he'd settled the matter.

"I beg your pardon?" If this was ghostly advice and logic, it hardly seemed worth making a special journey to earth to dispense.

"The Old Testament laws make it plain that someone with an eye defect shouldn't be a priest. I dare say the bishop isn't from the tribe of Levi either." The ghost polished his spectacles again; the lenses must have been almost worn through. "And they preclude lending money on interest. Read them, Mr. Church, however much it pains you. Read them and realise how many of them are broken daily by the people around you, without one of them being regarded as sinful. The world has moved on."

The fox carried on its eerie screeching, the wind rattled the windows, the fire crackled, all signs that life carried on as normal, even if the world had turned upside down.

"I've never thought of it that way." William's voice was as quiet as the rustling of the shifting embers.

"That's clearly true." The spectre smiled again. "Concentrate on what my master's son had to say and forget the rest for a while. You have to work out how to loose your own bonds. Let alone those imposed by the people around you."

"If I can persuade my conscience to let me proceed, then I'll take on society like a crack frigate would a stubby little pair of sloops. Although how I do it eludes me."

"A man of ingenuity and spirit can always find ways to loosen the bonds of the social order, yet still appear bound by them. Plenty of gentlemen who have found themselves with a similar dilemma have engineered a solution. It's a case of prestidigitation…" The ghost began to laugh, a creaking, hissing sound so infectious that William couldn't help join in.

"I don't think I quite grasp your meaning."

"Sleight of hand. An optical illusion. Call it what you will. A false impression that will fool the world, behind which you can live as your conscience would dictate, even if other folk's consciences might be appalled. Like your frigate, and the false colours it might fly chasing those sloops."

"The idea appeals. A *trompe l'oeil* which would make the Lady O'Neills of this world see nothing but what they wished to see. But I'm no painter." It all sounded wonderful in theory, yet the practicalities eluded him.

"That's what you were given brains for, Mr. Church, to figure out such things. Must I do all the work?" The spectre rose and bowed, impeccably polite as ever. "I may return, if my schedule allows. I beg that you will ensure I come back to a successful conclusion of the case. Time is not an infinite quantity in this place, however it manifests itself in our world. Please don't let the opportune moment pass."

"I will try my…" William realised he was addressing thin air. Even for a ghost this chap seemed pretty nifty, slipping between universes effortlessly.

Well, now he'd been told face to face. Make his mind up? In truth his mind had been made up not two days after harvest festival, he'd just not had the courage or moral certainty to speak up. Now he'd have to find it.

CHAPTER FOUR

The bells of St. Archibald's rang out wildly again – in two days it would be the last Sunday in Advent, and St Matthew's gospel would be proclaimed, the age old story told once more for anyone who had ears to listen. For those who had the wit to ignore the altercations about who had which pew and who set the flowers on the altar for Christmas Day, to the real message the Christ child brought, then Christmas truly was a season of joy. William Church pulled with renewed vigour, a great smile splitting his handsome face, his blue eyes dancing with sheer joie de vie. He had woken knowing what he had to do, and once the peal had finished serenading the icy fields and the barren trees he would be away to do it.

The last change sounded with a booming cascade and the bells fell silent at last. Hawthorne the verger produced a keg of beer, seemingly from out of thin air, and all the ringers drank deep. "We'll not sound the peal again until we're welcoming the New Year then?"

"Aye," William took a welcome swig of ale, "the canon likes the bells but he'd prefer Christmas week to be silent. Mr. Newington feels it's more reflective and I have to agree with him. Advent's a good time for thinking."

Murmured agreements came from mouths that were occupied with an excellent brew; the men would appreciate a rest from the hard work, too.

"Will you come along and take a spot of food with myself and the missus?" Mr. Hawthorne smiled over his pint. "It's a good wholesome broth she's made. Set you up perfect on a cold day like this."

"I'd love to, verger, but I have business to be about. Can I defer the invitation to another day? I would hate your wife to be offended." William produced the sort of smile that would ensure any woman would forgive him the refusal.

"No offence taken, sir. Another day it will be then. Let's secure the ropes and make all safe, then I'll be off home."

William helped with restoring the bell tower to its pristine glory, but his mind was already out of the building and away. As he put on his coat and hat, then carefully went down the little winding stair, his imagination was far away, striding along the path, knocking at a door, meeting the person he loved in an attractively laid out morning room. Speaking words he hoped would be well received. Expressing feelings he hoped would be reciprocated. *I pray I've read all the clues aright.* The looks that had been exchanged over dinner at the Newington's house were just the final set of proofs in his theorem ,and had spurred him into decisive action.

Maybe I would have taken the plunge without a ghostly nudge. Or, maybe we'd have all had grey hairs by then, and it would have been too late. The awful thought that the object of his affections might be wed, have offspring, be dandling a grandchild on their knee by the time William had plucked up courage to speak had been the final step on the road to decision. It would have to be now, or live forever in regret.

How could I have been so timid?

He decided to go over the field, rather than down the lane, vaulting the stile and striding over the crisp, hard ground. A robin called loudly from the bare hawthorn bush. The sky was bluer than it ever seemed to manage in summer when the haze spoiled the clarity. The crisp air made his nostrils tingle. It felt good to be alive in this, the best of all possible words on this, the best of all possible days. The sight of two bonneted figures coming along the lane confirmed he'd made the right decision regarding his route; now he'd got his courage in place, it might prove calamitous to be diverted into small talk, and the acceptance of a box full of mince pies.

Funny how he'd been bombarded with little offerings, which he'd passed on without a second thought, yet discarded the only one which really would have mattered. He began to wonder if there'd been more of the same, regular offerings for which he'd mistaken the provenance, little signs of affection, a nudge in the direction of *I am fond of you but have no other opportunity of acknowledging it.* And he'd probably ignored every one of them, for so long. Now that he'd been nudged from another direction, he could admit the truth. Every time he'd met his benefactor there had been a spark between them, some sort of electricity that arced through the air and made each exceedingly aware of the other. *Or so I now believe. Please God I'm not reading this all awry.*

William vaulted a second stile, into a magnificent garden. He strode over the lawns, whistling, almost leaping up the steps to the great front door, rapping the knocker firmly. The day was to be seized, and if it all turned out to be a dreadful mistake then he would have to hope that Mr. Newington could find him a nice little post out in Polynesia, or somewhere equally distant from Hampshire that wasn't on a regular postal route. The butler opened the door, produced, when he saw who was calling, the nearest thing he ever wore to a smile, and took William's card. He only raised his eyebrow very slightly when William asked to see not Miss Swann, but her brother. If he speculated for a moment about whether the visit was to ask Benjamin to give his sister's hand, he was too well trained to show his curiosity; that sort of conjecture would have to await his return to the servants' hall where he might seek the opinion of the cook.

The butler ushered the curate into the library, a room which smelled sweeter than many similar places William had been in. There was no dank, musty odour to suggest books which were more for show than for pleasure. Unloved and uncared for rows of leather bound volumes in a setting which rarely saw heat, air or usage. This library was a place of enjoyment and relaxation, perhaps a refuge from the constant companionship of a sibling, even from a beloved one. Someone came here regularly, and their choice of reading – if the scattered volumes were anything to go by – spoke of a keen sense of humour and interest in the world. *So far so good.*

The door swung noiselessly open. "Mr. Church. I wondered if you were here to see Beatrice, but Prior is certain it's me you require." Benjamin Swann's face lit up in a smile of welcome.

"You have such an interesting way with words. And it's William, remember? Or so I asked you to call me when you entertained us all at Whitsun, and many a time since."

"William, then. That was a magnificent evening; it's a long time since I've had such a brace of hares, and Prior excelled himself with decanting the port. I'm forgetting my manners, please take a seat." Benjamin took one of the chairs that sat in front of the fire, letting his guest take the other. "Is this a business call or merely social?"

"Perhaps both, perhaps neither. I…" the remark was left orphaned in the air, Prior having discreetly slipped into the room with a pot of steaming coffee and a plate of sandwiches.

"I took the liberty of ordering this." Benjamin smiled, indicating that he would serve the drink, and the butler could go. "I knew you'd be thirsty after all that ringing, and I guessed that a bottle of beer might be superfluous."

"Indeed – the verger saw us well provided for in that respect. This will be excellent, thank you. It was warm work in the tower, and cold ale was just the job, but I'm fair frozen from the walk over, so a hot drink is exactly what I could do with." William wished that he could put his other needs into words so easily and succinctly. "Benjamin, the evening we were the Newingtons' guests, and we had that rather odd visitor, do you believe he was a ghost?"

"Well, if he wasn't I have no idea what he was. Lawyers can't appear and disappear into and out of thin air and I rather think that a magician would have been more showy. I've assumed him to be a spectre of some sort and a heavenly messenger of some sort to boot. He certainly wanted to make his point."

"Have you thought about what he said?" William cradled his coffee cup in cold, clammy hands.

"I suspect that every one of us thought about what he said. It would take a very indifferent person not to be in some way curious." Benjamin seemed to find the fire fascinating, as if the solution to this mystery lay there.

"I wonder how many of us have been wondering if we were the ones being addressed?"

"Indeed, that's the conclusion I reached." William stared at the fire, willing it to give him the right words. He had been so full of courage ringing the bells and wandering over the fields, although now that he was here, finally grasping the nettle, he'd begun to lose his nerve.

"I believe he was addressing me on some particular points." Benjamin's voice sounded strained, something to give William encouragement, but there was no indication made of which points his friend had in mind.

"He certainly meant me. He was so adamant about it he returned later the same night." William grinned, amused to see the start his host had given. Benjamin always looked more handsome than usual when surprised or flushed. "This time I received the lecture, or whatever you'd call it, in the privacy of my own room. But it was none the less unnerving for that."

"What on earth did he say? Oh, I'm sorry." Benjamin held up his hand. "That was rude of me. The message must have been private."

"It was, although anyone might have heard it and been none the wiser. More of the same. Being told to buck my ideas up, just like the head master might have told me to, if I'd not been attending at school." William placed another sandwich on his plate, discussing ghosts and their messages clearly being an everyday occurrence and one for which a meal couldn't be interrupted. "And if I don't do what I'm supposed to, I'll receive the spectral equivalent to a visit to the head's study and six of the best. I am under notice."

"And have you," Benjamin's voice sounded strained and quiet, absorbed by the books and the growing tension in the air, "taken your lesson to heart?"

"I have." William laid down both cup and plate, suddenly too serious even for food or drink. "I have come to the conclusion – well, I came to the conclusion long ago, but this is a declaration of it - that whatever the expectation of the parish, I shall be refraining from asking for the hand of your sister or

Miss Ardleigh. I know that Miss Swann will be disappointed, but perhaps you would explain my decision to her. I couldn't embarrass her with an explanation face to face. That would make it obvious that I'd made some assumptions about her feelings."

"I think all of those assumptions were well founded." Benjamin held up the coffee pot to offer a refill, but was declined. "She thinks the world of you, William, although I wouldn't have you feeling any guilt about not obliging her. I'll take her to Bath for a fortnight and let her parade among the promenaders. Some handsome naval lieutenant will catch her eye, and your blue eyes will fade from her memory."

The reference to his eyes was welcome, giving William an extra spark of courage. "It's not just your sister I can't oblige. I won't be making an offer to any of the highly eligible ladies who seem to throng St. Archibald's. It is my expectation," he addressed the fire, the little flame of courage guttering, "that I will remain a lifelong bachelor."

Benjamin unexpectedly grinned, his striking features aglow with some unleashed emotion. "You've not only thought about that spectre's words – you've begun to talk like him." He reached over and slapped William's knee, a playful gesture which was out of character.

William grinned in return, the seed of hope in his soul beginning to germinate anew. "I'll simplify it then. I don't think I'm the marrying kind."

"Do you know, I think I'm the same, William. Miss Ardleigh is a charming thing and my opinion of her hasn't diminished by having her praises constantly trumpeted by my sister. She deserves a fine husband – all the lovely spinsters of St. Archibald's do. Could you not introduce some of them to that nice man over at St. Benedict's with whom you swap cakes and walking sticks?"

"I might just do that. He's under severe pressure from the rector to find himself a wife, and he wouldn't turn down such a wonderful choice of candidates." William lifted his cup to be refilled. "I should have thought of that for myself. He has the spare cakes and comforters, why not the spare affection?"

"Didn't you once tell me he has a private income to feather his nest with? The Ardleighs would be delighted to see their daughter well set up. Alas, I don't feel able to fulfil the role of the blushing bridegroom for them." They sat for a while, eating and drinking in a pleasant silence.

"I am sorry about your father's cane. I can't say it enough." William shrugged. "If I had known it was from you I would have cherished the thing, I..."

Benjamin raised his hand again, a gesture almost of absolution. "I should have brought the thing round myself, if I'd had any sense. It was a genuine mistake, and one for which I bear no grudge. Please, let us hear no more about it."

"Thank you." William sighed, happily then stretched out his legs until his boots and Swann's were just touching. "Choosing the bachelor life isn't the simplest option by any means. It won't be easy to keep the spinsters from the door, but I'll have to find a way. Have you any advice to give me?" He tapped his friend's foot with his own.

"I might suggest you begin by finding a house and a steady male companion to share your bachelor establishment with, but that would probably increase the volume of female traffic along your path. Twice the nectar to entice the bees." Benjamin returned the little nudge.

"At least then I wouldn't be short of companionship; lodging with a family like the Hattons is eminently comfortable and respectable, although it's not the same as having one's own fireside, and the company of one's choosing." Words were flowing easily now and although he couldn't put things exactly into the words he wanted to use – anyone might walk in through the door – then at least he could make his meaning plain.

"I would suggest you lodge here but my sister's presence would give occasion for talk, and raise her hopes rather too much." Benjamin leaned forwards, steepling his hands. "I have a cottage in the village, you know. It wants some work done but after that it would be ready for a tenant. I could chivvy the men along to have it completed no later than the end of January, should you be interested in a place you could call your own." Benjamin's eyes shone.

"And companionship? I could find a housekeeper easily enough, but…" William's gaze held his friend's, challenging him to just say the words that would confirm all his hopes had been rightly placed.

"I could visit, if you wanted, as often as you wished. I find your company more than pleasing – in fact, I cannot think of any person with whom I would rather spend my time." Benjamin nudged Church's boot again, with his own. "It wouldn't be unseemly, a landlord visiting his tenant or any man visiting his particular friend."

"A trompe l'oeil."

"I beg your pardon?"

"Something to deceive the eye. Sleight of hand." William smiled, clasped his hands behind his head, a head that felt it was about to explode from happiness. "Not my words – a little more advice from beyond the grave."

"Aha. That ghost goes up in my estimation all the time. One might apply his suggestions here," Benjamin's hand indicated the library and, by dint of it, the rest of the house. "If my sister marries, which please God will be sooner rather than later, I will be left in this big house forlorn and desolate." He grinned. "I'll need companionship, someone to help me buck up my flagging spirits. As curate, it would be your bounden duty to provide comfort to your parishioners."

"It would not be a duty to provide you with comfort, Benjamin." William's voice was hardly more than a whisper. "It would rank among the great pleasures of my life."

"As much of a pleasure as your beloved bells?"

"Indeed. Maybe more."

"Now that I can't believe." Benjamin leaned forward, gently touching William's elbow. "The first thing the ladies of St.

Archibald's should be jealous of is that carillon – they have far too large a portion of your heart."

"I could give up the bells, should it be required of me." William touched the hand on his arm, just briefly, although the contact spoke more than four dozen words might have. "I couldn't have my heart divided."

"Dear God, no." Benjamin tightened his grip. "I didn't intend anything like that. I was just…letting words tumble out. I can't say what I really want, not here, so I say things which are merely related. I speak of love for a set of bells, because I dare not speak of love for another person. "

"I've hoped, ever since you upbraided me about your father's walking cane, that's what you felt as well." William stroked the hand which clasped him, then let it go; they didn't need to speak now, meanings were abundantly clear. "If you are serious about the cottage, then I would be more than happy to accept your offer – both of your offers. But I would rather live alone than live a lie, Benjamin. Those words at dinner, I believed at the time they were a challenge to acknowledge the truth about myself. The second visitation was no more than a stroke of the whip to my rear, like I was a horse afraid to take a fence. I've taken it now."

"You will face the same sorts of prejudices that the vicar has, we both will." Benjamin's voice had dropped to a whisper. "Perhaps even more so given that there would be more to take issue with – if Lady O'Neill of Jarosite Mansion frowns on a dusky face, then she would have the vapours at the thought of…" he shrugged, sat back and nudged William's boot again.

"I will continue to pray, I will continue to search my four books, but I have to admit where I stand now, and you're the one I have to make my confession to, not Lady O'Neill. She, my dear friend, can keep her nose out of my affairs. Our affairs."

Benjamin left his chair to sit at his visitor's feet, his dark head barely a hand's breadth from William's knee. "I think we both stand in the same place, and it's exposed. Were I my sister I could take your hand at this moment, and no-one would say a word." He kept his own hands tightly clasped together, perhaps afraid they might commit all sorts of scandalous acts if not kept firmly controlled.

"Were you your sister I wouldn't want you to take my hand." William laughed then stretched out to touch Benjamin's black curls. He ruffled them affectionately, fingering a stray one. "I hope we will always share this same truthfulness from now on."

"Many married couples don't achieve the same candour." Benjamin reached up to touch the hand resting on his hair. "And how many people can even say they were wedded for love alone?"

"Don't start Canon Newington on that particular hare. He'd have you know that's the reason so many men break the seventh commandment." William squeezed the strong fingers which held his. "It can't be easy to share the marital bed with someone you have little affection for."

"Now, do I hear a curate condoning adultery?"

"You do not." William rapped his knuckles on Benjamin's skull. "You hear a man who despairs sometimes at the mess we've made of things. Society seems to have imposed all sorts of needless laws and expectations on things which should be simple."

"You should preach on it, next evensong." Benjamin turned, looking up into the curate's piercing blue eyes. "Only, not Leviticus. Please don't choose any of that as your text."

"Would I ever? I'm tired enough of hypocrisy. No…" William laid his hand on his friend's chest, keeping a decent distance between them. "I don't doubt your butler's discretion, but I can't read his mind. He'll be here for the plates and cups soon."

"It's a shame a man can't do what he wants in his own house." Benjamin lay his head, briefly, on William's knees.

"I won't keep a butler at that cottage. I'll have a decent housekeeper – Mrs. Newington can find me one – who can come in to clean and cook then leave me to my own devices. Then we can do what we want in my house. Your house."

"Our house."

William smiled, caressing those lustrous black curls again. "If we have to kiss behind a closed door then so be it. Rather a much desired kiss in the dark, than an undesired one in the light." He leant down and gently brushed his friend's brow with his lips. Benjamin's arm reached up to caress his friend's head then let it go, prudence conquering desire as it would habitually have to in this relationship. "The sooner I have that cottage ready the better. Until then perhaps all we can have is friendship."

William wrinkled his nose. "Unless you can persuade Beatrice to accompany Miss Ardleigh on a visit to the parish of Harmington in early January. They could fight over Mr. Regan, the curate, to their heart's content. He has that nice fortune of his own, and the excitements of the town would do them both good. There might even be some of the more eligible members of the military stationed there for a while, if their luck holds."

"The soldiers or the young ladies'?"

"Either or both, as long as they're out from under our feet. If Lady O'Neill could act as chaperone, then we'd be left to our own devices. And desires."

"Lady O'Neill? Not Mrs. Newington?" Benjamin tapped his friend's knee.

"Our lovely denizen of the rectory wouldn't give us any trouble. Probably encourage us. We need to remove the sources of outraged gossip."

"We'll never do that, William." Benjamin smoothed the fabric of his friend's trousers, just as they fell along his calves. It wasn't just his arms which were a mass of muscles. "Just like the way they talk about Mrs. Newington – someone will always believe she eats men's flesh."

"She survives the gossip. So will we." William's grave face suddenly broke into a smile. "You could start by having an accident on your horse. Oh, not a real one, only a reported one

— your gamekeeper will back up your story, muddying your clothes and helping you home."

"I don't follow…"

"A piece of prestidigitation. Spread the story that your injuries have left you unable to fulfil the duties of a husband. No-one would be so uncouth as to enquire too closely. It would put off the ladies and deflect the gossipers as well. You'd only be visiting me to receive a little pastoral comfort."

Benjamin grasped his friend's hand and squeezed it for a moment. "That's such a mad idea it might just work. I'll start planning my strategy immediately. Now all that remains is working out how you'll explain to those ladies why you can't offer them the position of curate's wife."

"I've had that plan in mind for a long time. I'll say I feel called to take a vow of celibacy for the foreseeable future, so I can concentrate on my vocation. It's an approximation of the truth that may serve very well." The squeeze of hands was returned. "If the accident line of attack doesn't come off you might have to employ the same thing with Madeleine. Now, it won't do to rouse Prior's suspicions. Lay the board for chess and we can pretend to play, if you'll have me stay awhile."

"*Have* you? What sort of words are those to use on such an occasion?" Benjamin lowered his voice — Prior could enter a room as silently as Toomhai Gamali had done. "For the first time I understand how the stallion feels when he comes to the mare."

"Then you'd best get your men working on that cottage, hadn't you?" William just managed to change his swoop towards his friend's lips into reaching for the white rook as the butler glided in.

"Didn't Mr. Church preach beautifully yesterday?" Madeleine Ardleigh sat at her friend's fireside, the roaring blaze keeping the cold at bay. Winter had struck with a vengeance, the wind more biting than the snow and January even colder than December had been.

"He has a way with Romans." Beatrice Swann picked at her embroidery, tackling an annoyingly knotted thread. *All members have not the same office; so we, being many, are one body in Christ.* Her brother had read the lesson, as a member of the Swann family always had the first Sunday after Epiphany, and he'd sounded as if he believed every word, as had the curate when he'd taken it as his text.

"All the different gifts we have to offer," Madeleine snipped off a loose thread from her work, holding it to the light to find any other flaws. "It's a wonderful thought."

Beatrice snorted – a ladylike sniff but a marked one. "He seems reluctant to acknowledge our gifts."

"Oh, I'm not sure he is. He was admiring my needlework on the altar cloth just the other day and," she added grudgingly, "he remarked to me that your flowers were beautifully arranged this Sunday. And he always says how wonderfully we all sing."

"He told me, too, but that's not quite what I meant." Beatrice stamped her foot then began to unpick a row of stitches. She wanted her tablecloth to be ready for Mr. Church's taking up residence at the little cottage her brother owned. "I'm beginning to think he doesn't appreciate all I, we, do for him."

"Now, why on earth should you think that?" Madeleine had never contemplated that the curate might be less than delighted with the flurry of gifts she showered on him. They were certainly of better quality than most of the offerings which the spinsters of the parish drummed up, although she suspected Beatrice outdid even her. "He always says 'thank you' so graciously."

"But that's all he gives us, isn't it? A 'thank you' and a flashing smile. Never an invitation to dine with him. Mrs. Hatton would be able to cook and act as chaperone, or he could ask Benjamin along, yet there's never a hint." Beatrice stopped, aware she'd spoken too freely this time.

"He's shy, that's all." Madeleine's words sounded so unconvincing, they hardly fooled herself.

"Who's shy?" Benjamin swung the door open, to feminine shouts of complaint that he was letting in a draught.

"Mr. Church." Madeleine arranged herself as attractively as she could on her chair.

"Is he? I'll have to take your word for that." Benjamin took a seat beside his sister. "Would you agree, Beatrice? Is my new tenant bashful?"

"Not when he's riding your second best hunter or teaching that team of bell ringers new ways of torturing our ears."

"I thought you liked the bells." Madeleine was horrified at the perfidious words. How could her friend have turned coat so readily?

"What we could do with in this parish is less noise and more," Beatrice seemed to be searching for the right word, "*action.* It's been weeks now and not a peep out of him. We were all there, we heard what Mrs. Newington's ghost said. And all we've seen since is more prevarication."

"Are you so sure the ghost addressed his remarks to our curate?" Benjamin's face wore a deceptively innocent look, which meant mischief. "He wasn't suggesting you girls take less time over deciding what dresses you're to wear?"

"My dear brother, if we weren't entertaining, I'd slap you."

"I really don't know what you expect of the man, my dear. He can't marry every spinster in the parish, so perhaps he's chosen to marry none. It can't be every man's lot to take a wife." Benjamin studied his boots.

"Oh." Madeleine flushed, conscious they'd strayed onto *that which couldn't be mentioned.* Mr. Swann still looked pale from his accident at the St. Stephen's day hunt and, although he'd never said outright what had happened, word had quickly spread around the parish. If anyone knew the truth of things it would be the gamekeeper and he'd, with as much discretion as an ordinary man could manage, disseminated the news about his employer's tragic injury. Sad to think there'd be no heir to this estate, not one of the direct line, anyway. Sadder also to think that she'd lost her second option.

"Thank you." Benjamin kept his eyes down. "You've been most understanding. I have decided to turn my energies to other matters. It is important for a man to be useful."

"Maybe you should take up this." Beatrice thrust the half finished tablecloth in front of her brother, her eyes bright with something which might be anger. "Perhaps Mr. Church would appreciate your handiwork more than ours."

"There's someone at the door with a cake." Mrs. Hawthorne pointed with her duster, in case the curate had forgotten where the front door was.

"A particular someone or just a chance passer by?" William emerged from under the table, where he was fixing a wobbly leg. This piece had graced his late aunt's dining room, a present from her own aunt on her wedding day. It had been lovingly tended and now looking entirely in place in its new home, alongside the slightly showier pieces the Swanns had provided for their tenant.

"Get on with you, Mr. Church. It's a lovely young lady with a yellow bonnet and a blue dress. Eyes like sapphires." Mrs. Hawthorne started to laugh.

William paled. "Would you tell her that I'm very grateful but I'm rather busy at present, and if she could leave the cake with you, I'll see to it…whatever is going on?"

Mrs. Hawthorne wiped her eyes on her apron. "It's that Mr. Swann. He's brought a bottle of something to welcome you to your new home, only he said I had to tell you it was one of the young ladies."

"I think I might have to kill him and you'll have to help me bury the body." William borrowed the duster to wipe his hands. "Although those girls will come, Mrs. Hawthorne and you – or Mrs. Wakeling when it's just her here – may do well to remember my answer so you can tell them. I can't be seen to have favourites in the parish."

"Of course you can't, sir. And there's been three lasses here already today, but I've cut all of them off on the path. Quite a pile of jam and scones on the kitchen table for you."

"Tell Mrs. Wakeling to sneak them home and give them to her next door neighbour. The one with the husband at sea."

"And what shall I tell Mr. Swann, sir?" Mrs. Hawthorne's smile filled her face with dimples.

"Dear me. I'd almost forgotten him." William made to roll down his sleeves then thought better of it. Benjamin would appreciate seeing his arms. "Mr. Swann," he said, even before he'd reached the hall, "to keep you waiting on the doorstep is unforgivable." They shook hands, grinning madly at each other - there'd been keen anticipation of this moment on both sides. They'd not been alone since they'd met over sandwiches and confessions; even when William had paid a visit post 'accident' Beatrice had hovered about, fussing over her brother and offering their visitor copious quantities of tea. "Come in, do. Mrs. Hawthorne could rustle us up a pot of coffee before she goes home. Keep the cold out."

"I'd appreciate that. I brought a bottle to bring you luck but I'm not sure I could face anything cold yet, after walking over in that wind." Benjamin thrust the wine forward. "At least you won't need to stand it in a cooler."

"Let's put it aside for later." William placed it on the deep stone windowsill then ushered his guest into a seat by the fire.

"That's better." Benjamin took off his gloves, rubbing his hands in front of the flames. "I was quite numb. That's a fine blaze going there."

"You must thank your sweep. He's got this drawing beautifully. Yesterday, I was afraid I'd be spending my first night here perished, but all the chimneys are excellent."

"Tried them all, have you?"

"Mrs. Hawthorne and Mrs. Wakeling have got every one of the fires going, afraid that if they didn't air every inch of the place they'd find me dead in the morning." William lazed back in his chair, then sat bolt upright. "You walked, you say?"

"I did, and I regretted it half way, when it was too late to go home."

"The verger is convinced we're about to have another blizzard. Mrs. Hawthorne is under orders to be home within the hour." The curate laid his hand briefly on his guest's arm. "I suspect it won't be quite so bad, but you can't walk back in it. You'll catch your death."

"Then you'll have to do your duty as a man of the cloth and put me up. From the marvellous aromas coming out of your kitchen I suspect there's at least a bit of bread for me to sup on." Benjamin settled into his chair as if he had no intention of going anywhere else before tomorrow at the earliest.

"Won't Beatrice worry about you? Won't she think you're at the bottom of a drift, somewhere?"

"I saw my gamekeeper's son, struggling up to the house with a gun almost as big as a cannon, which his father needed. I sent a message with him."

"And told the boy to get himself a pie from Prior's pantry, I suppose." William leaned forwards, narrowing the gap between them. "You're as generous as anyone I've met here, a quality I value very highly when the gifts are given without wishing for reward."

"In young Matthew's case that would be true. But how can you be sure that bottle of wine isn't offered in hopes of services returned? I haven't forgotten our conversation in the library."

"Neither have I. It's the first thing I think of every morning when I wake…"

Mrs. Hawthorne bustling in with tea and cakes put an end to any more confidences. "Might I be getting home now, sir? I'll take Mrs. Wakeling with me, and Mr. H. can see her home. It's going to be a nasty night, I fear."

"That's fine, thank you. And tell Mrs. Wakeling not to worry if the snow sets in and she can't get here early – I'm confident I can get the copper going, or at least set a kettle on the stove."

"That's no work for a curate. Mrs. Newington always says you need a mother to look after you, Mr. Church." The verger's wife smiled her dimpled smile and left.

"How odd." William poured them tea, steaming and aromatic from the shining brown pot.

"What is?" Benjamin took the cup and reached for a slice of cake.

"That Mrs. Newington said I needed a mother to look after me, rather than a wife. I hope it's just because she looks on me as no more than a slip of a lad, one who still needs protecting from shameless hussies. I can't believe she suspects, not such a respectable matron." William never seemed to take much notice of Jane Newington's provenance.

"Ah."

"And what does that mean?"

"I have a suspicion that Beatrice might say the same, mother rather than wife. There have been one or two remarks passed since my *accident,* which have left me wondering if she doesn't have an inkling about how I feel. How we feel." Benjamin laid down his cup and studied the fire.

"Tonight, if you should stay, will she suspect?"

"Something, if not all. She believes the story of my accident, enough to have told Miss Ardleigh, which she'd not have done if she still felt I could cut her rival out of your way. Still, whatever she suspects, she won't say anything, no matter how cross she is. The scandal it would create around Lady O'Neill's drawing room wouldn't make it worth her while." Benjamin shifted himself, sitting at his friend's feet, with his head on the man's knees. Strong hands caressed his ears and ran their sturdy fingers through his hair. "Once the weather's better I'll take her to Bath, tell everyone the waters will help my injury. Then I'll find her a nice chap, nothing worse than a commander with a quarter-decked sloop."

"Toomhai Gamali would approve of your pluck."

"Has he been again?"

"No, not since that evening when he spoke of magic tricks. It worries me sometimes - I half expected him to come along today and tell me whether he approved of our trompes l'oeiul."

"Maybe he'll come tonight – he seems to be fond of a good blaze." Benjamin rocked onto his knees, stretched up so that he and William were face to face. "Or maybe he'll wait until actions have followed words. Then he'll know that you've really decided to follow your heart." He leaned forwards, closing the gap between them to the breadth of a ribbon. "Have you really decided?"

"I have." William closed the distance completely, letting his lips just brush the other man's. "Have you?"

"Do you doubt it? I've even let the parish make game of my manhood, all for the sake of this." He swept his hand around the room, brought it back to rest on William's. "For your sake." He pressed his lips to his friend's, savouring the sweet taste of cakes and tea. The curate returned the pressure, pulling Benjamin close and just tasting the edge of his lips with a delicate tongue. The man's mouth opened to receive it, letting it play tenant in his mouth, finding a home there where it was welcomed and cherished.

"Hold." William reluctantly pulled back. "It's a filthy night, but we've no guarantee there won't be folk abroad. I've not even drawn the curtains, and we'll shine out into the night for anyone to see. I don't mind my maker knowing my business, but not my fellow man. Not yet."

"We could put out the light, let the fire bank down. Once the snow sets in, it would take a very determined or desperate man to come here. And if they were desperate it would be your duty to attend to them first, not me."

"I'd feel safer if we left this room, went somewhere we weren't quite so exposed."

"You said that all the rooms are aired. If we went upstairs we'd be both out of sight and earshot should some visitor decide their curate had ignored their knocking because he'd simply retired for the night and then came barging in to find you." The breathless anticipation and hope was evident in Benjamin's voice.

William rose, gesturing graciously towards the door. "Let's find out how well Mrs. Hawthorne has prepared my room, shall we?"

The guttering candle they'd taken to light their way up the stairs fought hard, even shielded by the curate's hand, against the draughts which sneaked around the front door. "I'm glad I stayed," Benjamin trod carefully; the stairs were old and unforgiving. "I'd have caught my death out there."

"I'm glad you stayed, too." William held the door to his bedroom open, allowing his friend to be first across the threshold. "And not just because of the risk to your health." He closed the door behind them, putting the candle holder down where it might have a chance of survival. He turned, taking the lapels of Benjamin's jacket to caress them with eager hands. "At last…" The words were hardly more than a whisper.

Benjamin leaned into the embrace, kissing William with undisguised ardour, now that there was no risk on them being seen. His tongue was impatient and strong, as predatory as the vixen which wreaked havoc among his pheasant chicks, as tender as the same animal with her cubs. "I've waited so long for this, William, and the last few weeks have been the worst." He received no more meaningful answer than another passionate kiss, one which seemed to come from the depths of his friend's being.

"We might be more comfortable were we to…" William indicated the bed, old but sturdy, beautifully made with an embroidered quilted counterpane speaking of softness and warmth.

Benjamin took him by the hand, led him over as delicately as a bridegroom might a bashful girl. One who knew nothing of what went on in beds except for sleep. But then, maybe they were both in that position. "I don't know if I should be the one leading. I'm not sure I'm more than a blind guide."

"Then it's the blind to lead the blind." They sat together on the bed, prim as two maidens, until William began to laugh.

"What would Beatrice think to see us now? There's not even a hint of scandal for her to fret over."

"Then we should amend that situation." A strong pair of arms wound themselves around the curate's waist. "I believe this might be the way to start." He pulled William closer, plundering his mouth again, the warm, moist taste of tongue and lips sweeter than port or syrup pudding. It seemed natural to roll themselves gently onto the counterpane, letting their bodies range alongside one another.

"I'm not sure we need these boots." William moved back, reluctantly, from the pleasurable contact.

"Surplus to requirements, definitely." Benjamin grinned, sitting up to discard his own boots, and jacket with them. "I suppose that most of this might end up surplus to requirements at some point."

William had thrust off jacket, stock, boots and stockings, letting his strong feet bend and turn to make strange shadows in the guttering light. "Lie down next to me again. Please."

"Of course." Benjamin flexed his neck, loosening any remaining cold or tension, then leaned back until they were side by side once more, the heat of the fire keeping them warm, although their smouldering ardour would have had the same effect. The kisses began again, soft and tender, heated and raw, mixed with exploration from eager hands.

"Oh." William gasped for breath as his friend's hand brushed past the front of his breeches.

"I'm sorry, I…"

"No apology required, my dear Benjamin. On the contrary, I should give you my thanks. Blind we may be but we've stumbled on the right road." He returned the contact, with more intent and precision, making the other man gasp.

"I see what you mean." Benjamin took his friend's hand away from where it was causing such intriguing sensations, "As long as you are absolutely sure you wish to proceed."

"You've started to talk like that ghost." William laughed, moving his hand firmly back to where it had been so contented to play awhile. "I am completely sure. I've dreamed often enough of this moment – guilty dreams, although now we come to it there's no remorse. I'll never have a wedding ring on my finger so I have no incentive to wait for the night of my nuptials." He began his predations again, gently insinuating his fingers under the soft material.

"I'm pleased that's your answer." Benjamin gently placed kisses on his friend's neck. "I'm not sure I could have borne it had the answer been otherwise. I've dreamed of this, too, with probably as much guilt as you felt. And I, too, have lost that feeling, except in regard to my sister. I wish she didn't fancy you so much."

"I'm sorry, but what else can we do? I can't not kiss you for her sake." William moved his hand away, reluctantly. He couldn't do this if the shade of remorse haunted his bedroom.

"I know. And I can't not kiss you either." Benjamin kept his word, kissing William with enough ardour to drive away any unwelcome spirits. "It's an old saying but a true one. What can't be cured…"

"Must be endured." The curate smiled, laid his hand back on his friend's breeches.

"I wouldn't apply the word 'endured' to my response to what you're doing." Benjamin's breath came shorter now, his voice deepening and mellowing. His own hand mirrored his friend's movements, hoping to bring him equal delight.

William swallowed hard, strange sensations beginning to run up his spine and down from his stomach. His fingers found their target, eagerly undoing buttons and strings in search of flesh.

"Would it be easier if we removed some more of these surplus items?" Benjamin's voice was hardly more than a hoarse whisper.

"Yes, if you'd be so kind. It's hard enough navigating uncharted waters without having to deal with obstacles. Oh." William had seen other men naked before – he'd sampled the delights of bathing often when at Oxford – but Benjamin was a magnificent specimen, much more so than any he'd seen on the riverbank. Especially in his current state of excitement. "I'm afraid I'm bound to disappoint you. I have nothing to offer that's anywhere near as splendid."

Benjamin's cheeks burned a sudden fierce crimson. "Whatever you have to offer will be more than enough for me." He carefully removed William's clothes, like a nurse might make a child ready for its bath. "See? Wonderful." He placed his hand on the object of his admiration. "Ready and willing to serve, as well. I expected nothing less."

"Always at your service, my dearest friend." William put his words into action, caressing gently and then with slow, deliberate strength, until neither of them could speak or think coherently.

"Thank you." Benjamin's voice, when he regained control of it, was low and soft. "I'm grateful beyond all measure to have shared that with you and not..." He left the sentence dangling, perhaps at a loss for something which wouldn't break the enchantment of the moment.

"A woman you didn't love but had married for duty? I agree entirely." William held his friend tightly, as if afraid he'd lose him to the world if he didn't cling fast.

"And is it possible you're as happy as I am?"

"Happy? Yes, more content than I ever hoped or thought to be. One small cloud on the horizon, although no bigger than a man's hand."

"My sister?" Benjamin held his lover close, as if he could squeeze all guilty thoughts from him. "Please don't worry about her, I'll do everything I can to make her as content as I am."

William kissed his friend's shoulder. "No, not Beatrice, bless her. It's the ghost. I can't get him out of my mind; I feel there's some unfinished business there."

"You need his benison, perhaps?"

"Aye, something like that. To be assured that I really have got it right, done what I was meant to do."

"Are two visits not enough? Must you be told so many times?" Benjamin fondly ruffled his friend's hair. "Just like a child needing constant reassurance after a nightmare."

"It's been a nightmare these last few years. I can't seem to believe that it's all come to an end and feels so...right."

"No bad dreams tonight, my dear." Benjamin rose reluctantly from their embrace, needing to wash and use the pot before sleeping. Prosaic, unromantic actions although they seemed natural now, as if they were a long married couple who knew and treasured each other's every deed, no matter how ordinary.

"Not with you by my side and the snow thick enough to put off all but the most determined visitor." William stretched, awaiting his own turn with ewer and bowl, anticipating sleep and perhaps another sweetly amorous encounter. "Did I tell you I love you, when we were..." he made an eloquent gesture.

"I'm ashamed to say I don't remember. Nor if I told you the same. But I do, with all my heart."

Benjamin shook the last lumps of snow from his boots, the bits which had eluded the scraper and brush.

"Made it home at last, then?" Beatrice came down the stairs, smiling and planting and a sisterly kiss on his cheek. "I'm glad you sent word with the boy or I'd have had Prior and all the rest of them out searching. It's been a nasty couple of nights."

"It has, and I'd have caught my death if I'd attempted to be out in them. Mr. Church has been kind enough to put me up." He looked sidelong at his sister, but if she was thinking anything amiss, she was keeping it well hidden.

"Miss Ardleigh is here."

"Oh." Benjamin felt himself colouring. "She's a brave girl, being out in this."

"She's been here two nights. On her way home from Harmington when the snow set in. Her coachman dropped her here then took the horse alone home. I pray that he arrived safely."

"So do I. It wasn't any sort of weather to be out in."

"No. I told her you'd decided to stay down in the village with your...friend."

Benjamin caught the edge in his sister's voice.

"I'm not blind, Benjamin, nor am I stupid. I can guess why neither you nor Mr. Church seem in any hurry to find yourselves a wife." Beatrice held her brother's gaze steadily.

"I shan't dissemble then." It was all he could say, thoughts of imminent disgrace whirling in his head.

"Not in front of me. However, as I said, I'm not stupid. I may not be happy about the situation, but I shan't be ruining my own prospects by making reference to it. I've still a chance of finding some half-decent man in this vicinity." A wan smile graced Beatrice's face. "Your secret is safe with me, it will have to be. Your lack on interest in the fair sex will be blamed on the *accident*, of course." She slipped her hand through his arm. "As much as I struggle to approve, I must admit I can't recall you being so happy, not for a long time. I wish you'd wave a wand and work the same magic on me."

"William, Mr. Church, recommends a trip to Bath and the pleasures of the promenade. We'll find you someone that's much more than half decent. Only the best for my sister." Benjamin kissed her cheek.

"No, Benjamin. You've got the best for yourself. I'll have to settle for something less."

They held each other close, out in the cold hall, as they'd held each other when their mother had died hard on the heels of their father. They'd faced one crisis together; they had the resources to deal with another. "Now," Benjamin kissed his sister once more. "You must help me face Miss Ardleigh. It's not going to be an easy time ahead."

Beatrice grinned, whispering, "She's not as clever nor as keen sighted," as they entered the room.

"Miss Ardleigh." Benjamin bowed. "I'm so pleased that my sister was able to help you last night. It would have been awful to be out in that storm."

"Are the roads passable now? I was afraid I'd be here for a week." Her voice suggested she was quite happy to be stuck a few days longer, now that the master of the house was home.

"There's been no fresh snow these past twelve hours and the village is seeing the start of a thaw. Unless it turns again, you should be able to make your way home by tomorrow. You'll take our carriage, of course." Benjamin settled himself by the fire, flexing icy fingers and trying not to think of two nights spent in front of the curate's hearth, nights of unbelievable bliss.

"Thank you. Is Mr. Church settled in his new abode? Beatrice says you found shelter with him."

Benjamin suddenly found the fire to be in need to rearrangement. He attacked a couple of ill-balanced logs with the poker as he spoke. "Mrs. Hawthorne and her friend have made sure he's got every comfort. We had bread, cheese and some of the late apples. What more could a man want? Oh, and," he added hastily, remembering the tales of what had been borne to the door, "some delicious scones and jam. We dined like kings."

"I hope that was our greengage." Beatrice wondered if the red on her brother's face was really caused by the fierceness of the fire.

"I think it was strawberry. Mr. Church's favourite, I believe."

"Is it?" Madeleine's eyes brightened. "I must remember. I always wonder what he would prefer."

"I'm sure Benjamin would be able to tell you." Beatrice wondered if her brother could turn any redder.

"Mr. Church seemed aglow tonight." Jane Newington slipped her arm through her husband's as they wandered home from evensong through the melting snow. "Such a wonderful sermon on Corinthians."

"One of his best, my dear."

Jane's throaty laugh began to bubble up. "If the number of sighs from the ladies was any measure it would outstrip all his past offerings. I've never heard such simpering or seen so many longing looks."

"My father had a mare, once, a fine creature, who wouldn't look at any of the stallions who were offered her. She seemed to have a fancy for the gelding in the next field and wouldn't entertain another suitor."

"I thought it was Mr. Swann who'd gelded himself?"

"Jane! Language!"

"I'm sorry, my dear, it's your strange idiom. Isn't the same word used for men as for horses? You know my grandfather had a gelded slave to look after his wives, it was the tradition." Jane laughed again. "I've always been a bit surprised the same system wasn't used here."

Canon Newington began to speak then held back. This conversation might last an hour and, knowing his wife's curiosity, wander off into castrati and Persian harems. Safer to stay within the parish. "I wasn't referring to Mr. Swann per se, although the same might apply - young women fretting over that which they can never possess. I mean Mr. Church and his vow."

"Ah. Gelding in name, if not reality."

"My dear, whatever has possessed you tonight?" Mr. Newington couldn't help laughing, imagining his parishioners' faces if they heard such stuff.

"Maybe it's Toomhai Gamali." She held his arm tighter. "What makes a young man take such a step? Do you think he's turning papist?"

Her husband shuddered. "He assures me not. He mentioned your friend Toomhai, though. Said he'd been mulling over our spectral visitor's words, and decided the only way forward was to eschew the comforts of the fair sex entirely. It has certainly inspired his preaching."

"Something has." Jane looked sidelong at her husband. "The 'wife-attenders' were said to be very insipid men, as if all their spirit had gone along with – I shan't say the words, dear, I've learned how easily embarrassed folk are on this poor backward isle. You may have given us cricket and Jesus, for both of which we're very grateful, but we could teach you a thing or two about enjoying the good things God has given the world."

"So you keep reminding me." Mr. Newington kissed his wife's brow. "And what was the point you were trying to make this time?"

Jane looked at her husband a long time before answering. "Just how the situation here so closely resembles many of the things which happened at home. Did I ever tell you about the 'wife-attender' assigned to my great aunt? It seems…" she launched into an amusing story of the trials faced by handsome men who were not quite as masculine as they once were, but still stirred up the affections of the women they looked after. It was her own piece of prestidigitation – the canon wasn't ready to hear what she really had to say, about another thing in which her people appeared to be more enlightened. Nor were many in these benighted isles, except perhaps two of the young men of the parish, who would welcome it.

"Very nice."

William Church jumped in his seat, then turned round, a huge grin lighting his face. "I'm glad to see you again." He'd have known where to turn, even if the distinctive voice hadn't come from the direction of the hearth. Toomhai Gamali loved his fireside. The apparition sat primly in the chair which was closest the door, Benjamin's favourite place to be seated.

"And I you. I believe I won't be seeing you again, this side of your taking the last journey, anyway, so I am pleased to find the satisfaction is mutual." As the curate had expected, the ghost took off his spectacles and began to polish them. Spectral visiting must be an extremely mucky occupation.

"Might I ask you what's very nice? The arrangement of this room?"

The ghost looked around, nodding steadily. "It is an exemplary sitting room. You have your desk in the best place to catch the light, and the various objets d'art are tasteful and well chosen. You have taste, Mr. Church. But that is not the thing I alluded to."

William wondered if Toomhai's fellow ghosts found him rather hard work to make conversation with. "I'd be grateful if you'd tell me what is was. It's most pleasurable to have things praised, although puzzling if one's struggling to know what's being lauded."

"I'm sorry. I meant the arrangement you have set up here. Very elegant. Very sensible."

William let out a huge sigh. "I'm so pleased to hear you say that. We…I…we've been so worried that we'd got it all wrong. It's not easy to do when you're a mere mortal and have to work these things out."

"We have things to work out too, Mr. Church. Heaven's no place for slackers." The ghost put his head to one side and produced a disarming smile.

"I'm glad to hear it. I'm not looking forward to being bored in eternity."

"You won't be. But before that you will have work enough. Your vocation and your life; that will be challenge enough to fulfil both of them with diligence and sense. Especially now you have more than one person to consider."

"You sound like Mr. Newington talking to those wastrel husbands who expect their wives to work like slaves, even when they're with child." They watched the fire together companionably, curate and spectre, like two old shipmates taking leave at an inn with no need of talk between them, the understanding running so deep. "I'll always consider him." William broke the silence at last.

"Quite right." The ghost's voice sounded reedy and thin, but that was to be expected as he was already nothing more than a vague outline, a reflection seen in a glass and darkly.

"Is Beatrice enjoying Bath?" William poured two glasses of hock, placing them on the little table where the weak afternoon sun could illuminate them best through the leaded cottage windows. Spring had arrived but an unnaturally cold snap had come along to blight the blossom and pinch tender shoots.

"She thinks it heavenly. She's found someone even more full of herself than Lady O'Neill and has been absorbed into the woman's retinue. A retinue seemingly awash with nephews and second cousins who have chosen to serve the king." Benjamin picked up his glass, inclining it briefly as if making a toast. "Soldiers and sailors."

"I'll drink to them, too. And to her success with them." The curate savoured the excellent vintage. "I've always liked your sister. Had my inclinations run otherwise…"

"She'd have had you like a shot. I suspect that's half the reason she disapproves; not just our attachment but the fact that I got you, not her." Benjamin's voice was mellow, with wine and affection. "Mind you, I always imagined it would be Miss Ardleigh who'd win your heart. Or perhaps I hoped that."

"Why?" William sipped the hock; he didn't want to over imbibe and risk any dulling of events later on.

"Can't you guess? Because it would have been agony to have you so close – a guest at my table, living in my house, perhaps – and have burned with desire. Better to have you half the parish away."

"I've always suspected the easiest way not to be led into temptation is to keep the wretched thing at arm's length." The gentle crackling of the fire created an atmosphere conducive to thought and confession. "Shall I tell you my greatest fear? That you'd propose to Miss Ardleigh and then ask me to perform the ceremony. The thought of joining your hands over the prayer book made my blood run cold."

"Colder than when we first saw Toomhai?" Benjamin laid down his glass, rose then took his place in his favourite seat – on the rug at William's feet, with his head resting on the curate's knee.

"By far. All the ghost brought was the unknown - seeing you married off would have been all too familiar." William ruffled his lover's hair. "Will we finish this bottle now or later?"

"Later?"

"Afterwards." William leaned down, turning Benjamin's face up for a kiss. His lips felt cool and tasted of wine; it was a heady combination.

"There'll be no afterwards until you've told me if Toomhai returned. Something's happened to make you even happier than you were the night of the snow and that's the only thing I can put it down to. Unless you've been offered a post as bishop's chaplain?"

"That wouldn't please me at all. Too far from here to the cathedral close." William's long, elegant fingers caressed his friend's temples. "Yes, he came back. And he gave me, us, a marvellous report. Top of the class."

"No wonder you're smiling like a cat that's got into the dairy. Or Beatrice when Lady O'Neill's praised her." Benjamin grasped his lover's hands, brought them to his mouth for a kiss. "Would he have come if the Hawthornes had been well? Ten at dinner instead of eight?"

"I've no doubt of it – and if not then, another time. He seemed quite determined to make his point." William outlined Benjamin's lips with his fingers, tracing the little lines and crevices of his handsome face. "I'll speculate all my life why we were chosen for such instruction, although I'll not complain about it."

"Quite right." He kissed William's fingers, stroking the palms as those same palms stroked the bell ropes. "Will we make the most of the sunlight pouring into your bedroom? It's been long enough since we were last here together, it would be pleasant to make love under natural light, and not the lamp or the fire's glow."

"Long enough?" William leaned down and kissed the lips he'd been caressing. "A fortnight, that's all."

"Too long for me." Benjamin returned the kiss with interest. "A few days is too long, to be honest. How Beatrice will cope when her boy in blue or red is away for months on end, I have no idea."

"Many women do. And not all of their husbands or sweethearts will obey the maxim about there being no married men south of Gibraltar." William leaned down again, tongue savouring the sweet, soft recesses of his lover's mouth. If kissing like this was a gentler, more innocent version of what was to happen later in their bed, then it was no less satisfying, at least for the present. They'd not taken the final steps yet, content with touch of hands alone, but the moment would come. Soon.

"I never thought I would object to the days growing longer, but it makes things so awkward." Benjamin broke the contact, drew himself up onto his feet and pulled his friend with him. "It's time to hide ourselves from the eyes of the world, and hope no-one will come knocking for the curate's services."

"I'd slip the bolt on the door but they'd know I was in, then. Best leave it and just trust that Toomhai's on watch." William took his friend's hand, scribing messages on it with his fingers as they mounted the stairs. The bedroom caught the full force of the afternoon sun, golden shafts turning to green as they forced through the beeches and gilded the old half-tester bed. "Look at that. As fine a bridal bed as you could wish for. And the nearest I'll have to one." Time had come to dispense with words; he wound his arms around Benjamin's waist, pressing his lips to the man's cheek. A trail of kisses was left along jaw, neck, ear, onto his hair – while William's stock was loosed and his buttons assailed. They'd seen each other naked before, by half light or the moon's silver glow, but never in the piercing beam of the sun, where nothing could remain hidden.

"I love you." Benjamin's words were hurried, almost feverish, reflecting his body's eagerness for naked flesh and soft sheets. The rate at which his hands were working, the first would be achieved very soon, William's shirt already discarded and the fine woollen vest under it soon following suit. "I cannot imagine a circumstance in which I would love anyone more."

"Neither can I." William loosed the buttons on his friend's breeches, found the places which gave them both such bliss to stroke and be stroked. "Now hush, let me see you in the light." He turned Benjamin – by now mother naked - to one side and the other, letting the sun play on his long, lean frame. He traced the peaks and troughs of light, admired the golden glow on the downy chest hair, his rosy nipples. "Perfect." William pushed his lover towards the bed, slipped back the covers and nudged him onto the clean linen sheets.

"I can't be perfect. That would leave no superlative with which to describe you." Benjamin had strong, lithe hands, using them expertly to excite his lover just enough, yet not to the point where control would be lost. There was plenty more to be done before then; barriers to be overcome, taboos to be broken. They'd pushed back the boundaries from that first night, when they'd been so eager and so inexperienced that barely a few firm strokes had achieved climax. They'd learned to take their time since then; pleasure lengthened was pleasure amplified.

"This evening," William's voice was hoarse, unsteady with emotion, "will the stallion come to...I was going to say to the mare, but I'm not sure the analogy is suitable. Will the stallion serve?"

A wood pigeon sounded out among the beeches, its soft call the only sound audible in the little room apart from the pounding of blood in ears, the fierce tympani of passion. "Aye. The stallion will serve or be served, whatever suits the mount."

"The mount," William burst into a smile which outshone the afternoon sun, "would like to be mounted."

Benjamin lay in contentment, echoes of pleasure sounding through his body, William's soft breath filling the air with a sweeter carillon than even his precious tenor bell could sound. A bright splash of colour caught his eye, yellow flowers in an elegant vase on the dressing table. "Do you have another admirer? Who sends you late winter jasmine?"

"The sprays of blossom? They came from the rectory garden, from Mrs. Newington, with a note wishing me success in my choices, whatever hurdles I have to overcome on the way."

"She said that?" Benjamin watched the last rays of sunlight catch the top of the copper beech. They'd finish the wine later, then return to this soft bed when it was pitch dark, perhaps to couple again or just to lie abed and listen to the owls. Either would be wonderful. "I always felt she was the most perceptive woman I've met. The canon is luckier than most men in his choice of wife."

"Maybe I have been more fortunate than even Mr. Newington. He had to travel to the far side of the world, across the whole social divide to find someone with whom to entwine his life." William laid his head against his lover's. "I found mine just the other side of the parish."

GREEN
RIVER

JARDONN SMITH

"Come sit over here, boy, and I'll tell you a story."

"Great-grandpa Ernest, I'm not a boy. I'm twenty-two years old."

"That may be, but in my head you're still a boy. And I ain't your grandpa, great or otherwise."

"I know, you're our great uncle, but we've always called you..."

"Yes, yes, your ma and pa feel sorry for me because I never had any kids of my own, so I put up with it. Uncle Ernie would've been much more fun. Don't you think?"

"Yeah."

"Doesn't matter now. Just sit there and listen. Record me on your digital do-hickie if you want. Put it in your thespians."

"It's a thesis."

"That was a joke, son. You will be hearing about a thespian of sorts before I'm finished."

"I'm ready."

"Good, and just so you know, back in my day a man's penis was called a pecker, a willy, a johnson, or a woody. We would at times use the word dick or cock, but only if we were drunk and talking nasty. Those two were nasty words back then. And another thing. Most people believed the dead liked to come out and wander around from time to time. Some folks were scared of it, but most just thought it was a natural thing. Listen to the songs from back in olden times and you'll know what I'm talking about. Got it?"

"Yes, sir."

"Now, let me get in my waxing-poetic frame of mind so I can make you a pretty picture. And don't interrupt me!"

PART ONE – SNAKES

The Gasconade is a gentle, spring-fed river. It flows from south to north, kind of a rarity for U.S. rivers. Beginning at its headwaters near Hartville in south-central Missouri, it twists and turns for nearly three hundred land miles, even though the total distance, if taken in a straight line through the air, is about half that. After meandering its way up from southern Missouri, the Gasconade contributes its sparkling color of emerald green into the muddy Missouri River near the center of its namesake state. It is a river ideal for floating, for swimming, for basking, and for touching. It's where Cecil Babcock and I first touched one another in places below the waterline, although there is some argument as to who touched who first.

Yes, the Gasconade River is where Cecil Babcock and Ernest Surbaugh progressed from simple touching to mutual hand jobs, to reciprocal blow jobs, to, well, you know where this leads. We were young, post-teenaged men. Still unsure of ourselves. I was twenty-two, Cecil twenty-one, and it took some rather monumental events in order for us to get where we got.

In very particular order they are: The Great Depression -- a severe economic collapse in the 1930's that at one point in 1933 saw the unemployment rate reach twenty-five percent. The Dust Bowl -- a massive erosion of farmland brought on by years of overuse and drought. Centered in Oklahoma, Kansas and eastern Colorado. This disaster just happened to coincide with and worsen the economic depression. The Works Progress Administration -- a government-funded program that put men to work for salary, mostly upgrading the country's infrastructure of streets, highways, bridges and water systems.

The WPA camp near the Gasconade River is where Cecil, myself, and about forty other men of our work crew were housed into four-man cabins. Our project was the U.S. Highway 66 Bridge over that river, the repair work on the bridge our reason for being there, plus widening and patching or resurfacing the highway for twenty-five miles in both directions, either side of the bridge.

I arrived at the work camp in early June, 1938, along with my Uncle Jack Surbaugh and my brother Raymond, who was three years older than I. Cecil came a day later and was assigned the fourth and final cot in our cabin. The place had once been a resort where folks stayed to fish and float the river, but had gone bust along with countless other businesses after the crash of 1929. The WPA bought the grounds, refurbished the cabins, built a dining lodge and a community shower house, complete with sinks and toilets. Also added was a fence and gate at the entry drive, closed but never locked, a garage for storing and maintaining the work vehicles and equipment, plus a small stage for end of the month, Saturday night dances.

This was the only time outsiders, including females, were allowed in the camp. A small orchestra was brought in for the event, paid for by townspeople who showed up to purchase a fifty-cent ticket allowing them entry to listen, mingle and dance. Finger foods and drinks were also provided, but no alcohol was allowed inside the camp.

Fifteen cabins separated by single-auto parking spaces were laid out in a semi-circle facing the river. Two cottages were nearest the river, along with a concrete boat-launch ramp and a roped off area in the water for swimming. The space cleared for our camp was surrounded by woods lush and green. Tall elms, oaks, sycamores and black walnut trees shaded every building, while dots of old-growth trees were left standing within the complex as well.

Locals had done the new construction work beginning early spring of that year, and many stayed in the program for the highway and bridge work. We Surbaughs were not locals. Neither was Cecil, and I'm sure that's why Cecil was assigned to our cabin. Highway work began the Monday after Cecil arrived. At six a.m. breakfast was served in the lodge, after which we piled into trucks and were taken west on Highway 66 to just east of a town called Lebanon. We spent the day patching holes, constructing new or leveling existing shoulders, and widening or resurfacing the highway. At two p.m. we loaded up for the trip back to camp, and after supper in the lodge some of the men headed for the river to soak and relax, including Cecil and myself.

The camp and its access to the Gasconade was about a mile down-river and geographically north of the highway bridge, and because Cecil and I got tired of the local hillbillies trying to scare us with supposed snake sightings in the water, he and I swam up-river toward the bridge to get away. Unlike those goofballs who swam in trousers, Cecil and I went naked like genuine hillbillies should.

"Cecil, you got any snakes over there in Kansas?"

"Not anymore. They all dried up and blowed away like the rest of creation."

We found us a nice spot north and west of the middle pier, one of three made of concrete, middle one in the river, two on the banks. With a current slow and relaxed, the water's surface was about chest-high, bed underneath soft and sandy, and water temperature cool enough to prevent a man's willy from showing much excitement. The sun had long ago disappeared behind the bluffs to our west, but enough daylight lingered so Cecil and I could barely see our underwater parts in blurs.

"Yeah, well, we've got plenty in Joplin."

"Any with poison, Ernest? Like rattlers?"

"Cecil, there's only one snake to be concerned with in the Missouri Ozarks. That's the Copperhead, and he don't like to swim much. There's a timber rattler, but he's a scaredy-cat and you hardly ever see him. Cottonmouths like the water, but they're mostly in the southeast part of the state. See? I know my snakes. These yokels from around here must think we're big-city sophisticates or something."

"Not me. I'm just a Kansas dirt farmer, but the dirt's all gone."

"And I'm just a Missouri factory worker, but the factory's closed."

We separated and swam for awhile as final glimmers of daylight faded to bluish-grey shadows. An occasional vehicle rumbled east or west across the bridge, rubber tires double-thumping when crossing its metal expansion joints. Our swimming hole was about one-eighth of a mile north of the bridge, its five-hundred-twenty-five feet of length nearly two hundred feet above us.

"So, Cecil, who did you leave behind back in Pittsburg, Kansas?"

"My entire family. They're on the farm about ten miles from town. Ma, my three brothers and two sisters. I'm the oldest."

"Is your pa in the WPA somewhere else?"

"No, he died last year."

"How so?"

"He was clearing brush. Hoped to plant wheat into some new earth. Tried to drag a log up a grade and the tractor tipped over on him. Crushed him like an ant underfoot, but at least he died quick."

"Sorry about that, Cecil."

His silence worried me, like maybe he was getting depressed, but then he playfully splashed my face with a slap of water. "Aw, he's better off. Sometimes I wonder if he didn't halfway do it on purpose."

"Why do you say that?"

"It wears on a man. Putting in a crop year after year, waiting for rain that'll never come, watching his little sprouts wither and blow away. I could see its effect on him, Ernest. Watched it happen day by day, sucking the life right out of him. Hell, a man can't even show his face in public when the only money coming in is from his wife's dressmaking."

"So, his dying made you head of the household?"

"Yep. After that year's crop burnt up, I told my brothers we'd try one more. That was this past spring, and it's going to waste like always. Can already see it."

"How come the WPA sent you all the way over here?"

"It's all they had open anywhere near me. Guess I waited too long seeing if the crop had a chance."

"You got the last slot. Did Mr. Morgan tell you that?"

"Sure did. The WPA man in Pittsburg told me the same thing. Said they were needing another man here who knew how to work on engines."

"Tractors and trucks?"

"Right. I can do it, so the agent called up Mr. Morgan and told him I was coming. Ma used what she had saved to purchase me a train ticket, but she was twenty cents short. The railroad agent loaned her the amount we needed."

"Nice fellow."

"Yep. His wife wears some of ma's dresses. I suspect she'll get one for free out of the deal."

Hard to believe this Monday-night swim was our first real chance at getting acquainted. Not because of any disinterest. We'd simply been too busy.

Cecil's physique was plenty exciting, although at the time I merely thought him a striking man. Didn't recognize any sorts of sexual attraction toward him, and would not have known what to do about it if I had. Such ideas were not part of my thinking process, not yet, but I was a bit jealous of his stocky frame, his height of five feet and ten inches, the abundant black hair on his legs and the small patch of it on his chest. His blue eyes were brighter than the sky itself, made even more brilliant by the healthy black hair atop his head.

I guess a man tends to admire what he himself doesn't have. A complete contrast to Cecil, my height at the time extended past six feet by one-quarter of an inch, head hair brown, body hair tan in color and sparse, while my frame was thin, and musculature sinewy. My eyes, also blue but of the slate-grey variety, rarely got noticed because of my nose. Hasn't changed much since then. Long, sharp and thin with its end almost at the same level as my upper lip, the tip of my nose curves toward me, and from the side view looks like a beak. I've been called hawk, eagle and buzzard by friends who know me, and by foes who think I give a shit. I always figured my compensation is the other body part similar to my nose, one that's equally long and majestic, and that's the pecker hanging between my legs.

That nose of mine is a good judge of character. Men who stare at it or keep darting their eyes away from it during face-to-face conversations are usually counterfeit. Got worries about their own faults, and are looking for some reason to bring me down to their level. Men who look once and let it go are usually men I can trust. Men I'll like. Cecil never paid any mind to my nose when we were handshaking our introductions in the cabin. Never lost his patience with my brother Raymond, either, like most men do.

The camp director, one Harold Morgan, a bright-eyed and kindly man approaching fifty years brought Cecil to our cabin on Sunday. We'd arrived and settled in the day before.

"Gentleman," Mr. Morgan rapped his knuckles on our open door, his bushy white brows raised high, his rosy red cheekbones protruding. "This is Cecil Babcock, from Pittsburg, Kansas, or thereabouts." They entered to our friendly hello's, as our director told us the obvious. "Mr. Babcock will be your cabin-mate."

After setting his suitcase and duffel bag on the floor, Cecil followed Mr. Morgan toward my uncle.

"Hello, Cecil. I'm Jack Surbaugh," he smiled with hand extended. "From Joplin, Missouri."

"Pleasure to meet you, Mr. Surbaugh. My train passed through Joplin sometime this morning."

"Yes, Pittsburg's not far from where we live."

"Another fifty miles west and you'd be living in Kansas instead. Isn't that right?"

"Or Oklahoma if we headed a bit south." Both men simultaneously released their grips and rested hands on their hips, as my uncle took charge. "I'm sorry to tell you, but you'll be surrounded by Surbaughs. These two are my nephews, Raymond and Ernest."

Turning toward Raymond, Cecil grabbed the hand waiting for him. "Hello, Raymond. I look forward to working with you."

After five seconds of silence, my uncle jumped in to explain. "Now, Cecil, you'll have to go slow with Raymond. Sometimes his words get lost in traveling from his head to his lips, so give him time. Raymond, say hello to Cecil."

With the reminder, Raymond used up another ten seconds and finally repeated, "Hello, Cecil. Welcome."

"Thank you, Raymond. This certainly is a beautiful spot."

Next came me, and like I said, Cecil passed my nose test. He settled into the final cot, and after Mr. Morgan took him on a tour of the camp's facilities, Cecil was ready for a nap. Hours on a train followed by a fifteen-mile car ride from the station where Mr. Morgan picked him up had Cecil worn out. He awoke at supper-time, walked with us to the lodge. Took a shower afterward, and by then all of us were ready for bed and our first day of work Monday morning.

Finally, our Monday-night swim allowed us to relax and converse. "Ernest, how did you Surbaughs get to the camp?"

"Uncle Jack's pickup truck."

"What kind of factory were you in?"

"It was Uncle Jack's factory. We made large blocks of formed concrete, specifically-designed for the construction of grain elevators. Curved slabs so heavy they had to be lifted onto rail cars by a crane."

"Wow! That was quite an operation. So, what happened?"

"Same thing that happened to you farmers. Not even Uncle Jack could have foreseen a drought like this. His clients were right in the center of the Dust Bowl, eastern Colorado, Kansas and Oklahoma. No grain. No need for new grain elevators. Banks cut off his loans, and he finally shut down the factory in March of this year."

"Is that when you signed up for the WPA?"

"Soon after. Uncle Jack had already been in contact with the agent. Like in your county, there wasn't anything open locally, but because of our knowing about concrete, Jack was able to get me and him set up for this project here."

"And your brother?"

"Right." Our conversation moved along quickly, which was a good thing. Helped me get through what I had to say. "Uncle Jack's always taken care of my ma and us since our pa was killed in the Great War."

"Was he your uncle's brother?"

"Yes, a couple of years older. Uncle Jack treats us like we're his boys. He lost both his wife and baby daughter to the flu epidemic a few months after ma got word about our pa being dead over in Europe.."

"The flu of 1918?"

"That's the one. Had us three funerals real close together. One of my earliest memories."

A shout interrupted any chance of me getting all sad. Came twanging from a hundred feet down-river. "Hey, you two! We just seen a giant black snake headed your way. Nearly ten feet long. You better watch it. Thing'll take your head plumb off. Take you under and drown ya."

"Virgil, is that you?" I'd met him at supper two nights prior. Virgil Shank, leader of the local clan. Real friendly until I told him we came from Joplin.

"Yep. I'm tellin' truth, now. Y'all better head for the banks, 'cause he's a-comin'."

"Virgil? You ever been to Joplin, Missouri?"

"No, I ain't."

"Well, we got black snakes there, too. Some of 'em *thirty* feet long."

"Naw, you don't neither."

Cecil made no effort to hide his chuckling, as I turned the tables on trouble-making Virgil. "I'm telling you true. Had me one as a pet when I was a boy. He bit me once, but didn't like the taste. Didn't hurt me much, either, so I figure I can handle any of the puny snakes you got around these parts."

"You're a liar, Ernest Surbaugh."

"So are you, Virgil Shank, so just get on back to your relatives and leave me be."

"Mister, you got a real smart mouth. I ought ta come up there and..."

"Mister, in case it's too dark for you to see, I can tell you that I ain't running. If you want some, come on up here and try me."

We waited, but heard nothing. "Can you see him?" Cecil whispered while I kept my eye on the dark speck of Virgil's head I'd pinpointed when the shouting began.

"Looks like he's going back down-river, Cecil. Guess he's not in the mood for it."

"He's probably fixing to fetch his buddies."

"Whatever. He and I are going to have it out sooner or later. Might as well be sooner."

"You can't take all of them on, and right now I can barely see you. They could sneak up on us, easy."

"They ain't coming up here. They know they'll get kicked right out of the program, and then where will they be? There ain't any other jobs around here."

"I think you're giving them too much credit for brains. We better go. If we're in a brawl we'll get kicked out, too."

"You go back to the cabin, Cecil. This is my problem. Virgil and I are coming to fisticuffs, if not over this, then over something else. He'll pick his spot."

"And his reason, as soon as he knows what will set you off. Right, Ernest?"

That would be my brother, Raymond, whose speech peculiarity made people think he was retarded, and therefore prime material for taunting. "You already figured that out, did you?"

"Sure."

"I will do what I have to do when it comes to protecting Raymond."

"I know. Don't worry, Ernest. I'm staying right here."

"This is nothing to worry about, but I appreciate you... Hey! Damn, Cecil. What're you doing?"

"Uh, standing over here. Why?"

"That felt pretty good. Want me to do yours?"

"What the hell are you talking about?"

"Squeezing on my pecker."

"I never touched your pecker."

"Sure you are. Here, let me return the favor."

"Ernest! I'm not even close enough to touch you or your pecker."

Putting the sound of his voice together with logic, I realized Cecil was telling truth. Too far away. "Well, who the hell's in the water yanking on me?" I reached down and grabbed my johnson expecting to feel a hand other than mine, but nothing was there. "What the...?"

"Damn it, Ernest. I done told you it isn't me, so there's no favors to be, um, well, I've got to admit that feels pretty good."

"Cecil, I'm at least five feet away from you."

I doubt if any two men ever exited water as quickly as Cecil and I did. My feet seemed to be treading in the sand, so I swam for it, and as Cecil and I climbed onto the bank-side, we reached for each other's hands and clasped on.

"What the hell was that, Ernest?"

"I don't know. You reckon it's coming after us?"

"Hope so. I kinda liked it."

At that moment, there was no doubt in my mind Cecil Babcock and Ernest Surbaugh would become the greatest of friends. We both burst into laughter and fearlessly returned to the river for play, dunking one another, wrestling each other, and touching.

"Guess the fish here think our peckers are big old worms, eh, Ernest?"

"Maybe it was a snake biting on us."

"Yeah, an old one that's lost his teeth." Cecil grabbed hold my woody, and I clutched his. Told him he could call me Ernie, if he liked. He did like, and we both enjoyed floating in the total darkness of the Gasconade River while jacking each other off. Twice.

PART TWO – THE JOY OF LEARNING

I guess it was no surprise that neither Cecil nor I were overly scared of whatever had played with our peckers in the river. Curious, yes, but fear is when you don't know if you'll have a roof over your head come week's end, or if you'll ever again have a coin in your pocket. Fear is sharing the last chunk of bread and one fried egg with your ma and brother, not knowing when you'll get your next bite of food. That's just the short list of what we Surbaughs and Cecil Babcock had been through.

Of course, we weren't alone. Every man there had seen tough times, and because there was a sort of brotherhood in that respect, we all settled down to our routines with no more conflicts. Virgil Shank and I were satisfied with cold stares and no words whenever we were forced into close contact, such as the shower room, dining lodge or on the work site. Same goes for his two sons and the rest of his kin. All told, they numbered seven, with Virgil the oldest and somewhere around forty years. He had worked with the Missouri Highway Department as a laborer in building the Gasconade River bridge back in 1922, information Uncle Jack finagled out of the camp's director, Mr. Morgan. They all came from an area in and around Sleeper, a community of less than a hundred people about twenty miles northwest of our camp. For these folks, the Great Depression hadn't done much to change their lifestyle. They were dirt poor regardless of economic conditions. Lived in the woods of the Ozark Hills in shacks they built themselves, subsisting on wildlife they could hunt, chickens they raised and whatever puny vegetables they could grow in rocky soil.

The WPA program for them was something to do, a change of routine, and it was no surprise that after our first paycheck at the end of June, several of them left camp and never returned. Virgil stayed. So did his sons, but after learning from their first attempt that Cecil and I were willing to fight and could not be intimidated, they kept to themselves, swam down-river by the camp and let us be.

Fortunately, the Shanks were the only clannish men there. All the other fellows were good-natured and easy-going. Cecil became friends with many of them and so did I, which meant we weren't always doing things together, nor running in a pack like the Shanks. Swimming by the bridge was not an every night thing for us, as many types of card games and domino contests took place at picnic tables scattered throughout the camp.

Every day saw us working the highway in closer proximity to the bridge, as we gussied up Highway 66 from west to east. Uncle Jack's main duty was to mix and test the concrete, asphalt, and hole-patching materials. I drove heavy equipment, either a dump truck, steam roller or grader. Cecil looked over the truck engines at day's end. During the day, he and Raymond worked hand shovels, and this is how Cecil first learned of Raymond's special gift – his hands.

Whereas his speech and movements from one spot to another were painfully slow, Ray's hands were lightening quick, accurate and talented. It might take him five minutes to scoop a shovel-full of gravel or tarred rock from the back of a truck and take it to the hole being filled, but once there, he could have his material in the hole distributed evenly and leveled perfectly in five seconds. First day out, Cecil wasn't paired with Ray and hadn't seen what Ray could do, but the second day he was near enough to take notice. Third day, Cecil finagled it with the foreman to team with Ray so he could deliver the material to the hole for Ray to manipulate with his shovel. Saved Raymond the steps. Preserved Ray's energy for the talented part of the job, a skill neither Cecil nor any other man could match. Together, the two of them became the A-number-one team in preparing holes for the steamroller.

In 1938 the Fourth of July fell on a Monday. Our first wages had been paid out the last Friday in June followed by a Saturday night dance, and on Friday night before the Fourth, we'd all showered and were piddling before it was time for supper to be served in the lodge. Cecil was at a table outside the lodge playing four-handed pitch. Uncle Jack visited with our crew foreman over at his cottage while Raymond and I lounged in our cabin.

"Ernie?"

"Yes, Ray?"

"You... gonna... dance... "

The end of his question was obvious, but I'd never interrupted him. Not when we were children, not now, not ever. Sitting in my undershorts on the mattress of my cot with my back against the wall, I massaged my bare feet and looked up at Ray with a gaze serene, waiting while he stood above me.

Our cabin was rough wood, no finishing, small and rustic and outfitted with the following from front to back: one front door with two small windows on either side; four cots with their long sides nestled against the walls, two on each side, foot of one touching the head of another, Jack and Ray on one side, Cecil and I on the other; one writing desk next to the foot of Ray's cot with side drawers, a kerosene lamp on top and chair in the middle; dresser of drawers with mirror at the foot of my cot; one tiny stone fireplace built into the back wall and two small windows on either side; and on the floor a metal bin for fireplace wood and a piss bucket for middle-of-the-night needs.

"... tomorrow... night?"

"I don't think we're having a dance tomorrow, Ray. Dances are the Saturdays after payday, and we just had one last week. I think tomorrow night is a celebration for Independence Day."

After a ten-second delay, his next question. "Will... there be... ..."

He couldn't think of the word. I could always tell because he'd curl his eyebrows and frown, his eyes drifting distant and to the floor. If I saw this, I'd fill in the blanks for him. "Fireworks?"

He nodded.

"That's what I heard, Ray. First there'll be a special supper in the lodge, and then fireworks as soon as it's dark."

"Ernie?"

"Yes, Ray."

He lumbered toward the desk about five paces away. Opened a drawer. "I've got no color."

"You don't? Let me see," I strolled to the desk as he reached for his satchel and opened it. "Down to the nubs, aren't you?" I plucked one of his colored pencils from his bag, held up the half-inch remaining. "What have you been drawing, Ray? Show me."

Like I said, the perplexing oddity about Ray -- whereas the connection from his brain to his mouth took forever, signals to his hands were instant, faster than normal men, and the result of whatever his mind told his hands to do was a finished product near perfection. The walls of his room at our ma's house were lined with paintings created by his skilled hands.

Landscapes, faces, beasts, machines or any combination of elements that popped into his head. He could put a pencil to a napkin at a diner and within five minutes show me the spitting image of whatever human within his sights he chose to draw. Every facial line present and correct. Size and shape of eyes, nose, ears and mouth a near-to-exact duplicate. Even more curious was his memory. He could draw a subject in the present, or reproduce something he'd seen hours, days, or even weeks earlier.

Ray took out a stack of papers from the desk drawer, set them on top for me to enjoy. "Hey! This is our work crew."

He nodded.

I scrutinized each one, nearly a dozen drawn in pencil on standard, eight-and-a-half by eleven sheets of paper. Scenes of men with shovels, men driving trucks and heavy machinery, every detail present and in color. Raymond had duplicated the exact shades of our WPA-issued uniforms – dark grey trousers with light grey shirts. Our orange hard hats shined brightly in sunlight, and even though we all dressed the same, our body shapes and faces were distinctly identifiable for each worker depicted. I could even recognize myself as the man in the seat of our steamroller. "These are beautiful, Ray. So, are you planning to draw the fireworks show?"

He nodded.

"Are you out of paper, too?"

He'd learned to exhibit his answer rather than speak it when possible, and he lifted out the few remaining sheets in the drawer. Same as I'd vowed to protect him from smart-ass remarks best I could, I also made it my responsibility to keep him stocked with paper, colored pencils and a sharpener. Back home, I supplied him with oil paints as well. "All right, Ray. Let me talk to Uncle Jack and see if we can use his truck tomorrow. Or maybe he'll go with us, but first I'll have to ask Director Morgan for a pass to wherever the nearest town is that would have what we need to buy. OK?"

He nodded with teeth showing, confident I would come through for him.

The newly-built lodge was a beautiful facility made of native black walnut. Beneath its vaulted ceiling were six long tables also of walnut, each seating twelve men in table-matching, individual chairs. In one front corner was a supply store stocked mostly with toiletries, cigarettes, and basic clothing like socks and underwear, open for one hour per day after supper and manned by Director Harold Morgan. He fastidiously scrutinized and accounted for every item while deducting from upcoming wages whatever a man purchased. He'd also accept cash.

On the back wall of the lodge was a huge stone fireplace, dormant in July, and along a side wall was the kitchen. Run by a full-time staff of three who were on WPA wages like us, they served our meals on trays at a window, where we'd line up to grab and sit. Behind the wall everything was modern and electrified – a long grill, ovens, refrigerators and freezers. Even had a fire-stoked grill for charbroiling and a giant vent fan to suck out smoky air.

Barney the cook only cooked, while the other two cleaned our trays, metal utensils and porcelain dishes, plus they scrubbed our shower and toilet facilities daily. The lodge was the only building with electricity. A gas-powered generator in its own little room at the back of the building supplied power to the kitchen, to the brand-new washing machines in a back room next to the kitchen, and to Mr. Morgan's office which was adjacent to the opposite side wall of the lodge. He had electric lights and the only telephone on site. The stage and dancing area outside the lodge could also be lit up.

After finding Uncle Jack and confirming he'd like to take his pickup on a Saturday road trip, I visited Director Morgan's office to ask where we should go.

"Lebanon should have a store selling those things. Would you like to see a map?"

Hanging in frames on the wall to his left were city maps, all the Missouri notables along Highway 66 from St. Louis to Joplin, including Lebanon. While I memorized a route to its downtown, Mr. Morgan made out the pass for us to leave camp next day. Business finished, I stepped into the lodge.

"Baby Surbaughs, your uncle thinks I should go to town with you tomorrow."

Our crew foreman, Forrest Barton, plopped down his tray and joined us for supper. A burly, barrel-chested man in his middle-forties, his dark brown hair sparkled with specks of silver, a bit of flesh peeking through on top. With his shirt sleeves rolled back above his elbows, his gorilla-like, muscular forearms were two-times wider than mine when pressed upon the table. His paws were scarred from hard labor. They laid flat with plenty of meat on his strong fingers. His eyes equaled the chocolate-brown color of the paper wrapping his fat cigar, and a cigar was always with him, either stuffed in his shirt pocket or clamped in his molars, lit or not.

"Mr. Barton," I welcomed him, "that will be a hoot. We baby Surbaughs and Cecil here will ride in the bed of the pick..."

"No need for that," he cut me off, removing the spit-saturated cigar from his mouth and slapping it down onto his tray. "We can all pile into my Buick. Plenty of room."

"All right. That sounds even better."

We were too hungry for talking, at least until a few bites were swallowed and Forrest remarked, "Well, gentlemen, I reckon by middle of next week we'll be ready to start on the bridge."

"Forrest here helped build it," Jack piped in. "Back in the twenties."

"1924, to be exact. That's when we finished it."

Cecil wondered, "Were you a foreman then, Mr. Barton?"

"Oh, hell no. Just a laborer. Did what they told me, but I will tell you this. Something didn't seem right about that bridge. You know that feeling you get? Like things ain't what they're supposed to be? Well, that's a feeling I had the whole time we worked on it." He sat up straight, puffed his chest, put his thumb in the middle of thick chest fur exposed by his unbuttoned shirt buttons. "And by God I was right. There's no way its deck should be crumbling like that. Only fourteen years old. Me and Jack have been talking about it."

"I figure they used a bad mix of concrete," Jack analyzed. "Contractor probably trying to skim the county."

"Could be, or the girders beneath aren't right, but I guess we'll find out when we get up there. No use fussing over it now. Right, Jack?"

"Right. It's a holiday. Let's chow down, get a good night's sleep, and take Raymond shopping in the morning."

We did devour silently for awhile, but Forrest liked to talk. "I haven't been to Lebanon since I was here before, except passing through on my way to our camp."

"Are you from this area, Mr. Barton?"

"Name's Forrest when we're relaxing, fellas, and no, Ernest, I come from Kansas City, born and raised."

Cecil asked, "How did you get into the highway-building business?"

"During the Great War in Europe. They threw me in with road crews. Building temporary bridges for movement of ground forces and transports. Running the big Cat graders to level off ruts in the dirt roads. After the war, I took what I learned and got into road building."

"How did that work?" I wondered. "I mean, how did you end up here in the Ozarks?"

"Well, it's like this." He swallowed what he'd been chewing, forcefully wiped his mouth with his supper cloth, stuck his cigar into his jaw and fired it up with his Zippo lighter. "With the growing number of people owning automobiles, there was a national effort to connect the old dirt pathways made for horses, pave them over and make them into continuous highways. This road here was once known as Missouri 14. When we got finished, it was officially designated as the Missouri stretch of U.S. Route 66. Each county paid for their own sections, and a man could sign up at any state office. Be put on a waiting list for assignment to a county where there was work. Since my wife contracted the influenza and died on me while I was overseas, I didn't have any strings keeping me at home. I took whatever came up anywhere in the state, and believe me, there were plenty of choices. Last I checked, there's only six counties in the entire state where one Forrest Barton hasn't worked on their highways."

"You know, Forrest, Uncle Jack lost his wife same as you did." Instantly, I wished I hadn't chosen that subject to follow up on. After all he'd just said, with one simple nudge Forrest Barton would have told exciting tales of his experiences in the Great War, or some of the more interesting road projects he'd worked on, or anything not involving death. I guess I was in awe of this man, his manner, his appearance, all of him, and my intimidated brain wasn't quite functioning properly.

"Well, damn it, Ernest, your uncle done told me that." His tongue maneuvered the cigar between his right molars and he chomped down hard. "Lost his daughter too," he growled, "so I guess Jack's one up on me." A couple of sucks fired up his cherry, and then he removed the stogie from his mouth. Wedging it between his first two fingers, he waved it at us while talking. "That there epidemic of 1918 was a horrible, horrible thing. Forty million people died from it. Made the Great War seem like child's play, but by God, there's no use sitting around moping about it." He scooted his chair away from the table. Clasped both hands to the back of his head and stretched, his heavily-muscled chest thrusting forward until I thought he'd pop off what few shirt buttons were fastened. "Now, look here," he sat straight up with fingers spread atop his thighs. "Things are rough out there, but in here, we've got solid meals every day and money in our pockets. Let's think of good times and celebrate the birth of this great nation. I'll see you at breakfast, and then we'll go to town."

With that, Forrest Barton stood, took his tray and marched to the kitchen area. Shook hands with Barney the cook and his assistants, apparently thanking them, and then exited the lodge. Everything the man did had an effect on me. The way he walked, his head held high, spine erect, chest and eyes straight forward. Certain men are born to inspire others, like generals, kings and statesmen. Forrest Barton was such a man, at least for me, and when we got back to our cabin I asked Raymond to draw me a picture of him.

"In... black?"

"Yes, Raymond. I know you're out of colored pencils, but that's fine. He should be in black and white."

As Ray sat down to create, Cecil entered looking a bit dejected.

"Card game over?"

"Yes."

"I take it you lost."

"Let's just say my partner lost it for us."

"Sounds bitter."

"Ah, hell, I don't mean to be. He's a nice fella, but he prefers to talk instead of focusing on his hand. Not important. Only a game. What are you and Ray up to?"

"Ray's using the last of his paper to draw me a picture. Thought I might go for a swim and let him be. Wanna come?"

"Sure."

On average, Cecil and I hit the swimming hole four times a week. Found us a trail along the east side of the river that emerged from the woods near the bridge, and used it so we could avoid the Shanks who monopolized the swimming hole by our camp.

The night was overcast and pitch black, but by now Cecil and I knew every step. We stripped and waded in, heading for the west side beyond the middle pier. Vision no longer needed, I knew precisely how Cecil looked. After four weeks of good eating and hard labor, his stocky frame now had meat on it, and because I was feeling frisky I wasted no time in getting my hands on him.

"Come over here. I'll give you a shoulder rub."

Using my voice as his beacon, Cecil drifted over and stood with his backside in front of me so I could dig my fingers into his trapeziums. Got my thumbs rubbing his shoulder blades and made sure my woody rubbed on him somewhere, too.

"Damn, that feels good."

"Which? My hands or my hard pecker?"

"Both. How come you're so horny?" He reached behind and clutched hold of me, gave my willy a squeeze.

"Don't know. Must be the holiday."

"And we get paid to do nothing on the Fourth."

"Heck of a deal, ain't it?" I wrapped my arms around his middle and hugged.

"Whoa, careful there," he warned. "Don't wanna make me lose my supper."

"How about down here? Got anything you wanna lose?" I grabbed his johnson, soft as a noodle. "How come you're so *not* horny, Cecil?"

"Aw, I dunno. I'm kinda down tonight. Missing home, I guess."

"Well, just think how happy they'll be when they get those twenty dollar bills you sent. And the letter you wrote telling them next time will be five times more."

"I know. Wish I could see ma's face when she opens it."

"Yeah. She'll be happy, and you should be too. So come on, let's go to our yanking place and I'll make you happy."

That was the bank on the west with soft mud and scattered pebbles. The place where we could lay with our bodies just under the surface and our faces above it, where Cecil could sprawl and gaze at the sky while my hand stroked him off, and where he could do the same for me after he'd finished. We'd never planned the order of it, that's just the way we'd been doing it, but when we got there, something took hold of me. Yes, Cecil was an attractive young man, a force to be reckoned with, but on this night another man also was on my mind. A man who Cecil might look like twenty years down the road. My imagination of Forrest Barton naked, and my reality of Cecil Babcock naked, doubled my excitement.

No plan, no forethought, I got on my knees right between his thighs and put my mouth onto his pecker. All I got from Cecil was a surprised and breathy, "Oh," even though it came from a far distance, like out of a fog or a tunnel, as though I was in some sort of dream. What I also got was instant reaction from him. His willy swelled to full strength, and he wiggled himself further onto the bank so his groin was in the air, not water.

That same mysterious force guided me to service him. No fears of choking. No worries of cutting him with my teeth. An angel, a teacher, or perhaps merely intuition, prompted me to plant my hands into the mud and work my mouth on him as if I'd done it a hundred times before.

My tongue wrapped around his penis while the roof of my mouth clamped down, crushing him in between. Invisible hands clasped the back of my head, forcing my lips all the way to his pelvic bone, drawing me away from him ever so slowly as my tongue wet-scraped the underside of his pecker. Those same hands twisted my head one way and another, guiding me to orally stroke on him. Down to his pelvis, up to his corona, my tongue and lips and plenty of spit glided along the length of his shaft. Unseen hands calibrated my pace, gradually gaining speed. Invisible fingers clutched my chin, slowly tightening my jaw and squeezing him. Crushing him more and more while stroking him faster and faster.

He arched his spine, raised up his chest, sucked in his belly and groaned his warning. "Oh, God, Ernie. I'm nuttin'," he said, and as his seed filled my mouth, my angel opened my throat to accept his flow. No gagging, no drooling, no slowing or lessening of my oral strokes and squeezes. It's as though another person took over for me, an expert, a professional with skills only years of practice can bring, and as the grand finale to my other-worldly, first-time performance, I swallowed every gooey drop of his seed.

The unexplainable energy driving me vanished, sucked out by a vacuum. Exhausted, I collapsed, my head crashing onto Cecil's belly, the rest of me sinking in the mud between his legs.

Both of us breathed hard, collecting ourselves and recuperating. His one hand rubbed my shoulder while the other massaged my scalp, and here we stayed for the longest time.

Cecil was forced to awaken me. I'd been dozing until he raised up, gently lifting my head in his hands. "Let me try you, Ernie."

Those were the final words spoken between us. Cecil performed on me same as I'd done to him – flawlessly, fearlessly, and without hesitation. We had no desire to discuss our experience. Either we were both liars and had sucked on peckers before, which we both knew was not the case, or something seized hold of us that night and caused us to satisfy one another with skills unimaginable. Could have been lust, or love, or something even more powerful.

Whatever, the bottom line is, Cecil got over his being homesick.

Awaiting me in our cabin was Raymond's drawing of Forrest Barton. He'd captured the man perfectly from the middle of his torso to the top of his head, including the cigar clamped in his teeth. Raymond's re-creation of him sitting at our supper table showed fine details of every curled hair on his chest, exposed by his top three unbuttoned shirt buttons just like he'd worn them. Another of Ray's treasures for me to keep. Tucked away in one of several folders where I kept all the gems Ray had gifted to me over the years.

Part Three – Happy Birthday

"Holy cow! Look at the horizontal bars on that grill." Cecil didn't bother hiding his excitement over Forrest Barton's automobile.

Neither did I. "How about those side vents! A spare tire cover on each side? Dang, Forrest. She's a beauty."

"That's the Buick Roadmaster, boys. Lots of chrome and plenty of engine. Pile on in."

Sleek and shiny black, a six-passenger with trunk-back and... "Leather upholstery, too?" I hesitated stepping into the car, as Forrest stood waiting with door open. He'd spiffed up for our trip. Brown wool trousers held up by same color suspenders, and a crisp white shirt with only the top button unbuttoned. A cream-colored straw hat was tilted handsomely atop his head, its brown band matching his cigar.

"Of course it's leather," he beamed. "Hope you all washed your behinds." He moved to the front, folded back the hood. "You might as well look at this 320 engine now, rather than expecting me to describe it while I'm trying to drive."

"A straight V-8, Forrest?" Cecil's interest and skills with engines went beyond farm and heavy equipment, thanks to a class offered at his high school.

"Yes-sir and look down there at the wheel well."

"Spring coils?"

"Something new on the Roadmasters. Coil springs all around, so these crappy Missouri back-roads won't jerk our spines out of whack."

Even Uncle Jack was impressed. "It's one helluva car, Forrest."

"It's better on the inside, men, so let's stop yammering and get to riding."

Gliding was more like it. Once we left the rutted lane connecting our camp to the highway, we felt like we were floating on air.

"Now we can enjoy the work we've done the last few weeks." Forrest chomped on his cigar, driving with both hands on the wheel as we hovered atop Highway 66 westbound. I'd finagled the back seat behind Uncle Jack who rode shotgun, leaving Cecil in the middle and Ray behind the driver. This gave me my best view of Forrest's right side and the upper half of his face in the mirror. Every now and then our eyes would meet. His sparkled. He was proud of his automobile. Why shouldn't he be? He earned it. Highway building is hard, outdoor work. Hot as hell, or cold as the polar caps. Supervising a crew to properly perform that work takes even more skill, and Forrest Barton deserved to own a car of such caliber.

He conversed with Jack, pointing to and admiring places on the highway we'd fixed until we reached the outskirts of Lebanon and he asked, "What did you say we needed to buy here?"

"Colored pencils and paper," I answered with Raymond's drawing of Forrest Barton fresh in my mind.

"What are they for?" Forrest wondered, looking in the mirror at me.

"So Raymond can draw pictures. In Joplin we get what he needs at the drug store, so if you know where there's a..."

"Naw, that ain't no good," Forrest butted in. "That's cheap shit. Raymond, are you talking about artistic drawings?"

We all waited, as Jack had already told Forrest about Ray's manner, and no sooner had Ray said yes than did Forrest announce, "I know just the place, if they're still in business. Right next to the newspaper office. Get some quality pencils so you won't use them up so fast."

Inside Lebanon's city limits, the highway made a sweeping turn to the southwest, where Forrest pointed to the left. "Lookee there. It's the Cedar Crest Motel. Many a night did I poke the horse-toothed waitress who worked at their restaurant, back when we built this highway."

That dampened my spirits for about five seconds. So what? He never remarried. Didn't mean a thing.

Soon, Highway 66 intersected with Highway 5, where Forrest turned right and headed for downtown. "Looks to me like they're fixing for a parade." Wagons attached to farm tractors or horses were lining up on the highway, along with shiny, convertible automobiles. A policeman directed traffic over one block, a right turn and then a left before we could continue to Commercial Street. Forrest stopped at the four-way, looked both ways to get his bearings, and then saw it. "Connor's Printing Supplies," he beamed. "Right there."

One right turn and half a block later, he'd parked it and we all stepped out. "We better hurry," Forrest suggested. "They're probably going to lock up and watch the parade."

The place was a print shop where they made posters and banners. Had their own printing press for people needing announcements, invitations, auction fliers and such. One wall was nothing but shelves filled with supplies to make any sort of graphic items imaginable, and unlike the boxed kits we'd always bought, these pencils were in open-topped boxes, one color per box, and every color under the rainbow stacked side-by-side.

While Ray plucked what he wanted from the boxes, Forrest joined the rest of us looking at paper. We picked out three different weights from medium to heavy and joined Ray in plopping it all down on the counter. Purchase complete, Ray's new supplies dropped into a box provided by the store clerk, we scrambled back to Forrest's Buick so we could get out of there before the parade trapped us.

Forrest took a detour before leaving Lebanon, stayed on Highway 5 and pushed south of 66. Nobody asked where he was going. We figured whatever he had in mind could only be another adventure. He pulled into a lot with a building and sign saying Beardsley Packing Plant. Forrest drove around behind the building, backed his auto near to an open-door loading dock, parked it, got out and opened Ray's door.

"Come on, baby Surbaughs and Cecil. Time for you to earn your fare."

We followed his lead as he flattened his palms on the dock's floor and deftly swung both legs up until his feet were at the same level. With a spin and spring of his legs, he stood and headed into the plant. "Charlie still here?" he asked the first employee he saw, got a yes and finger pointing direction. "Charlie? I'm Forrest Barton from the Gasconade camp."

"Yes, sir. Come for your T-bones?"

"That I did. Brought my own labor, too."

They were in cold storage, fresh, not frozen. T-bone steaks cut and trimmed to twenty-two ounces, individually wrapped in plastic and packed in boxes of eight. Forrest whipped out a roll of cash to pay for six boxes, as we stacked them into two's and toted them to the edge of the loading dock.

"Now, men, we need to get these to camp as soon as possible," Forrest stated as we packed the boxes in his trunk-back. "Barney's going to keep them refrigerated until it's time to grill 'em up for tonight's big wing-ding."

"So, that's why you were talking to Barney last night," my fist nudged his bicep.

"Yep. Wanted to make sure he had all the peripherals ready to go."

"Like what?" Cecil asked.

"The usual. You'll see. Come on, let's get."

North on 5 and east on 66, Forrest glided us out of Lebanon. Passing the city limits sign, he floored it. A runaway on a straightaway, his engine purred like a kitten as we hit seventy miles an hour, eighty, ninety, and then he slowed it for a curve.

"This is one beautiful ride, Forrest," Cecil complimented. "Thirty-five or eighty-five, it all feels the same. Smooth as butter."

"Well, for fifteen hundred bucks, it ought to do something."

Uncle Jack finally broke his silence. "Forrest, when did you make arrangements for the steaks?"

"Harold and I called it in a couple of weeks ago. It was his idea. Figured on doing something special eating-wise before the fireworks show."

"Worked out great for us," I noted. "Riding in a Buick's better than the bed of a pickup."

"Hey, if it wasn't for the steaks, I couldn't have brought you. Did you see how those men were looking at us when we pulled out? A lot of resentment there, because you know none of them can leave the camp without written permission from Harold. I can't wait to see their change in attitude when we show them what's in my trunk-back."

Jack asked, "Some of them did go home for the holiday, didn't they?"

"Sure. I think between those on leave and those who quit, we've got about thirty men in camp."

We'd learned early on that a sharp highway curve to the south and another one back to the east meant we'd reached the bridge. After crossing it, an eighth of a mile brought us to the dirt road on our left leading back to camp.

Sure enough, several men drifted toward the lane as we stopped and I got out to open the gate. If looks could kill, the eyes of those men watching us enter would've shot holes straight through us. They followed us to the lodge, where Forrest parked it near the kitchen's service entry, got out and opened the trunk-back. "Fellows," he bellowed as they hovered nearby. "Somebody go get Barney and tell him his steaks are here."

The dozen or so within hearing distance all came running, while others shouted the news so all in camp could hear. "What's them fer?" asked one of the baby Shanks while pointing to Ray's box of pencils and papers.

"That's some stuff we bought for us." I answered.

"What's it fer?" he asked again, reaching in to grab a pencil.

"Drawing pictures," I replied while lifting the box and handing it to Raymond.

"Huh, pitchers, that's stupid."

"Just a way to pass the time, same as playing pitch or dominoes."

"Huh, a stupid way to pass the time, if you ask me."

"Right. I heard you the first time." Standing tall with chest forward, I waited to see where he wanted to go next. The other men were long gone, having grabbed the boxes of steaks and following Forrest into the kitchen for delivery to Barney. Even Cecil and Jack had drifted off somewhere, so it was Raymond and I standing behind the Buick, with the baby Shank named Marvin giving me a dumb stare. Strolling up behind him still several paces away, daddy Virgil and baby Henry Shank.

"Lookee here, pa," Marvin guffawed, pointing at the box Raymond carried. "This'n here draws pitchers." He showed Virgil the pencil.

After a glance at the pencil, Virgil stepped toward Raymond. He peered into the box, and then stepped back with a glare at me, his eyes sharp and beady, one side of his mouth turned up in a smirk. "Come on, son. Let the baby draw his pitchers." His eyes still on me, Virgil added, "Don't wanna offend these high-falutin' Surbaughs. Ass-kissers, ridin' around in the boss's fancy car."

He waited, hoping I'd make a move, and my hand came forward all right, but with fingers open. "I'll take back that pencil, thank you."

Marvin offered it, but forced me to step toward him to take it, which I calmly did while keeping my eye on Virgil. He turned to the side and walked away, his neck straining so he could stare back at me with a snarl of crooked teeth. Following him, Henry and Marvin gave me the same look.

Situation averted, again, for now.

Forrest had exited the kitchen. I don't know when because I was looking elsewhere, but before he got into his car Ray and I thanked him for taking us to town. Even offered to wash his Buick and he said yes. First, Raymond and I headed for our cabin. "Where's Cecil?" I asked Uncle Jack, who sat on his cot looking blankly at his stocking feet on the floor.

"Cecil?" He looked up slowly as though shaking loose from some deep thought. "Oh, uh, I think he said he was going to look for a game of pitch."

"Hmm, I've been meaning to ask him if he plays seven or ten point pitch. I could go for some ten point myself. Remember how we used to play ten point, Uncle Jack? You'd come over and ma would break out the cards. You'd partner against me and Ray. I remember many a cold night we'd sit at the kitchen table by the stove and..."

"Ernie?"

"Yes, Ray."

"... I'm going to... draw the car."

"Wait until we clean it up first, Ray. How's that?"

"... Dirty first... then washed."

"Oh, sure. That'll work. Go on over. I'll give you time to draw and then we'll wash it. OK?"

With Raymond gone, I joined Jack on his cot. "What do you think, Jack? Should we show some of these fellows how real pitch players do it?"

"Aw, I don't know. Can't remember how to play." His eyes were again looking at his feet.

"It'll come back once we've played a hand or two. What do you say? After Ray and I wash Forrest's car, we'll see if we can..."

"Don't feel like it, Ernest. In fact, I'm thinking I might leave camp and head back home."

"What? Why? You were in high spirits last night. What happened?"

"No energy today, Ernie. It's hard on me being up there on that highway, in the heat. Guess I'm spoiled from working inside my factory so many years. Besides, I miss home."

"No, you don't. You miss ma."

Jack didn't even try to hide it. Finally looked up from his feet and turned toward me. "Yes, I miss her, too."

"Did you and ma think you'd been fooling me and Ray all these years?"

"Well, we tried."

"Uncle Jack, it's only natural you two should be together. What other woman's going to take care of you when you get old?"

"I can't think of any others I'd want to take care of me... now or later."

"Seems to me this camp is where you ought to be right now. Get some money saved so you can start up a new business and, uh, perhaps get married. Eh, Uncle Jack?"

He perked right up, glad to get my positive response to a tricky situation. "Think I'll help you and Ray wash that Buick, and then we'll find us a game of pitch."

Turned into a four-man operation, as Cecil saw what we were up to and joined in. Since we'd noticed a can of wax in his trunk-back, we told Forrest to open it up so we could wax and buff that beautiful, black finish.

After Cecil found a partner who didn't talk so much, his team took on me and Uncle Jack in ten point pitch. Ray stayed with the Buick, drawing it when spiffed up, and then walked down to the river bridge using our secret path and made a few renderings of the scenery there before supper-time.

Our meal was superb, the fireworks a dud. "The big show will be Monday," Harold explained while all men devoured grilled T-bones and sides in the lodge. "Just a teaser tonight."

Cecil and I watched Saturday's fireworks from our river place near the bridge. Practiced our sucking skills by doing each other at the same time. "You want on top or bottom?" I asked him.

"Under you, so I can smell your butt."

"It ought to smell like spring-fed water."

"Or fish," he chuckled.

"Oh, I get it."

Picked up right where we left off, like we'd been doing it all our lives.

Sunday and Monday we stayed close to home, with family. Played hours of pitch at the picnic table in front of our cabin with Cecil and his partner, one Frank Decker from Waynesville, a town in Pulaski County about thirty miles east. Frank's situation was similar to most in the camp, his former employer a closed down shoe factory. Like us, Frank took the game seriously, was damn good at it, and valued how it made the hours pass like minutes. Sometimes Uncle Jack would step out to go visit with Forrest, or just to stretch and take a break, and Ray would be my partner. Used his fingers rather than his mouth when it was time to bid, and had a sharp mind for remembering what cards had been played. Night-time didn't stop us, a kerosene lamp providing all the light we needed.

Monday night's fireworks display was quite a show. Harold and Forrest took their boxes by canoe across the river and lined everything up on the west side, while we watched from camp. Every man there appreciated what the WPA did for us in celebrating our nation's birthday, but I'm sure many of them would have preferred being elsewhere for the holiday.

I wasn't one of them. I liked being in a camp with so many men, especially two. Cecil I knew first-hand, and Forrest, well, for now, just being around him was enough.

PART FOUR – TOUGH GUY

Forrest was wrong about us reaching the bridge mid-week. Wednesday late we found a section one mile west where the ground beneath had sunk. Forrest wanted it to be re-enforced with compacted gravel and a concrete bed beneath, so we broke up the pavement one lane at a time and redid the entire, two-hundred-foot section, which took up all of our Thursday and half of Friday.

As we approached our two p.m. quitting time on Friday, we stood near the west portal of the Gasconade River Bridge. The concrete curbing had crumbled. Fist-sized nuggets laid at the side of the roadbed and the iron rods shaping the curb were exposed.

I heard Forrest say to Uncle Jack, "It's only the west side doing this. From the middle pier east its performing as it should."

"Well, let me grab a couple of pieces. My boys and I will look them over tonight." Jack walked along the bridge's north rail in the lane we had closed to traffic and picked up some concrete nuggets for the short ride back to camp. "Here, Ernest," he handed one to me as he passed, and we all started loading up equipment to end the day.

Things were pretty quiet in camp that night. Forrest had pushed us hard to finish the unexpected flaw and everybody was bushed. Saturday morning, however, we all woke up refreshed. Card games and swimming commenced, and since Jack and I hadn't seen Forrest at breakfast, we stopped by his living quarters with our concrete findings.

His place wasn't like our cabins. It's what resort owners would call a cottage if they were pushing their amenities – honeymoon cottage if it was a hard sell. Up two steps and onto his little porch, we knocked on his door around mid-morning, but heard nothing.

"Wonder where he is?" Jack looked around. "His car's here."

"He's probably sleeping late."

A voice from inside huffed, "That's right, I was." The door swung open and there stood Forrest Barton in nothing but a sheet, held in his fist and positioned just above his crotch. "How's that concrete, Jack?"

"Uh, best I can tell, it's a good mixture," Jack said, handing a nugget over. "Proper grade for roadway curbing, so I'd say something else is causing the deterioration."

"Well, I'm going to have Harold call his state man in Jefferson City when he gets back on Monday," he returned the concrete sample to Jack. "See if we can get some of Missouri's structural engineers down here to inspect our bridge.

"Harold's gone?" Jack pursued.

"Went home to St. Louis. Wife's sick."

I asked, "So, you're in charge of the camp, too?"

"Pretty much. Tell you what, we'll just patch up the east side of the bridge and move that direction up the highway until they're finished looking it over. Thanks, Jack. See you later." We turned to go, but as my foot hit the ground Forrest said, "And thank you, Ernest."

"Oh," I stopped and turned. "You're welcome."

Again I tried to leave, as Jack was several steps ahead of me, but Forrest asked, "Ernest, did Raymond show you the pictures he gave me?"

"Nuh-uh."

"I got 'em up on my wall. Come take a look."

"Jack, I'll catch you later," I waved him on, as Forrest stepped aside from the doorway, one hand holding his sheet, the other pointing to pictures of his Buick, a dusty version and a shiny one. Forrest's place was different on the inside, too. In a rectangular room, dish cabinets took up part of one wall, along with a counter-top, drawers and a sink with hand-pump for, I guess, water from a well somewhere. With dark green shutters on the windows and floral designs painted on white walls, the room had a happy-homey feel to it.

Ray's pictures were taped to the opposite wall above Forrest's bed. Not a cot like ours, his was a two-person bed on metal frame with wooden head and foot rails, the horizontal-rod types. He closed the door and joined me for a look at Ray's pictures. "Talented, ain't he, Ernest?"

"Yes, he is."

After a few seconds of silence followed by a clearing of phlegm from his throat, he casually walked to the table in his kitchen area and I turned to watch. His bare legs and feet preceded the wadded up sheet, his hairy butt uncovered, his strong knee-bones protruding and legs bowing outward a bit, their muscles well-defined and covered with dark brown hairs. "Left my stogie over here somewhere." He fumbled through papers and assorted clutter. "Or maybe not. Do you see it on my bedside table?"

"No, Forrest." .

"That figures. I couldn't find my undershorts, neither." He seemed unsure of himself. Fidgety. Out of sorts. "It's why you had to wait for me to answer the door." Turning toward me, his eyes scanned the room for a couple of seconds before he said, "Ah, the hell with it." He dropped the sheet. "If you see 'em laying around somewhere, toss 'em to me."

With his decision to go naked finally made, Forrest Barton's self-confidence was restored. He stood with hands on hips. Took a deep breath. Expanded his chest. Arched his back a little, and exhaled with a whistling sound through his teeth. "So, uh, you got any special talents? Like your brother?"

"Probably got some I don't know about yet. Does that make sense?"

"Makes perfect sense." He strutted to a window. "Tell you one thing." He closed the shutters. "I sure like how you diffused that situation with them Shanks the other day."

"Ha, yeah, but the day's coming when..."

"I know," he slammed shut the shutters on the other window, locking his front door along the way. "I've already told Harold about the Shanks." Moving past me he closed shutters on two back-wall windows. "They are trouble waiting to happen." Finished with his security measures, he stood directly in front of me with a foot of separation between us. "You handled it like a man ought to, Ernest. I like that." He slowly slid both hands along his rib cage, and in the same movement reached toward me, clasped his paws onto my shoulders. "I like you, too, Ernest. Does *that* make sense?"

My arms under his, I slid *my* hands along his rib cage, pulled him toward me. My face met his chest, my lips burrowing through mounds of fur until they reached his sternum. His hand moved to the back of my head and he held me there so I could kiss him, smell him, press my face into his pectorals and tickle my nose in his chest hairs. Forrest sighed when my lips brushed his nipple. Gorilla tits. As a boy I'd seen such an ape. A male gorilla named Phil at the St. Louis Zoo. Its tits were tiny and perfectly round with tips nearly an inch long. My gorilla named Forrest had nipples similar, but his tips were nowhere near an inch. A quarter-inch, and so very suckable.

How I ended up on his right one, and why I stayed for so long cannot be explained. I'd never before considered a man's tits as anything extraordinary, just dots of flesh that were there to add symmetry. No real function like a woman's, but when I felt his body shudder and knees nearly buckle, Forrest's nipple became a magnet to my mouth. He turned, but I could not let go. I kept sucking as he sat on his bed, followed him when he pivoted on his butt and laid down. When he threw his arms past his head I switched my mouth to his left tit, used my thumb to rub his right, still moist with my spit.

Another deep breath and exhale from Forrest included words. "Ah, Ernest, take off your clothes."

Done in record time, I laid on top of him, crushing his stimulated penis and mine between our abdomens. My lips pressed his. I forced him to open so I could pluck his tongue with my lips and suck on it like I'd done his nipples. His tongue tasted fresh. Not the sour of morning wake-up. Like mint, as though he'd prepared for me. Like he knew I was coming. Like he'd laid around all morning, dreaming, knowing I'd show up, knowing I could be enticed, knowing I wanted to eat him alive.

Forrest finally fought back. His lips clamped onto my tongue and he sucked on me, and when my fingers squeezed his pectorals and my thumbs rubbed his tits, he bucked. His hips raised us both. His penis poked my belly, and then he lowered his hips and wrapped me in his arms. I slid mine under his shoulder blades and my fingers clutched his trapeziums. With our mouths locked together, we took turns sucking each other's tongues. My chest and abdomen glided atop his, as shuttered windows brought sweltering heat to the room. Sweat lathered us, lubricated us, gave us fever, and I abandoned his mouth to devour his chest. My tongue and lips frantically slurped and licked his masculine sweat. Despite his arms wrapping me in a tight hug, I slimed him with my spit. He tried controlling me. Squeezed me in an attempt to tame me, but I could not be slowed.

My face assaulted his pectorals. I smeared his brine into my nose, onto my cheeks and mouth. The air, hot and filled with moisture and beastly odors, plus the taste of manly muscles and wet-matted fur set me afire, drove me to savagery. With my arms I bolted upward, breaking his grip from my torso as I rose to my knees. Grasping his wrists, I pinned them beyond his head and brutally attacked his nipples with my mouth. The right one, the left, I sucked and licked on them with my lips sealed to his flesh. I touched him with my teeth, as he moaned and groaned and turned his head side to side. I let go of his wrists but he kept his arms past his head. Reached for the horizontal rods of his head rail and grabbed hold. My hands slid under him, raised his chest, brought his tits to me so I could ruthlessly suck on them. Left or right, I played no favorites. Involved my upper teeth, pinning his sensitive tips of nipple flesh between my sharp incisors and slimy tongue.

I munched on him. A hungry infant slurping for milk, and he liked it. His growls and grunts said so. His slightly open jaw with teeth exposed said so, and his frantic penis incessantly slamming against my belly said so.

As did his breathy words, "Mm, god damn, suck those things, baby Surbaugh."

We were men gone mad. Crazed by wet and heavy heat. Insane with lust. Drowned by sweat, and with his brains boiling, my man-beast planted his feet to the mattress and vigorously thrust me into the air, off the bed and onto the floor. Pouncing on me, he grabbed the back of my neck and forced me to stand. Wrapped me in his arms and squeezed out my insides while smothering my face with his mouth. His wet, salty lips and slimy tongue lathered my forehead and mouth and gigantic nose with his frothing spit. Crushed by the gorilla, I collapsed in his arms. Surrendered as he tossed me onto his bed. Laid helplessly as he plucked a jar off the table. Made my limbs numb when he grabbed my ankles and draped my legs atop his shoulders. Relaxed best I could and told him, "Yes, Forrest," as he slathered my asshole with cold cream from his jar. I first rejected, and then accepted his rectum-penetrating finger. Repeated my reaction when a second finger entered me. Made ready for his woody as a third finger joined in, formed a cluster equal to the diameter of his pecker – his three fingers, his glorious penis, all the same.

"Yes, Forrest. Try it," I answered the question on his face, his eyebrows, his one-sided smile asking if I was sure.

His fingers left my rectum and dipped into cream, clutched his johnson and stroked it. Jar tossed aside, he pierced my anus in a manner completely contrasting to our build-up. Hesitating with purpose, Forrest entered my rectum slowly, gently. He studied my face before coming forward. With his corona inside my portal, he waited for my grimace to subside, inched his way further in. A painful expansion, a bloating inside me, slowly transformed to pleasure. An unnatural invasion became something beautiful, a dominating presence, a connection between me and the man I desired. He shared his strength with me. He became a part of me, and the quickly-accepting muscles in by rectum worked with him, not against him. I invited him in, dared him to come forward and crushed him inside me when he did. His pelvis made contact with my buttocks and my rectal muscles locked him in their vise. Squeezed his three-finger diameter down to that of a twig, and then I relaxed on him.

How quickly I'd learned to accept him, to stimulate him, and I wondered if my ghostly river friend, the one who'd prodded Cecil and me into our explorations, was now helping Forrest and me work our way back to our previous frenzy.

Droplets of sweat rained from his forehead onto my belly, as he pressed forward, his hands planted to the mattress on either side of my ribs. Displaying his confidence in me, he pressured me further. Moved his hands near my arm pits, forcing my spine to a severe curve. His face hovered above my chest. His hips thrust forward, retracted and returned while his knees flexed, pivoting left and right, higher and lower. He paid a price for his deepest penetrations. My inside muscles crunched him, drained the blood from him, brutalized his swollen penis with every ounce of my strength, and yet, he kept coming back for more punishment. Relished his pain, as he poked me from all directions, intensifying his pace.

My hands reached for his face. I cleared his forehead and eyebrows of sweat. I licked my fingers, tasted him. Wedged my fingers into his armpits. Licked again for a different taste. As he increased speed, his face turned red. His eyes glazed over and glared into mine. His mouth showed pleasure. His tongue licked his teeth, while an ecstatic panting of deep-toned growls accentuated the powerful thrusts of his hips.

I reached for his belly. Dug my digit into his navel. Drew a line the length of his stomach. Licked my finger clean, and as he plowed into me with strokes frantic and deep, I took between my fingers and thumbs both of his tits. Squeezed them. Twisted them and tripped his trigger. With shards of his working-man sweat pouring from his ruggedly-handsome face, he clenched shut his eyes and drove his wood into me. Short strokes, rapid-fire, Forrest Barton came inside me. Showered me with his seed, his smells, his sounds, and his brute strength.

Pure. Male. Animals. We were so very, very hot.

"Damn it, Ernest," he held steady on all fours, as I let go his tits and wiped brine from his face.

Pulling his head toward me, I kissed his cheeks, nose and forehead before asking, "What?"

"Now," his panting separated his words. "I can't decide for sure." His penis turned to mush, slipped out of me, left my rectum tingling with fire as my legs fell to the mattress. "But, I'm afraid…" he collapsed full-bodied on top of me, peppered me with kisses from my forehead to my chin. "I like your talents better than Ray's."

His mass nearly crushed me. Buried me into the mattress and smothered me in his cocoon. Forrest imprisoned me under his massive rib cage, his solid and bulky muscles, as his pectorals and abdomen undulated against mine, both of us slick as grease. Wedging his mighty arms under my shoulder blades, he squeezed them together while his clawed fingers massaged my drenched scalp.

"Lucky me," I gasped, shallow breaths all I could muster. Pressing his big ears with my palms, I steadied his head so I could stop him from pecking me and force him to kiss me. Seriously. Our mouths opened wide and locked together. Our tongues, slimy with froth, tied knots, twisting and curling and scraping against one another, exciting our taste buds. Our saliva glands opened their gates, thinking it time to devour, and as his manly-tasting spit streamed down my throat I nearly choked.

My convulsions broke off our kiss. Forrest raised on his elbows, his face hovering above mine, his chocolate-brown eyes scanning my face, and after a lingering lick along the bridge of my nose, he offered, "How about a drink of water?"

"Sure, and a towel."

He left me atop the sweat-soaked mattress, grabbed towels from the back of the room and together we wiped our cream away. Next came two glasses of water. The hand pump at his sink worked.

"Is that from a well, Forrest?"

"Yes. It's between this cottage and the next, where Harold lives. Oh, and look at this," he handed me my glass of water and I followed him to the back wall, where in one corner was built a tiny room. He opened the door, revealed a toilet. "This works, and after what I just fired into your behind, I suspect you'll be using it soon."

I didn't understand what he meant, but then a rumbling in my lower bowels educated me. "I better try now."

After I'd finished and flushed, I joined Forrest in sitting on the side of his bed. "Found your cigar, huh?"

"Yep. On the table over there, like I figured." Half of it already burned, he lit and puffed on the remainder. "Saw my shorts, too, under the bed."

"Leave them there."

"Gladly." Removing his stogie with his left hand, he draped his arm over my shoulder, bent toward me and kissed my neck. His lips nibbled my cheek and chin, moved onto my chest as I sat up straight. Squeezing my thigh with his right hand, he slid it toward my groin, grabbed my already-responding woody. "Damn, Ernest," he interspersed his words with kisses to my chest and stomach. "That is one long pecker you've got there."

"Yours is fat, mine's like a hose. Didn't know if I could take yours, being my first time and all."

"I know. Didn't hurt you, did I?"

"Nope. You were smart. Waiting for me like you did."

"That's because I knew you'd be smart enough to stop me if you needed to." His hand stroked on my corona, as he raised up, kissed my mouth, and then eyed me. "Ernest, I want to try. My mind says yes but my ass says no. I'm like you. Never been the taker, just the poker."

He'd given me opportunity to learn of his past. Who had he poked? When? How many? Men, women or both? Who cared? The only Forrest Barton of concern to me was the one with his hand on my pecker. The man who wanted me then and there. Grabbing the back of his head I kissed him hard on the mouth, and then whispered, "It's hotter than hell in here, Forrest."

"I know. You want me to..."

"Just how I like it. Hot room with a hot man on a wet bed. I know I've got a monster hanging between my legs, so maybe you should do it to yourself."

"I don't follow you."

Breaking free of his arm, I crawled onto the bed and laid on my back, hand-stroking my johnson. "Try sitting on me. That way, you control everything."

The advantage of having a man atop me who drove me insane with lust was I could last for hours if need be. Half an hour is all I needed – all he needed. With his knees straddling me, my penis and his asshole cold-creamed, Forrest made several attempts to insert, as my fully-charged pecker stayed firm for him. I made him keep his cigar clamped in his molars. The image I wanted, but pity the cigar as he forced the head of my penis past the rim of his ass. His teeth chomped, face contorted, and a vociferous grunt of pain rattled the room. Forrest, however, was no sort of man to give up a challenge, and so he kept me there just barely inside his anus.

I waited for him. Like I said, half an hour and Forrest had accepted my entire length. Carefully glided himself up and down my pole, and learned to like it. His twinkling eyes confirmed it. His grin and his slobbers tinged brown with tobacco enhanced it. Only then did I think of myself. I wanted to be back in my cocoon. I needed his incredible mass of sturdy bone and muscle to bear down on me.

"Turn around," I told him, knowing that with my length he could maneuver and still keep me inside.

"All right." Forrest manipulated his right knee onto my belly. "Hurt?"

"Real good."

His left leg moved in small increments – shin atop my thighs, knee in between them and then outside my left leg. Lifting his right knee off my belly, he pivoted to complete his rotation.

"Now, Forrest, do me backwards." He fine-tuned his position, rode my woody until he could comfortably take my entire length. Satisfied, I said, "Kick out your legs. Sit on me with your heels on the mattress." He obeyed, and I raised up, hooked my arms under his and brought him back. Laid down with Forrest atop me, my pecker deep in his rectum. "Grab hold of the head rails."

He reached for the rails and I had him where I wanted him. His muscular back crushing my chest, his solid mass pressing me down into the curve of the mattress, I was smothered in his cocoon. With new layers of sweat saturating us both, Forrest was skewered, his limbs in a four-way sprawl, his hands grasping the rails as though bound to a device of punishment. His mighty chest rose high into the air, his hard belly was stretched and sunken while my over-sized pecker brutalized his rectum.

I sneered in his ear. "How does it feel, tough guy?"

"Ah... it, uh..." his breathing was rapid, diaphragm compressed. "Like you said... hurts... real good."

"What are you going to do about it, tough guy? Here you are. Stripped naked. Stretched out. Impaled by my ten-inch spear. How will you survive it?"

The atmosphere of punishment created by my words, coupled with his very real discomfort, brought the desired effect. He struggled. His scrotum clenched, convulsed, and his rectum crushed the life out of my penis. "You... rotten bastard," he groaned.

His words were music to my ears. I increased the pressure on him. Curling my fingers into claws, I dug into his belly. "Mm... you are one strong son of a bitch, Forrest Barton. You truly are. Damn belly of yours is hard as concrete." I kneaded his stretched abdominals, clutching into his rock-solid wall of vulnerable muscle, as his insides spasmed around my imprisoned penis. He planted his heels into the mattress and raised himself. Arched his spine and lifted off of me. The friction of his rectum gliding up my shaft caused me to twitch and contort until he abandoned his struggle and collapsed, again atop me, burying me into the mattress.

"Give up, Mr. Barton?"

"Never. Damn you."

"Then you leave me no choice." My fingertips turned into butterflies fluttering the length of his belly. I began below his navel, worked toward his rib cage ever so slowly. Atop his elevated chest, I continued toward his pectorals, and his moan told me he knew where I was going. "Are you sure?" I asked him. "Must it come to this?"

"Oh, no," he groaned. "You wouldn't. Not that. Anything but that."

"Yes, that," I snarled, taking his horrifically stretched tits between my fingers and thumbs. He jolted. He gasped. His rectum savaged my helpless pecker as his scrotum rapidly clenched again and again. I pinched and twisted his tits, knowing what he would involuntarily do to my wood — everything I needed him to do, incessantly crushing me in his hot vise. I tormented him so he could brutalize me, and with a feigned attempt to escape his punishment, Forrest Barton arched his back, lifted off of me and slammed back down. He repeated his move, writhing up and down, his sweat and my sweat flying in all directions as he skewered himself, his rectum afire, his hot friction bringing me to explosion. My nuts contracted and let go, my moans of orgasm matching his groans of pleasurable pain.

What kind of love-making is this? What the hell did I ever do to deserve an excitement like this? What kind of man would put up with this? Follow my every request and desire to thrill me at levels such as this? A confident man, an adventuresome man, a man who, despite his impenetrable outer shell, is a lonely man. Or was.

After my pecker calmed down enough to slip out of him, Forrest rolled off me, grabbed hold of me and put me on top of him. Exhausted, we hugged and kissed and fell asleep.

Forrest Barton's fur-covered pectoral is the best pillow my face has ever known.

PART FIVE – COOL DOWN

"Do you reckon we missed lunch, Forrest?"

"Terribly. It's after two."

"I'm starving."

"So am I. Let's go swimming."

"Huh? You didn't even have breakfast. You must be..."

"Yes I did. Barney fixed me a platter before any of you men showed up."

"So, you weren't sleeping when Jack and I knocked?"

"Yes I was. Taking me a nap."

"And waiting?"

"Maybe."

"Maybe my ass! Well, you got what you were waiting for, but I'm still hungry."

"That's the best time to go swimming. Let's find your gang, take them all with us and cool down a bit.

Donning trousers and boots, I carried my shirt and he never put one on. A game of three-handed rummy was in progress. Raymond, Jack and Cecil sat in temporary sunlight at our cabin's picnic table, beams shining through a gap in the overhead trees. Cecil played while stripped to the waist; Ray and Jack wore their singlet undershirts. All three glistened with sweat.

"Cecil?" I asked. "Where's your partner, Frank?"

"I decided he's not comfortable here."

"What do you mean by that?"

"He made a remark to Ray that didn't sit well with me, and I told him to get lost."

"That happens."

"Where've you two been?"

Forrest handled it. "Ernest put the leather treatment to my upholstery, and I helped."

Jack eyed Forrest with disbelief. "Took two men four hours?"

"More like five," Forrest convincingly chuckled. "We did a bang-up job, and as you can see, we got over-heated, so we're heading for the river. Grab your trunks and let's hit it."

Raymond shook his head no; Jack spoke it. "Not me. I'll burn to a crisp."

"No, you won't. I brought sun lotion. Put away the cards and quit your arguing."

"Right," I backed him. "He's our boss. Remember? Gotta do what he says. Ray, you can take your pad and pencils. Make a picture of us swimming by the bridge. Uncle Jack, you *will* be in the picture, so come on."

Cecil needed no prodding. He and I led the way, our group moving single-file along our secret path. Emerging on the eastern bank, we all stripped to our undershorts, Ray and Jack keeping on their singlet shirts, Forrest and Jack sporting their straw hats. Passing around the bottle, we slicked our faces, necks and shoulders with lotion, helped each other apply some to our backs, and stepped in while waving to the pair of fishermen in their flat boat near the middle pier. They returned our wave, pulled up their anchor and paddled up-river, apparently worried we might scare away their quarry.

"Hold it, Ray," I stopped him from sitting at a spot from where he planned to sketch. "Our swimming hole's near the western bank. Hold your satchel up high and we'll wade you across."

Jack was curious. "How deep is it?"

"About waist-high here. Up to your armpits over there."

"Well, get going before I change my mind."

Cecil led the way, followed by Forrest, while Jack and I flanked Raymond in case he lost balance. Once he was safely across, he left the water and found a boulder fallen from the bluffs above, used it for his seat and began his sketching of us. Ray soon indicated he had our image stored in his brain, and so we scattered and swam, floated, or simply stood quietly absorbing the beauty all around us.

"What do you think, Uncle Jack? Ain't this a glorious spot?"

"It certainly is, Ernest. This is one fine river. Water's refreshing as it can be."

"This is a better swimming hole than down at the camp," Forrest joined us. "Just look at those bluffs to the west." He removed his hat, took out half a cigar and book of matches from its inner headband. "Sunshine on the moss makes them look like skyscrapers."

"Green skyscrapers?" I joked.

He fired up his stogie. "Emerald. Like jeweled towers of a great city."

Cecil left the water and visited with Ray, looking over his right shoulder at the sketching pad while rubbing his left shoulder with fingers. Returning, he reported to us, "Ray said he likes this view of the bridge better than from the east side."

I asked, "Did he show you his drawing of us?"

"No. Said he'd finish it later."

"Men?" Forrest butted in. "Have you been over by that pier?" he pointed west.

"No, Forrest," I answered. "We always come at night after supper."

"Well, see, that's a good way to get belly cramps," Jack chuckled.

"I don't wanna get too close to that middle pier," Cecil added. "I've heard you can get sucked under water."

"That's true, son," Jack agreed. "Currents can be tricky."

"Jack, how about we go take a look at it?" Forrest asked. "I'm no engineer, but I do know cracks when I see them."

"Might as well, Forrest, since we're down here."

We floated halfway and then drifted to the western bank-side so we could walk in water waist deep. The terrain under us was mostly soft and muddy, but every now and then a coin-sized rock would dig into someone's foot, causing a flinch, an ouch, and a quick step elsewhere.

"Jack, what do you think?" Forrest chomped on his stogie, as we stood in water forty feet from the western pier.

"Can't see any cracks. You?"

"Nope. How about you two?"

"Looks solid from here," Cecil said, and I concurred.

We stood there five, maybe ten minutes before Jack noted, "Does look like it's leaning a bit, but that could be us, where we're standing."

Forrest agreed. "Yeah, no way to tell. OK, we've seen it. This here ain't our responsibility. Just thought if we saw something major I'd have Harold report it when he calls the state office Monday morning."

"Hey, Ray! Where you going?" I'd caught movement in my peripheral vision, turned and saw Raymond nearly to the middle of the river with his satchel over head.

He stopped, faced us and dragged his finger across his throat.

"Finished?"

He nodded and continued his journey, while we waded a bit further up-river until we could see the southeast side of the pier. With no damage visible, we headed back for our swimming spot, Cecil and I dog-paddling in the down-river current and getting there ahead of the other two.

"Are we coming back tonight?" Cecil whispered. "After dinner?"

"Sounds like a plan, and I'll bring some lotion."

"What for? Afraid you'll get moon-burn?"

"No, I want you to poke me with your woody."

"You talking about your behind?"

"Shush, here they come."

Forrest and Jack floated toward us from Cecil's backside, when all of a sudden Cecil jumped halfway out of the water.

"Hey!" he turned, shouting at them. "Which one of you goosed me?"

They looked at one another, perplexed, Jack stating, "We weren't close enough to goose you."

Forrest warned, "Now, Jack, don't be twisting on my titty."

"I ain't twisting..." Jack's eyes widened and he dropped his jaw. "Somebody's yanking on my undershorts."

We stood four corners and facing each other, each of us more than arm's length apart. With a grin, I informed them, "Now, he's yanking on my shorts. Down to my ankles. With a wink toward Cecil, I announced, "Men, I suggest we stand here and let the cards play out. Right, Cecil?"

"Yep. We've been getting visits like this during our night-time swims."

"What's the deal?" Forrest wondered. "Are there spooks in this river?"

"Must be," Jack said. "There goes my shorts all the way down. Holy mackerel! It's got hold of my pecker." Jack looked into the water. His eyes of surprise turned to bliss, as he grinned at me. "Ernest, there's not a damn thing down there, but," his eyes rolled to the heavens. "good God almighty, I'd swear there's a mouth sucking on me.

"Well, shit! That ain't fair," Cecil complained. "All we ever got was hand jobs."

Jack's grin was a mile wide, and my advice was for him to close his eyes and enjoy. We three watched as Uncle Jack stood there twitching, moaning, and dreaming. Masturbation without the work, that's what a blow job is, and when it's done right few pleasures in life can match it. Jack's responses indicated he was getting a good one. When he nutted, the poor man nearly collapsed in the water, but he recovered, extremely happy, and then submerged. Left his hat floating in the current. Popped back up just in time to grab it before it floated out of his reach.

We waited to see who'd be next, but nothing happened.

"Cecil? Anything over there?" I asked.

"Nope."

"Forrest?"

"Nuh-uh. Never even pulled down my shorts. Guess I ain't to this spook's liking."

We gave it another five minutes or so, and then broke up and swam. None of us talked about it, but I always figured Jack was the one in sore need of some affection while we were not. Nobody'd been taking care of Jack or Raymond, which got me to wondering when Raymond might get his. He needed to spend more time in the river, and that's all there was to it.

PART SIX – MORE SNAKES

Half an hour later we headed over to the east bank, sat on a boulder and drip dried in the sun awhile before putting on our boots. About mid-way along the trail my eye caught something bright blue off to the side in undergrowth. "Looks like Raymond dropped a pencil." Checking first for poison ivy, I reached down, grabbed it and we continued to our cabin. After Forrest said his goodbye until supper-time, we three entered and found Raymond at the desk piecing together torn sections of paper.

"Ray? What happened?" I looked over his shoulder at a patchwork drawing of the bridge. The backs of his hands and arms were scratched, knuckles and fingers cut and red.

His delayed answer, "Fight."

"Fight? With whom?"

"Shanks."

"God damn it," I reached for his satchel. At least half of his pencils were missing, as was the one new drawing pad he'd taken with him to the river. Guess our secret path wasn't secret enough. "I will kill those sonsabitches," I stormed for the door with satchel in hand until Cecil and Jack stopped me.

"No, you don't," Jack scolded. "We're going to do this proper. Going straight to Forrest and let him handle it."

Of course, Jack was right, and given time to calm down, I realized Raymond didn't seem to be in such bad shape. Other than his hands, there wasn't a mark on him, which led me to believe it hadn't been much of a fight. "Sure, Jack. That's the thing to do. Cecil, you stay with Ray while we go report this."

Cecil didn't need to stay with Raymond, because soon everybody was running toward the boat-launch swimming area. Howls and screams of terror were coming from swimmers in the water. "Snakes! They're everywhere. Oh God, get 'em off me."

Three men, Virgil, Henry and Marvin Shank, flailed in the water clawing at their heads, faces, chests and shoulders, each man shrieking at the top of their lungs. "I can't stand it. Black snakes. They're all over us. God, please. Somebody help us."

Nobody made a move because there wasn't a snake in sight. We all stood around the boat launch and at bank-side, curious, dumbfounded, and for the most part, unsympathetic.

"Why don't you get out of the water?" A man in front of me shouted.

"Yeah, there ain't no snakes up here," added another, as a small bit of chuckling spread and blossomed into roars of laughter. With the Shanks making their way to the bank, still screaming and doing battle with their imagined serpents, the entire crowd took their shots.

"Hey, bring them snakes up here. We'll skin 'em and cook 'em up for you."

"Them black snakes make good pets. Keep 'em around the house so rats don't eat what little food I got for myself."

"Keep the birds from shittin' on your roof, too."

"And your vehicle, if you still got one."

"I keep a snake at home so my wife will stay in bed at night, in case I wake up needin' a screw."

The teasing continued as the Shanks reached the boat ramp, still hollering and spinning in circles with their arms flailing. Exiting the water, they got plenty of help from the men closest to them by way of hands slapping their arms, chests and heads. Still, the Shanks wouldn't calm down. The slapping got forceful, including a few fists. Men quickly lost their patience with such foolishness, prompting Forrest to intervene.

"Here, now! Everybody get back. Go on, get back up the ramp away from these men."

With Forrest standing between the Shanks and the rest of us, Virgil, Marvin and Henry finally came to their senses a bit.

"What the hell's wrong with you?" Forrest growled.

Virgil, quivering and panting for breath, his flesh white as a sheet, answered. "Something was after us out there." His trembling finger pointed to the river.

"There's no snakes in that water. Have you gone plumb crazy?"

"Oh, yeah? Then what happened to my boys? Just look at 'em. There's marks all over 'em."

Sure enough. Marvin had a black eye and purple bruise on his ribs; Henry's upper lip was cut and his nose appeared a different shape than last I'd seen it. "No snakes did that, Virgil Shank," I stepped forward. "Raymond's fists did that, and you know it."

"I'm telling you, snakes were after us out there." Virgil, still shaking, kept an eye on the river like he expected a school of serpents to come after him again.

"Then how come there are no scars on *you*, Virgil?" I pointed, as Virgil stood in his drenched trousers, shirtless and barefooted.

"I, uh," he scratched his head, confused.

Forrest took charge to straighten everything out. "Ernest, what do you mean it was Raymond's fists?"

"These three jumped Raymond on his way back to the cabin. You'll have to get his story from him, because we'd just found out when we heard this commotion and came running over here."

"Raymond, what about it?" Forrest waved for him to step forward, and immediately noticed Raymond's hands. "Let me see." He took Ray's wrists, raised his hands for inspection. "Been punching on faces, Raymond?"

He nodded yes.

"Tell me what happened."

Here was an instance where all the men had to put up with Raymond's faults, like it or not. He told of how the Shanks jumped him from the woods along the trail. Of how Henry leapt onto his back, while Marvin threw punches from the front. Of how he flipped Henry off his back and proceeded to pound both of them with his fists, using Forrest and myself to replay his punches in slow speed. Raymond's acting-out fists were scary enough. I'd have hated to be at the ends of them for real. Continuing, he told of how Virgil dumped contents of his satchel to the ground, picked up and tossed pencils every which way as far as he could, and ripped to pieces the three drawings Raymond made while we were swimming. Lastly, he flung the pad of paper toward the river.

"Ah-ha! Now I get it," Virgil Shank pointed his bony finger in Ray's direction. "You're the one who got them snakes after us. Put a curse on us. That's what you did. You're a demon from hell, Raymond Surbaugh. Drawing them pitchers. Casting spells on us."

"Virgil Shank," Forrest huffed. "I think you've lost your mind, but it doesn't matter because you'll have to leave the camp. All three of you."

"Don't have to tell me twice. Wouldn't stay for no amount of money. This place is wicked, long as he's here. Come on, boys. We're getting out."

Everybody cleared a path as the Shanks marched single-file up the boat ramp. We followed them to their cabin, hovered nearby while they loaded up their old truck with their belongings. Took about five minutes.

"Harold will mail out a check come Monday," Forrest told Virgil. "He'll pay what's due the three of you."

"We don't want it. Money here's cursed. Everything's cursed. Don't believe me, take a look at this." He handed Forrest a torn sheet of paper and headed for his truck with one final warning. "Rest of you men better get out, too, if you know what's good for you. Evil spirit's a-gonna kill you all. You'll see."

With the Shank's dilapidated, flatbed truck sputtering and backfiring its way to the gate, the rest of us crowded around Forrest for a look-see.

"Get back, damn it!" he barked. "I can't breathe." He moved through the throngs and headed for a picnic table.

Stepping onto the bench and then table-top, he held up the torn sheet.

"Now, men, this here is a drawing of our bridge, or what's left of the drawing. Raymond Surbaugh drew it today while we were down there swimming." He looked at it, held it once again for all to see. "So let's forget all this silly talk about curses and spooks. Virgil Shank thought he was going to scare Raymond Surbaugh and it backfired on him. His boys got their asses whupped because of him, and he was trying to save face by making stuff up about snakes and demons and all that other horseshit. That's all there is to it." Forrest stuffed the paper in his trouser pocket, pulled out his watch for a look. "Now, by my time it's five after six, and Barney gets his feelings hurt when nobody's there to eat his grub. So, come on, it's time for supper. Let's go eat."

And that, as they say, was that. Forrest Barton cleverly diffused the situation, and wisely sat at a table other than ours. He ate quickly and visited all tables, including ours, as men were finishing up. "Be at your cabin in thirty minutes," he whispered. "All of you."

Little did I know just how smartly Forrest had played his hand, not until he stepped in, told Cecil to hang around the door so nobody would peek through the windows, and plopped down that crumpled paper on our desk.

The torn piece was the right-side, lower quadrant from Ray's entire picture. West side of the bridge. Standing in the water looking at the pier was Cecil, myself, Jack and Forrest. To the right of us at the base of the western pier, the figure of a man, shadowy and vague, drawn in blue. Its body from head to thighs crawled out from beneath the pier, the rest of it between the ground and the pier's concrete as its clawed fingers dug into the dirt.

"Raymond, what is that?" Forrest put his finger near the shadow.

"... What... I saw."

"Is that the first time you've seen it?"

He shook his head no.

"Was it there when you drew the second picture?" I asked, knowing the first was of us in our swimming hole, which would not show the bridge. "The one you were putting back together in the cabin?"

"... Below." Ray's finger pointed beneath the pier.

"What about when you drew from the east bank the other day?" I continued. "Was it there then?"

He nodded yes, and Forrest suggested. "Well, Raymond, I'd like to see those pictures."

And to think, I could have seen them at any time, had I not so thoughtlessly failed in asking Raymond to show me. First time I could remember ever not asking him, and it made me feel ashamed. In this case, I also felt very stupid, because from the east bank Raymond saw the man's figure completely under the pier. A much smaller rendition from further distance, the shadow was several feet below in what appeared to be a natural, cave-like space made of rock. The figure laid on its side as though sleeping. In another version, it stood as though stretching and yawning, while in a third drawing its hand appeared to be waving. Waving at Raymond!

The other drawings from Raymond's first visit were of the bluffs. Their green moss looking very much like Forrest had said. A city of emerald skyscrapers, but devoid of any human figures. Suddenly, I remembered the drawing he'd made during our day's swim.

"Raymond, did you finish piecing together your other picture of the bridge? The one from today before we swam down to look at the pier?"

He shook his head no. Held up two fingers.

"Two pieces are missing?"

A yes nod.

"Is the man in that picture?"

Another nod, and a finger pointing down.

"He was in his cave?"

A yes, and Forrest asked. "Is that one of the missing pieces?"

Of course it was, and now we had a problem. Somewhere out there in the woods was a section of Raymond's drawing of the bridge with a spook underneath the western pier. We had to find it before someone else stumbled upon it, otherwise there'd be a mass exodus, or worse, a riot, along with demands for Raymond's head.

Jack said. "It's nearly dark, but you and Cecil better go look."

"We'll take the lamp."

"No," Forrest objected. "You've got to do it sneaky. If you can't find it tonight, we'll have to look at the crack of dawn."

Fortunately, as far as we knew, nobody besides us and the Shanks had been on that path, or even knew about it. Cecil and I could walk every step, dark or otherwise. All we had to do was stay on it and look for anything white.

"It's dusk. White ought to show up pretty good. Right, Cecil?"

"Hell, you guys. When do I get to look at the pictures? I don't even know what's going on here."

"Sorry, about that. Come take a look. I'll watch the door."

Forrest joined me, while Jack and Raymond explained the pictures to Cecil. There were a few men meandering about, but then our cabin was just one in a semi-circular group so that wasn't unusual.

"Think they're suspicious, Forrest?"

"Oh, they're curious, for sure. I just hope they're not superstitious. How did you like the way I kept that figure covered with my thumb when I was showing off Ray's drawing to all of them?"

"Yep. Sure fooled me. Do you think it's the same spirit that's been playing with our peckers?"

"After what happened today, I'm sure of it."

"Hey, Forrest! I'll bet that thing took off after them Shanks. That's why it only played with Jack's woody and left us standing there."

"Hmm... could be, but it sure was a long time before it made them think snakes were after them. Wonder what it was doing in between time?"

"Don't know. Maybe it was watching the Shanks go after Ray, but couldn't do anything until Virgil and his sons got into the water by our camp."

"Oh, I get it. Like the thing can only stay in the river or its cave."

"Right."

"Well, I'll tell you something that's got me real curious."

"What's that, Forrest?"

"How did a pier get built on an open-air rock formation like that? There were two geological men on-site when we were constructing that bridge. If there is a cave under there, they should have..." Forrest jolted back like he'd been electric-shocked.

"Forrest! What is it?"

"I think I know who that is under there."

"Who?"

"Can't remember his name. You and Cecil go find those missing pieces. I'll be in Harold's office making some phone calls, and don't worry, I'm keeping Jack and Raymond with me until you two get back."

With our eyes scanning every direction, Cecil and I crept along the path seeing nothing but dark green and shadows. Our fruitless search continued until we emerged from the woods at river's edge. Water flowed. Crickets rubbed their legs together. An occasional vehicle crossed the bridge. Sounds which left us feeling hollow and defeated.

"Guess we might as well go back, Cecil. Look one last time."

"Well, uh, since we're here, do you think it's dark enough?"

"Oh, hell, I ain't in much of a mood for it. Besides, I didn't bring that lotion."

"Damn, Ernie! You're just a tease. Leading me on that way."

"Sorry. Didn't mean to be. Just all the things that've happened."

"Yeah, I know." We stood looking at the river. Couldn't see much, other than the concrete piers. Moon wasn't high enough and the sun long-gone, but still we stood silently thinking the same thing, confirmed for me when he asked, "You reckon that thing's in its hole? Or in the water waiting for us?"

"Hard to say. After its busy day, it's probably taking a nap under the pier."

After several more seconds of quiet, Cecil said, "Ernie, do you see what I see?"

"Pretty sure I do." In the water, at bank-side near the western pier, a patch of white. "Shall we strip?"

A minute later we were wading across the east side and headed for our swimming hole. From there we followed the same path and dog-paddling method as before, making our way toward the pier. "God damn, Ernie. Look at that!"

Ray's drawing pad hovered above the water, dry as a bone, with two small pieces sticking out from under the cover. I peeled back the top and there were the two missing sections, one depicting the figure sleeping in its cave from Ray's western bank perspective. Scratching my head, I pondered, "How do you suppose it got these two pieces?"

"Don't know, unless they came near the river after Virgil Shank tore Ray's picture apart. Close enough he could grab hold of them."

"Or maybe my idea that he can't leave the river is hogwash." After securing the two pieces under the pad's cover, I spoke to our friendly spirit. "Thank you, mister. We don't know who you are yet, but Forrest Barton is working on your behalf. And believe you me, Forrest Barton is a man who gets things done."

Cecil added, "We sure enjoyed what you did to them Shanks, too!"

"That's right. My brother Raymond is beholding to you for..." Our ghostly friend put its tongue to my asshole, causing me to first bolt, and then giggle. "Hey, Cecil."

"What?"

"Is your johnson still looking to give me a poke?"

"Sure. Let's get this back to the cabin and you can..."

"No need for that. I'll just set it over here on the bank. Mister Spirit will keep it safe for us, and I suspect he'll take care of our lotion problem, too."

That's not all he did. As I dropped to all fours with my hands and knees sunken in mud, my spine just below the water's surface, he sucked on me while Cecil plugged my behind. I should've been sore. Hell, I'll admit it, my ass was raw from my stint with Forrest, but as Cecil stood tall and proud with his hands on my hips, his pecker inside me felt slick as snot. Fat and fulfilling, too, like a round peg in my hole. A perfect fit. A night-time river-fest. A pleasure-filled three-way with a studly farmer and a talented spook. Damnedest thing I ever did experience and one I'll never forget. Who would?

We bid our friend goodnight and headed back to the cabin, where Forrest, Ray and Jack were waiting for us.

"Got it!" Cecil excitedly plopped Ray's pad on the desk and proceeded to tell them what happened. All of it, from odd beginning to ecstatic end.

"What did you three find out?" I queried.

Forrest explained. "I called the Laclede County Sheriff's Department and had them look in their files for missing persons, 1922."

"Did you get his name?" I truly was anxious to know who'd just recently sucked on my willy.

"Clarence Hoover," Forrest looked at his notes. "Thirty-two years old. Geological surveyor with the Missouri Highway Department. Officially reported as missing person on August 3, 1922. Mr. Hoover's partner on the Gasconade River Bridge Project, Edward Page, stated Mr. Hoover left the site Friday, July 28, for weekend visit with his family in Warrensburg, Missouri. Wife, Marie Hoover, called July 29 inquiring of him, reported he never arrived. Automobile never found."

"So, you think he never left here?"

"Don't know what to think, Ernest, but the talk around our crew at the time was that he'd up and quit. Didn't think anything of it then, but a week later saw an article in the Lebanon paper reporting his having disappeared."

Cecil asked, "What happens now?"

"Well, nothing."

"Nothing?"

"We will go about our business repairing the east side of the bridge's roadbed, and when we can work on the west side, we will."

I found this hard to believe. "Forrest, don't you want to look for the cave?"

"Yeah," Cecil backed me. "See if there's a corpse in there?"

"No."

That answer seemed wholly inadequate and caused me irritation. "I don't understand. Seems to me if the thing can seep out from under the pier, there must be way in. All we've got to do is look at Ray's pictures, get our steam shovel down there and..."

"Collapse the bridge?" Forrest snapped.

"Ernest, what the hell's wrong with you?" Uncle Jack jumped on me hard. "All of a sudden you're an expert on everything. Yes, sir, just ask the genius," he waved his arm toward me as though introducing me on a stage. "He's a structural engineer, geological scientist, police detective, and psychic-come-philosopher in the world of spirits. All bundled up into one package named Ernest Surbaugh. Cecil? Do you have a question for our expert? How about you, Raymond? Forrest? Anything you need to know? Ernest is the man to ask."

"All right, I get it," my head justifiably drooping, my pride sufficiently checked.

"You're embarrassing me, boy. Thought I taught you better than that."

"You did, Uncle Jack. I just got way too excited. I am sorry."

"And?" With eyebrows furled, Jack jerked his head toward Forrest, who most definitely deserved my apology.

"Mr. Barton, forgive me. Jack taught me long ago a man should stick with what he knows and do it right. Period."

"There you go," Forrest resumed his good nature. "We know concrete and asphalt. Leave the rest for the people trained to do it. When Harold gets back I'll have him call in some geologists. If they find a cave, and there's a corpse inside, they can report it."

"While we do what we know," I beamed.

"Right. Building highways," Cecil seconded the thought.

"And keeping that thing in the river happy until it's all played out," Forrest completed it.

"You wanna go tell it what we're up to?" I hoped Forrest would say yes so I could get him naked and alone with me. "I'm sure it'll come listen if we're in our swimming hole."

"No, Ernest. I prefer the living." The look Forrest gave me could only be understood by me, and I knew he'd be finagling a way for us to hook up again real soon. "Ray, could you draw me a picture of the bridge, but without the cave underneath and its shadowed figure?"

Ray nodded yes and got busy drawing, while Forrest collected all of Ray's pictures featuring our spook and put them in a folder. "Jack, come with me to Harold's office and we'll lock these up. You two keep your eyes open and we'll be right back."

Seems Forrest was concerned the other twenty-odd men still in camp were getting restless. Hours had passed since Virgil Shank's superstitious rants, and despite Forrest's deft calming of them at the time, Virgil's words had been allowed to fester. Men with idle hours on their hands get to talking, starting rumors, and I began wondering if I might have to defend Raymond from some sort of lynch mob. The tension in camp was heavy, or so it seemed to me.

I should have known better. Could have saved myself the worry. Once Raymond finished his special picture, Forrest looked it over and told us to follow his lead, as we spread word for all men to gather in the lodge for a meeting.

Under electric light, Forrest slapped the new drawing onto a table and told all present to look it over while he talked.

"Men, Raymond Surbaugh drew this picture of our bridge the other day, and his Uncle Jack and I got to looking at it, thinking maybe something is wrong with our western pier. Like maybe there's a sinkhole underneath it, or perhaps a cave. Now, I ain't much of a swimmer, but the Surbaughs and Cecil Babcock took me down there today and helped me get to the pier. Sure enough, looks to me like it's leaning a bit. Men, I'm no smarter than you are when it comes to education. Everything I've learned about highway building, and bridge building, came from working with men who are experts. Men who went to college and can do the engineering mathematics to figure all these things out. That is exactly who we're going to call in here to look this thing over. And we're going to call men who can do land surveying and figure out what, if anything, is under our pier that might be causing problems. Any questions so far?"

Forrest whipped out his Zippo and lit his cigar stub. Maneuvered it between his molars and clamped. Hearing only mumbles amongst the men, he continued. "What we're going to do come Monday morning is repair the surface. We'll start above our middle pier and work our way east. We will continue east on our highway every day until the experts are finished with their findings. If that's not until we're plumb to Waynesville, then so be it. When it's time for us to fix the western half of our bridge, we will do what needs to be done."

I was learning a bit of leadership skills from Forrest's speech, noticing how he kept using the word, "our," a point he now drove home with his spit-saturated cigar held between finger and thumb, his arm waving it through the air for emphasis.

"Those of you thinking there's some sort of spooks haunting this river and our bridge, let me assure you that if there is such a thing, it is on our side. Those of you who think some of your team members are possessed by demons, well, that's just an old-fashioned way of thinking. There ain't no demons in this world, except for the ones you make for yourself. What we have here is a very talented artist, and without his drawings we never would have noticed the problem with that pier. Maybe there isn't a problem, but by God, thanks to that picture we are going to find out."

He paused, puffed on his cigar, removed it and spit out a flake of tobacco. "Until our job is finished, this Gasconade River Bridge is our bridge." His cigar pointed the direction. "Highway 66 is our highway. From this side of Lebanon to this side of Waynesville, it belongs to us, and we are going to make her the best stretch of highway between Chicago and California. Ain't nothing going to stop us, no way, no how. Those of you who are scared, those of you who wanna go back to your life of being broke and hungry and stupid, now's the time to get the hell out. The rest of us have got a job to do."

Such a rabble-rouser! Why, the man should have been a preacher or a politician, and whereas I expected the men to gather around Forrest Barton, pat him on the back and verbally confirm their loyalty to him, they did so in another way. They approached Raymond. Formed a circle around him. Got in line, shook his hand and thanked him for his picture.

It's an odd experience when you realize you're in the presence of a leader, a man who can inspire others to their full potential. It's even more numbing when that man is someone you've experienced in an intimate way.

I suddenly realized Forrest Barton's importance to me as a human being was a thousand times more meaningful than my desire for him as an object of sex. Make no mistake, his physical presence demanded attention. His mighty chest preceded him when he walked. His strong, rough, working-man hands could easily make their statement with fisticuffs. Scars on them proved he had done so many times, and yet, his words were his most powerful weapon. His demeanor, his thoughts, his attitude toward life and those around him, these were the traits he implemented to fight his battles. Forrest Barton led by example. Here was a man I could truly love with every ounce of my being until the end of our days, if he would have me.

Because Forrest Barton was a dominating figure, a man amongst men in my eyes, I would leave it up to him. I would give him the clear facts – no vague platitudes, no maybe this or I think that – I'd tell it to him straight. I loved him. I was willing to devote my life to him. He could accept me or he could punch me out. The decision would be his.

PART EIGHT – HARD WORKING MAN

If there were lingering doubts as to the good intentions of our river ghost, they were squelched by a Sunday morning surprise. At the boat launch in the water was a school of catfish. Catfish don't swim in schools. Some were blue and some were channel cats. Not the bloated-with-grease, fishy-tasting kind. These were all between fifteen and twenty inches, and as soon as the men got Barney down there agreeing to fry them up if we could catch them, they all flopped themselves onto the dry concrete. Committed suicide they did. We picked them up, tossed them into buckets and commenced to filleting each and every one. Forty-plus catfish, two fillets per man served up for breakfast.

After our morning meal, Cecil and I strolled our secret path looking for pencils. Clad in long pants, long-sleeved shirts and gloves to protect us from poison ivy, our two-hour search produced two-thirds of those missing. We presented them to Raymond. Told him we'd make another search after we rested a bit, but he shook his head no, said he had all the colors he needed and thanked us for our efforts.

Everything Forrest said would be done was done. Yes, the pier was leaning because it had settled atop a cavernous rock formation, part of which had collapsed from the weight of the pier and therefore was not level. Inside the cave was a corpse, taken by the Laclede County Sheriff's Department for an autopsy. The pier was held up with hydraulic jacks while engineers filled the cave with concrete and leveled out first the pier, and then the steel girders it supported, movement of which created so many cracks on the western end of roadbed we had to completely shut down the highway for a day. Every bit of the old pavement was broken up and hauled away, from east portal to west, and then we laid down new concrete topped with the latest type of petroleum-based asphalt. County and state engineers were so pleased with the result, they had us do the same for the entire stretch of highway. "From this side of Lebanon to this side of Waynesville," Forrest had said, and until the interstates started replacing the two-lanes with four in the 1950's, our section of U.S. Highway 66 was the construction model followed by other contractors along its entire 2400-mile route.

Getting back to July when we worked our way east while the engineers figured out the bridge issues, our dance that month wasn't a dance at all. In fact, I had to explain it to Raymond.

"Ernie?"

"Yes, Ray?" We lounged in our cabin after Friday's work. Showers taken, we awaited supper-time while Cecil and Jack were out socializing.

"Are you going to dance tomorrow night?"

"I doubt it, Ray. They're bringing in an entertainer. I marked it for you."

He strode his leisurely lope to the desk and looked at the wall calendar. "Bert..."

No surprise he couldn't read my scribbling. "Mr. Lahr is one of those song and dance men from Vaudeville days. Been in a few movies, too. We heard him once on the radio. Remember?"

"No."

"Well, we did. Beamed out of KVOO in Tulsa. He was singing songs and doing comedy bits. Making all sorts of funny sounds, like 'nyoing-yoing-yoing.'" My impression of Mr. Lahr was lame, but good enough to jar Ray's memory.

After the normal delay, he tossed back his head with a guffaw. "Yes! Very funny man."

"And I hear his facial expressions are even funnier, so we're in for a real treat. You ought to take your pad and pencils. Make some drawings and give them to Mr. Lahr, or one of the people traveling with him."

That is exactly what he did, but because slow-moving Ray nearly made us late, we got some piss-poor seats at the extreme right of the stage, which actually turned out to be fantastic seats.

There was no backstage, so Mr. Lahr's makeup man sat next to me with dry towels and jugs of water at the ready. Crispin Huck was his name, a friendly man of thirty years who'd grown up in Los Angeles, born to parents who'd worked behind the scenes of filmdom's beginnings. He'd been with Mr. Lahr since 1931, when the entertainer appeared in his first Hollywood film.

The benefit to us was that between routines Mr. Lahr would rush over for a swig of water, and then Mr. Huck toweled off his face. They went through a dozen towels the first set alone. Sure, the night was sultry as could be, but it wouldn't have mattered had we been in a deep freeze. The man was an explosion of energy, and I do believe the hardest working man in show business. Dressed in a trim black suit with crisp white shirt and bow-tie, his outfit instantly wilted as he danced and sang to phonographic records. During comedy routines he wildly flailed his arms, contorted his face and bugged his eyes with hilarious expressions. Best of all, his voice. Incredible. He made sounds I didn't know a human could produce. Animals, automobile horns, factory whistles and all sorts of undefined oddities. Mr. Lahr was an amazing performer in superb physical condition. Had to be in order to do the things he did, and all for an audience of perhaps fifty – we WPA men and a few of the government hot shots from Laclede and Pulaski Counties.

Another advantage to us, during his third toweling, Mr. Lahr asked Ray what he was drawing. Didn't have time to wait for an answer, and so he leaned over me for a look, dripping sweat all over me and Ray's picture. From then on, it was clear Mr. Lahr was mugging for Ray. Spent much time turned toward stage right, but being the professional he was he'd cover all the stage and angles so everybody could enjoy. After the first, forty-minute set, Mr. Lahr and Mr. Huck walked over to a tent by their traveling entourage of autos so Mr. Lahr could change outfits and rest a bit before set two.

Returning with a new stack of towels and more jugs of water, Crispin Huck reclaimed his chair next to me, leaned over and spoke to Ray. "Mr. Lahr would like to see your previous works, if you have any. Which cabin is yours? I will stop by for pictures you would like to show and deliver them to Mr. Lahr."

"Third from that end," I pointed my answer, explaining, "Raymond's words sometime take the long route to his tongue. Please don't think he's rude. It just takes him awhile to answer. On the other hand, his hands are lightening fast."

"And very talented."

"I know."

"Ernest, thank you for telling me, and Raymond, you take all the time you need to answer. Mr. Lahr has never seen anyone who can draw his facial expressions so accurately, or quickly."

Ray pointed toward our cabin. "Third... from... that end."

One might expect that Mr. Lahr's second act might be more subdued. After all, how much stamina is required to maintain the energy of his first act for another forty minutes? Plenty, but not only did he equal the first act, he surpassed it. The man had stage presence few have. My admiration and respect for him grew stronger with his every move, every word, every melody and every expression. His merely standing to speak with us, his tiny audience, between numbers caused me tingles. Do you think he phoned it in? He most certainly did not. He gave our paltry crowd every bit of his talent. Treated us no differently than if we'd been sitting amongst throngs in Carnegie Hall.

After the show, we quickly headed for our cabin so Ray could pick out his samples. He chose them without asking my opinions, as I laid each one into a new folder. We were made to wait five minutes for Crispin Huck to arrive. We waited another fifteen for Mr. Huck to return. The longest few minutes of my life, as I dreamed of where this might lead. It was all I could do to contain my excitement, while Ray sat casually, either unaware of the possibilities or too deep in thought to care.

"Raymond, Mr. Lahr very much enjoys your work." Crispin Huck took the chair offered him and laid the folder upon the desk top. Opened it. "He is particularly fond of this one. What do you call it?"

"... City... of... Emeralds."

I bit my tongue, wanting so badly to explain the picture's subject and how the title came to be, and fortunately Mr. Huck spoke before I made a fool of myself.

"It is beautiful, Raymond." Crispin Huck stacked the drawings into their folder, stood and faced Ray. "Do you also paint?"

"... Not here... Oils... at home."

"Wonderful! Do you think you could paint mattes? The backdrops used for Hollywood movies?"

"... Like... picture backgrounds?"

"Yes, Raymond. Exactly that. Mr. Lahr recently signed a contract to appear in a new film. Production will begin in September, and he requested I ask if you would like to come with us to work on this film. We are traveling Highway 66 all the way to the west coast and will stop along the way to entertain men in WPA camps just like this one. We will arrive in Los Angeles third week of August, and Mr. Lahr believes your talents would be perfect for making some of the mattes used in his movie. What do you think, Raymond?"

As I marked time about to pee my pants, we waited for his answer. "... Now?"

"We will leave in about thirty minutes. Now, keep in mind there is no guarantee you will be hired, but Mr. Lahr will do everything in his power to see that you are. He is very excited with your work, and his is no small role in this film. He will have plenty of clout with his request on your behalf."

Ray, thankfully, nodded yes just as Cecil entered, Jack several steps behind him. Ray pointed to Cecil. "... Can... he come, too?"

Crispin Huck turned, looked at Cecil, scrutinized the gleaming in Ray's eyes and his charmed grin. "Can he use a hammer? Buzz saw? Build things?"

Another nod from Ray.

"Yes, he can come if you wish, but he will be on his own as far as securing employment. Fair enough?"

Cecil had no clue as to what was happening, as Crispin Huck shook hands all around and reminded Ray the caravan would depart in thirty minutes. In fifteen, both men were packed and waiting around the line of Cadillacs to see which one they'd be riding in.

I was glad they were ahead of schedule, because I sure as hell had some questions before they got away from me. "Didn't know you two had, uh, gotten to be such good friends."

Cecil chirped. "Ernest, old buddy, you aren't the only fellow around here who knows how to swim."

"How long have you been..."

"Never mind."

"Did our friendly spook get you and Ray..."

"Never mind. All you need to know is, Ray's everything you are without that scary nose."

Apparently, drawing wasn't the lone activity taking place when Ray hiked to the river.

With a finger scraping the length of my beak and a friendly punch to my shoulder, Cecil bid me farewell. "Thanks for everything, Ernie. It's been gallons of fun, but only a fool would turn this down."

"And only a fool would pass up a chance at my brother. Goodbye, Cecil, and may all your dreams come true."

I tried to shake his hand, but all he wanted to do was hug me, and we did. As for Raymond, neither one of us could think of much to say, or maybe we could and I was stricken with his syndrome of not being able to get words to my mouth. Our hug lasted a long, long time, causing us both to sweat from exchanged body heat, and my whisper in his ear, "I love you, brother," was repeated by Raymond to me with one additional word – forever.

When in doubt, keep it simple and true.

With not an ounce of shame in me, streams of tears blurred my vision when the line of Cadillacs exited our gate. Unbridled joy will do that to a man.

Part Nine – Dis-invite

"Well, son, we're getting close to the place where your Uncle Ernie can say as they do in Hollywood, that's a wrap. Besides, Nurse Diesel will be coming around soon with my brain-bending pill. Now, there's one film Raymond never worked on, but for nearly fifty years Raymond Surbaugh helped design and create hundreds of mattes for dozens of movies."

"What about Cecil Babcock?"

"He didn't get to work in Mr. Lahr's film. First, he had to join the union and it was too late for that movie, but he did join up and worked construction for some later movies, building sets and whatever. Like me, World War II interrupted whatever ideas he had about a career, and I don't know what happened to him afterward, or if he even survived it. We lost contact with him."

"Did he and Raymond stay together up until then?"

"No, no. Ray wasn't like me in that regard. I think he simply enjoyed getting his willy sucked on while his mind drifted off to some faraway place. You know how artists are. Kind of spaced out half the time. Ray loved women. Married a solid one and started a Surbaugh line out west, as I'm sure you know."

"Of course I know, Uncle Ernie. I'm named after him."

"Indeed you are, son. Let me see if I've got this straight. Your father married one of their daughter's daughters. Right?"

"Correct."

"Well, then, that means you might have a small percentage of Ray's talent for making pictures. Do you?"

"I've done some drawings."

"Oh? Let me see them."

"I didn't bring any with me."

"All right. Bring them next time. I promise I will be objective and truthful with my opinions."

"There's going to be a next time?"

"If you want. After all, my life didn't end at a WPA camp in the Missouri Ozarks. There's World War II, my post-war career, and a whole bunch of stuff betwixt and between."

"Like Forrest Barton?"

"Yes, Ray, every bit of it included Forrest. Every minute was because of him, and for him. I will proudly tell you of our life together – now. You see, Raymond, I enjoy talking with you because you youngsters don't have all the hang-ups of my generation, or even those of your parents. It wasn't easy carrying on a relationship of nearly forty years with another man. Forrest and I constantly had to make up stories about why we were living together, and watch our every move, every word at our workplace. That's just the way it was, but when that man is the love of your life, you do what you have to do."

"How did you find out he felt the same way about you?"

"Oh, my! That didn't take long at all. I was lonely with Ray and Cecil suddenly gone, as you can imagine, but work on the bridge and highway continued as planned while the engineers did their thing with the pier. So, I was kept occupied and tired at the end of the day. Like our first time in his cottage, Saturdays became Forrest and Ernie day. With Harold back in camp, Forrest didn't have to worry so much about what the other men were up to, and we wallowed in his bed for awhile before heading to the swimming hole by the bridge."

"Did the spirit try to play with you two?"

"Yes, it did, and that's how I learned Forrest Barton was my man. He told that thing, 'Now, lookee here, I appreciate what you're trying to do, but we don't need it. I prefer the company of flesh and blood. This man right here is named Ernest Surbaugh,' Forrest stood behind me and wrapped his gorilla arms around my chest, kissing and breathing on my neck. 'He makes me feel things I ain't ever felt before. I'm not sharing him, and I'm never letting him go. Ever! So, go on down the river and find some other peckers to play with, because this one here belongs to me.'"

"Wow! Uncle Ernie, that is totally awesome!"

"Yeah, well, he had a gruff way of saying things, but there was never any doubt about his point being made. Anyway, we'd brought plenty of lotion, and we spent the rest of the afternoon standing in chest-high water plugging each other in the ass. Funny, people would go by in a canoe or flat boat, and we wouldn't even separate. We'd just turn and face them, wave and pretend like we were giving a shoulder rub. Get back to screwing once they were out of sight."

"Did Clarence Hoover go down river and play with other peckers like Forrest told him? Or did he..."

"Clarence Hoover?"

"Yeah. The friendly, horny ghost."

"Holy crap! I forgot that part. See? That's what happens when I don't get my pills, which by the way my nurse is late. That is so unlike her."

"What about the ghost?"

"Hmm? Oh, right. Turns out the corpse in the cave wasn't Clarence Hoover, but a man named Zeke Gulch."

"Who was Zeke Gulch?"

"An old retired colonel who'd long ago bought a large tract of land which included a speck across the river from where our camp was. Back before there was anything built there, before the Great War. The reason he was in the cave is because that bridge should have been built down-river, north of the bluffs, not south. Remember I told you how when heading east the highway made a sharp turn to the south before turning east for the bridge?"

"Yes."

"Well, Zeke Gulch and Clarence Hoover were both murdered over a kick-back on a land deal."

"I'm listening."

"The county was all set to pay Mr. Gulch for his parcel of land where they wanted to build their highway and bridge, when all of a sudden the other surveyor, Edward Page, comes up with a new route for the bridge to cross up-river, south of the bluffs. This was property belonging to Hickory Gale, and guess to whom Mr. Hickory Gale was related?"

"Who?"

"Virgil Shank. A cousin. Well, Clarence Hoover had already determined that was a bad spot to build the bridge, because he'd seen the cave underneath where the western pier would be. He'd also told Zeke Gulch of such, and Mr. Gulch was fixing to file a complaint with Laclede County over the change. Since Edward Page was expecting to receive from Hickory Gale half of what the county planned to pay Hickory for his property, the kickback I mentioned, Page and Hickory murdered Zeke Gulch in his cabin north of the bluffs. Put him in the cave and sealed it with rocks, and as you know, the pier was built right on top of poor old Zeke. Since he lived like a hermit deep in the woods, nobody reported him as missing. Ever."

"What about Clarence Hoover?"

"Clarence Hoover did indeed leave for home on that Friday evening, but he didn't get far. Virgil Shank and some of his kin were broken down on the highway to Lebanon, not far from Sleeper where they lived. Not really broken down. They just parked their old jalopy on the highway and flagged down Clarence so they could whack him on the head. Killed him, put him in his car and drove it to their place. With Clarence's corpse inside, they buried the auto deep into the dirt of a lonely field."

"So, Virgil Shank got his cut too, and helped build the bridge knowing there was a dead man under the pier."

"As did Edward Page. He's the one who talked. About a year after the investigation began, the Laclede County Sheriff got to looking into his financial records, found a bank draft made out to him from Hickory Gale. A bank draft, for Christ's sake! How stupid is that? Anyway, Hickory Gale died in 1925, less than a year after the bridge was finished."

"Didn't get to enjoy his loot very long. Did he?"

"Well, maybe he made the mistake of floating the river to look at the bridge. That's where they found him. Drowned very near the western pier."

"Zeke's revenge?"

"That'd be my guess. Of course, all of this came to light long after Forrest and I'd finished our project and moved on to our next job site. Uncle Jack, I'm happy to say, went home to Joplin and married our ma. Saved up enough money and got a bank loan to start a new concrete factory. This time specializing in sections for bridge supports, as in highway bridges."

"Something no economic depression could shut down."

"Right you are, Raymond. Oh, look, there she is! You're late. Got my memory pill ready?"

"And you're fiber pill, Mr. Surbaugh."

"Fiber pill? Woman, I've done told you a red apple takes care of that. One a day isn't just some old wives tale. Did you hear me, Ray? Do like I say. The acid in an apple is an antacid in your gut, and the peeling keeps the rest of your innards cleaned out so you can shit a nice, comfortable turd."

"I'll remember that."

"Are you ready for me to take you back, Mr. Surbaugh?"

"Yes, nurse, you can walk with me to my room, not that I need your help. See there, Ray? The Veteran's Administration takes good care of me. And why shouldn't they? I did my time. Who says government-run health care doesn't work? Don't believe it, young man. They're scamming you because it'll cut into their profits. Big companies, I'm talking about. And speaking of the VA, I've got one more thing to tell you. Got time?"

"Yes, Uncle Ernie."

"Zeke Gulch got a proper burial with full military honors. Forrest and I attended, and I've still got the obituary if you ever care to see it. We also drove up to Warrensburg for Clarence Hoover's funeral. Figured since we played our part in catching his killers, we should close it out by offering our condolences to his wife and kids. Edward Page, Virgil Shank and his kin died in

Jefferson City, state pen. Forrest Barton died in my arms, and that, Raymond number two, is a wrap."

ABOUT THE AUTHORS

STEVIE WOODS is a Brit living in the Northwest of England and though Stevie would love to be able to write full-time she has to resort to a day job, though she's counting down to the days until she can finally give it up and concentrate on doing what she really wants!

A long time avid reader of romance with a dash of adventure, Stevie only stumbled over 'slash' pairings a few years ago and was an immediate convert. Having dabbled with writing on and off for years, it wasn't long before Stevie was tapping away on the keyboard inventing stories around two hot guys, gaining her first publication in the summer of 2007.

Stevie likes reading stories with a good strong plot and believable characters and does her best to create them in her own work.

Stevie has a soft spot for historical settings but also thoroughly enjoys SF and Fantasy, Paranormal and Contemporary, finding the similarities as intriguing as the differences. Stevie already has several novels and short stories released by Torquere Press and Phaze Books.

Stevie is happy to hear from her readers via
http://www.steviewoods.com

CHARLIE COCHRANE primarily writes historical gay mysteries/romances, although she has to admit that her favourite short story is the little one she wrote about gay werewolves. She started writing relatively late in life but believes she draws on all her hoarded experiences to try to give a depth and richness to her stories. She also reckons that an East End upbringing and a Cambridge University education gives you an unusual view on life.

Her ideal day would be a morning walking along a beach, an afternoon spent watching rugby, and a church service in the

evening, with her husband and daughters tagging along, naturally. She loves reading, theatre, good food and watching sport, especially rugby. Charlie can be found on the internet at:
http://www.charliecochrane.co.uk

JARDONN SMITH resides at this web site: http://www.jardonnserotictales.com. There you will find free short stories and book excerpts both in text and audio mp3, plus the latest info on past, current and future book projects. Also at the site is info on books by Jardonn's alter ego, Jasper McCutcheon, same erotica concept featuring manly heroes, but female/male, as opposed to Jardonn's male/male.

THE TREVOR PROJECT

The Trevor Project operates the only nationwide, around-the-clock crisis and suicide prevention helpline for lesbian, gay, bisexual, transgender and questioning youth. Every day, The Trevor Project saves lives though its free and confidential helpline, its website and its educational services. If you or a friend are feeling lost or alone call The Trevor Helpline. If you or a friend are feeling lost, alone, confused or in crisis, please call The Trevor Helpline. You'll be able to speak confidentially with a trained counselor 24/7.

The Trevor Helpline: 866-488-7386
On the Web: http://www.thetrevorproject.org/

THE GAY MEN'S DOMESTIC VIOLENCE PROJECT

Founded in 1994, The Gay Men's Domestic Violence Project is a grassroots, non-profit organization founded by a gay male survivor of domestic violence and developed through the strength, contributions and participation of the community. The Gay Men's Domestic Violence Project supports victims and survivors through education, advocacy and direct services. Understanding that the serious public health issue of domestic violence is not gender specific, we serve men in relationships with men, regardless of how they identify, and stand ready to assist them in navigating through abusive relationships.

GMDVP Helpline: 800.832.1901
On the Web: http://gmdvp.org/

THE GAY & LESBIAN ALLIANCE AGAINST DEFAMATION/GLAAD EN ESPAÑOL

The Gay & Lesbian Alliance Against Defamation (GLAAD) is dedicated to promoting and ensuring fair, accurate and inclusive representation of people and events in the media as a means of eliminating homophobia and discrimination based on gender identity and sexual orientation.

On the Web: http://www.glaad.org/
GLAAD en español:

http://www.glaad.org/espanol/bienvenido.php

SERVICEMEMBERS LEGAL DEFENSE NETWORK

Servicemembers Legal Defense Network is a nonpartisan, nonprofit, legal services, watchdog and policy organization dedicated to ending discrimination against and harassment of military personnel affected by "Don't Ask, Don't Tell" (DADT).The SLDN provides free, confidential legal services to all those impacted by DADT and related discrimination. Since 1993, its inhouse legal team has responded to more than 9,000 requests for assistance. In Congress, it leads the fight to repeal DADT and replace it with a law that ensures equal treatment for every servicemember, regardless of sexual orientation. In the courts, it works to challenge the constitutionality of DADT.

SLDN
PO Box 65301
Washington DC 20035-5301
On the Web: http://sldn.org/

Call: (202) 328-3244
or (202) 328-FAIR
e-mail: sldn@sldn.org

THE GLBT NATIONAL HELP CENTER

The GLBT National Help Center is a nonprofit, tax-exempt organization that is dedicated to meeting the needs of the gay, lesbian, bisexual and transgender community and those questioning their sexual orientation and gender identity. It is an outgrowth of the Gay & Lesbian National Hotline, which began in 1996 and now is a primary program of The GLBT National Help Center. It offers several different programs including two national hotlines that help members of the GLBT community talk about the important issues that they are facing in their lives. It helps end the isolation that many people feel, by providing a safe environment on the phone or via the internet to discuss issues that people can't talk about anywhere else. The GLBT National Help Center also helps other organizations build the infrastructure they need to provide strong support to our community at the local level.

National Hotline: 1-888-THE-GLNH (1-888-843-4564)
National Youth Talkline 1-800-246-PRIDE (1-800-246-7743)
On the Web: http://www.glnh.org/
e-mail: info@glbtnationalhelpcenter.org

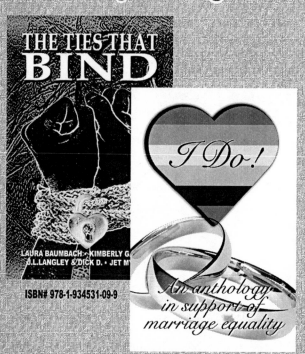

Stimulate yourself.
READ.
www.manloveromance.com
THE HOTTEST M/M EROTIC AUTHORS & WEBSITES ON THE NET

LaVergne, TN USA
10 May 2010
182149LV00001B/17/P